The

'I don't want six ladies to swoon over me,' Pedro said. 'I want you to love me, Teresa.'

'But I do! I do! I love all my family. You are my dear cousin.'

'Only that? No more than cousin? Teresa, is it only as cousin you think of me? Only as that?'

'You have no right to discuss such matters!' Teresa cried, the ready colour flaming into her face.

If you only knew, her thoughts ran, how great is the capacity for evil in me! If you only knew what it is like to be gnawed day and night by temptations I don't even understand, by impulses tearing at me like wild beasts. The idea of marriage fills me with horror. I know that my destiny is to be different. But how . . . ?

Available in Fontana by the same author

Elizabeth the Beloved
Katheryn, the Wanton Queen
Joan of the Lilies
Anne, The Rose of Hever
Princess of Desire
Henry VIII and His Six Wives
The Woodville Wench

MAUREEN PETERS

The Cloistered Flame

Collins
FONTANA BOOKS

First published by Robert Hale & Company 1971
First issued in Fontana Books 1974

Made and printed in Great Britain by
William Collins Sons & Co Ltd Glasgow

AUTHOR'S NOTE

Although presented as fiction, this book is based closely upon the life of St Teresa of Avila. All the characters really existed, most of the incidents have been recorded, and many of the conversations are adapted from Teresa's letters and books.

To simplify matters, I have anglicised part of the original names, so that Maria de San José becomes Marie of St Joseph — and so on.

I would like to express my sincere thanks to Monsignor D. McDonnell, Vicar-General of the Arch Diocese of Liverpool and Superior of the Carmelites of Liverpool, for so generously giving up his time in order to discuss various theological aspects of the work, and for lending me books.

I also wish to thank the Mother-Prioress and Community of the Carmelite Monastery, Up-Holland, for their warm hospitality, and for the loan of books from their library; and the Mother-Prioress and Community of the Liverpool Carmelite Monastery, for their courteous welcome.

Finally, I would like to thank the Chief Librarian and staff of the Crosby Branch Library for the trouble they have undertaken in hunting down books that have proved useful in my extensive research.

The soul sometimes leaps out of itself like a burning fire that has become one whole flame and increases with great force. The flame leaps very high above the fire. Nevertheless, it is not a different thing but the same flame that is in the fire.

Teresa of Avila

PART ONE

THE SPARK

CHAPTER ONE

For Don Alonzo Sanchez y Cepeda it was the favourite time of day. The blaze of golden sunlight had deepened to a warm orange streaked with crimson, and long purple shadows blurred the walls and turrets of the little town. In this brief interval before late afternoon slid into night, there was time to relax and reflect. The library was a pleasant place in which to do both. It was a long, low-ceilinged room with arched windows leading out to a narrow terrace, from which the walls fell sheer to the plains that stretched beyond Avila to the cities of Granada and Salamanca.

Within the room, lamps waited to be lit in the alcoves. The shutters were folded back against the panelled walls and gleams of sunlight irradiated the polished floor, the delicate woven rugs, the Venetian goblets from which important guests were invited to drink, the narrow shelves where Don Alonzo's books were ranged.

He leaned from his high-backed carven chair and ran the tip of a well-manicured finger along the spines of blue and green and purple. Many happy hours had been spent in the perusal of these volumes. The *De Officiis* of Cicero, the *De Consolatione Philosophiae* of Boethius, Seneca's *Proverbs*, had excited and nourished his thoughts. Education, provided it be directed to spiritual ends, was a desirable thing. It was his intention that every member of his family should learn to read and write. In that way, a person need never be lonely.

It never occurred to Don Alonzo that he was sometimes afflicted by a vague consciousness of his own solitary state. As he sat in his beautiful room which looked out to the wider world from the enclosed world of his native Avila, he seemed the epitome of a proudly self-contained Spanish grandee. His spare frame was encased in a stiff doublet of scarlet and gold, with a narrow pleated ruff of white lawn and breeches of doe-skin. His black hair was cut short, and showed, as did his pointed beard, flecks of white, thick as the snow that lay on the roofs of the town in the cold season. His face with its high cheekbones, jutting nose and humourless mouth reflected his pride in the conscious superiority of his race. He and his brother, Francisco, who occupied the adjoining mansion, were of Castilian blood, pure, hidalgoes, free from the taint of Moorish or Jewish origin.

Their two houses occupied one side of a square, in the centre of which a wide plane tree afforded shade for gossiping women on their way to market. Two walled orchards separated one house from its neighbour, while the backs of the buildings formed part of the town walls with their nine gates and eighty-six towers. Occasionally, if he rested his hand on the sun-warmed stone, Don Alonzo could sense an imperceptible throbbing as if the life blood of Avila were contained in its protective battlements. A hill-town, he reflected, that had repelled the Moorish invaders, expelled the Jews, and now lived its own secret, subtle life high above the plateau through which the Adaja river wound a wayward feminine course.

His thoughts had taken an uneasy turn. Women, he decided gloomily, were odd, contrary beings. He would never begin to understand any of them, and yet he had been married twice. His first wife, Catalina, had been a stolid, placid woman, who, having presented him with two stolid, placid children, had died in the same quiet, well-bred way she had lived.

As a stepmother for Juan and Maria, he had chosen a beautiful girl of thirteen and treated her with great generosity, and she had given him strong and healthy children. Beatriz was twenty-seven years old now, and the high spirits and outbursts of merriment, which he had sought to quell early in their life together, had been disciplined into a cool and remote gentleness.

There was a discreet tap at the door, and at his 'Come!' the object of his thoughts entered. Turning in his chair to watch her as she glided across the floor, he felt irritation mingle with his admiration. Why, he wondered, did she insist on dressing always in black? Although her skin gleamed like ivory against the jet velvet of her gown, he would have liked to see some colour about her. Only the week before he had presented her with a dress of apricot satin trimmed with tiny roses; and she had thanked him and hung it in her closet with all the other garments she never wore.

'Why don't you ever wear your pearls?' he demanded, abruptly.

'Do you wish me to put them on, Don Alonzo?' she asked, giving him, as she always did, his formal title.

'I should order you to adorn your beauty,' he said, trying to wrap a compliment in the mild jest.

'Then, if it pleases you, I will get them,' she said, stiffly.

'Not now, Beatriz. Sit down and talk to me.'

She seated herself obediently on the companion chair to his own, and, folding her narrow hands, fixed her dark eyes attentively on his face.

'I have received an offer for Maria,' he said.

'From whom?'

'From Señor Martin de Guzman y Barriento. He is of an excellent family.'

'She is too young,' Beatriz said.

'Past seventeen,' Don Alonzo protested. 'At that age you had borne two children.'

'Does she wish to marry?'

'How should I know?' Don Alonzo blustered a little. 'Every girl wishes to marry, doesn't she? Unless she has a vocation for the religious life. You've seen no signs of that in Maria?'

His wife shook her head.

'Well then, where's the objection? She knows Señor Martin and seems to enjoy his company. And there have been no other offers. Maria does not attract suitors.'

'She is a good, gentle girl, as dear to me as my own daughter,' Beatriz said, with a shade of reproof in her voice.

'Then why deny her a husband?'

'I would like her to wait a little, to be certain of her own mind,' Beatriz said, slowly.

'You talk as if they were going to be married next week!' Don Alonzo said, testily. 'A two or three year betrothal was what I had in mind. They can meet during that time, learn about each other. Don't you approve of that?'

'Yes, of course. May I tell Maria?'

'Mention it to her, but there must be nothing official until the settlements are drawn up. Now, it was you who sought me out, so you must have something to tell me or did you merely crave my company?' he asked, hopefully.

'I have a request, Don Alonzo,' she said.

'Yes, Beatriz? Don't be afraid to ask me.'

She hesitated, flexing her hands and then said, abruptly, 'I do not wish Jeronima to come here any longer.'

'My brother's girl? Why not? Has she been rude or disobedient?'

'She is sly,' his wife said. 'She tells lies and encourages the others to laugh at her cleverness. She has a bad influence upon Teresa. The child admires her and tries to imitate her way of speaking and moving. It worries me to see Jeronima watching Teresa, as if the little one's sweetness were something to be sucked out, and destroyed.'

'Nonsense! Jeronima is, how old? – eleven? You talk as if she was a calculating woman of twenty! I'll grant you she has a fawning manner, but that's no reason to forbid her the house. And it would not be practical when only a garden separates Francisco's house from ours.'

'I have nothing against the others,' said Beatriz, quickly.

'If we allow them to run in and out as they choose, we cannot forbid Jeronima,' Don Alonzo decided. 'What possible reason could I give my brother that would not hurt him? It is not easy for a widower to rear nine children. As for Teresa – if you spent more time with her, instead of burying yourself in that foolish poetry, she might begin to imitate you, instead of her cousin!'

'You are right,' Beatriz said meekly. 'I will try to improve.'

Her eyes were defeated and Don Alonzo put out his hand consolingly.

'You are a good wife,' he said.

'It is my duty to be,' she answered, and his hand dropped to his side again.

A bell clanged through the great house.

Dona Beatriz rose in a graceful, fluid movement, coughing a little as she did so. She had been troubled with a dry irritation of the throat and pains in her back since the birth of her seventh child the previous month. Sometimes she felt so weary it was an effort to stir from her room. On these occasions, when Don Alonzo was absent on business, she would bribe the children to be quiet with candied nuts and story books, while she lay on her bed, and devoured the tales of chivalry and erotic verses of the Provençal troubadours, that made life so much more exciting than she had ever found it to be.

Her family was already seated down both sides of the long trestle. At its foot, the de Cepeda confessor read his Breviary and darted an occasional, quelling glance at any child who had begun to chatter too loudly. Servants moved about the room, setting on the table baskets of bread, wooden bowls of lettuce and endives, pyramids of grapes and figs, and carafes of red and white wine. The lamps had been lit, and a pleasant scent of roast veal came from the sideboard where the joints were being carved.

Grace over, the children resumed their places under the watchful eye of their father. Juan was not there, having joined the king's service in order to win the coveted spurs of knighthood. Maria, lint-coloured hair bound tightly into its coif, was cutting meat into small pieces for the little ones.

Hernando and Rodrigo, tall lads of twelve and eleven, with insolent eyes and curling black hair, sat together. Next came seven-year-old Teresa, with her stool pushed as close to Rodrigo as she could get it. Opposite them, three-year-old Lorenzo was poking two-year-old Antonio in the ribs. Close to them the year old Pedro banged his spoon happily on the table, while a little apart from the rest, the baby Jeronimo lay, tightly swaddled, in his wooden cradle.

'Father, is it true that volunteers have been called to put down the riots in Valencia?' Hernando asked.

'Quite true. Civil strife must be quelled before Spain is strong enough to campaign against the French.'

'Diego says that boys of twelve have been accepted,' Hernando said wistfully.

Don Alonzo gave his son a quiet look of sympathy and shook his head.

'If Hernando goes to war, I want to go too,' Rodrigo began, and broke off, staring at Teresa's round face, which had flushed scarlet.

'Is anything the matter, my child?' Don Alonzo asked.

'She doesn't want Rodrigo to be a soldier,' Lorenzo shrilled. 'She doesn't want Rodrigo to fight the French.'

'Nobody from this household is going to fight anybody until their educations are complete,' Don Alonzo said. 'Sit up, Lorenzo. Castilian gentlemen do not slouch. Teresa.' His glance softened. 'It is your duty to love your brother, but excessive devotion to one member of your family is not only unfair to the others but may even divert you from the love of God.'

'Is it not possible to love God through people made in His image?' Maria asked.

'In some ways,' agreed the family confessor, 'but we must never forget we are but pale reflections of the Divine Reality. Poor, fallible creatures doomed to die.'

'But God goes on for ever and ever, doesn't He, Father Vicente?' Teresa demanded, through a mouthful of veal.

'Indeed He does,' the priest agreed. 'But it is as well to finish chewing what is in your mouth, little one, before you speak.'

'For ever and ever and ever,' Teresa muttered, hastily swallowing her food.

The phrase fascinated her. It was hard to imagine a single year when one was only seven, but when she tried to think about eternity she felt herself grow smaller and smaller in the midst of a vast and powerful space. And somewhere in that space God moved. Well, she and Rodrigo would know all about it very soon.

Don Alonzo smiled indulgently into his beard. He was proud of all his children, but Teresa was his favourite. She would be a beauty, he thought, despite her small, plump figure, for her skin was as white as her mother's, and when she smiled three dimples puckered her cheek.

Later, they knelt together for evening prayer. Father Vicente had chosen to read a passage from the Passion of St Perpetua and St Felicity, and the family ranged themselves in a semi-circle around him, while those servants not engaged in active duties knelt behind. As the chaplain read out the account of martyrdom, Teresa listened intently. So that girl at Carthage long ago had also worried about her father before she walked out to face death in the arena among the wild beasts. Perhaps some of the pain of martyrdom lay in leaving those whom one loved best. She wondered if Rodrigo felt the same, but when she peeped from beneath her long eyelashes, she could discern nothing in her brother's face but a barely suppressed excitement.

The reading of the day was over, and the recitation of the rosary began. Half-concealed by her mother's voluminous black skirt, Teresa knelt demurely, the cool beads dripping through her fingers down to her pink dress. She loved this end of the day, with the lessons learned, the small naughtiness forgotten, the family circled in harmony under the quiet lamplight.

This was the last time she would kneel among them. Ahead lay the journey to North Africa and then martyrdom, for when the savage Moors learned she was a Christian they would undoubtedly cut off her head. Then her soul and Rodrigo's, for she and her brother always did everything together, would fly up to the glories of heaven.

They had talked about it often and agreed it was much more

exciting to die violently for the faith than to gain heaven after a lifetime of good works.

The devotions over, Don Alonzo stood up to bid the children and the servants good night. As his younger daughter paused before him, he bent to kiss her cheek.

'You are a trifle overheated, Teresa. Are you well today?' he asked.

'Yes, Father. Perfectly well.'

'Be a good child then and say your private prayers with care.'

'Yes, Father.'

Teresa hesitated, and then flung her arms about his neck and pressed her face into his doublet.

'Gently, Teresa,' her mother admonished, and the child drew away reluctantly and followed the others.

'She has a loving heart,' Don Alonzo said, looking after her.

'And a passionate nature,' said Beatriz, and looked for a moment as if she were regretting her own lost youth.

Teresa slept in a wide, curtained bed with her half-sister, Maria. It was pleasant on cold nights to snuggle close to the older girl, and let the sound of her breathing hold at bay the silence of the dark room.

Tonight she stood docilely while Maria unfastened her stiff bodice with its pointed collar and puffed sleeves of silver lace, and the skirt with its rows of lovers' knots. As the gown fell in a froth of pink, her plump little shoulders emerged, clad in a white shift. Maria unloosed the hairpins from the mass of curling dark chestnut tresses and reached for the silver-backed brush.

'Maria,' Beatriz said, from the doorway, 'may I have a few words with you?'

'Yes, of course, Mother.'

Maria set down the brush and went towards the black-robed figure, pulling the door close; a sign, as Teresa knew, that she was about to indulge in some private and boring conversation.

Another door led from the bedroom into a narrow corridor beyond which the boys' rooms were situated. Teresa, who hated sitting still, opened the door and looked out in time to see Rodrigo padding towards his own quarters.

'Is everything ready?' Teresa hissed.

Her brother paused and nodded.

'And we'll meet at dawn, by the side-gate.'

He nodded again but something in his face caused her to ask anxiously, 'You will really be there, won't you?'

'I said I'd come with you, didn't I?' the boy asked, in a nettled tone.

'And we'll go to Africa and become martyrs?'

'If you like.' Rodrigo hesitated and then burst out, 'Wouldn't you like to run away to sea instead? We might get to the New World, to the Indies.'

'You said we were going to Africa,' Teresa protested.

'Perhaps they make martyrs in the New World,' her brother suggested, but she shook her head and stamped a small, bare foot.

'I want to be a martyr in Africa,' she insisted. 'You promised, Rodrigo. You promised!'

'It's such a long journey, and I'm not sure of the way,' Rodrigo began doubtfully.

'We just keep walking south until we get there,' Teresa assured him, with the confidence of complete ignorance. 'I've got a big bag of raisins so that we won't be hungry and you may have the fattest ones.'

Rodrigo, who could never stand out against his adored sister for long, took a deep breath.

'I'll be ready before dawn,' he whispered, and scurried to his own quarters as Maria re-entered the bedroom.

'Teresa, close the door and come away from the draught.'

'I was talking to Rodrigo.' Teresa submitted to the ministrations of the hairbrush.

'Plotting some mischief?'

'Oh, no,' Teresa assured her truthfully. 'Rodrigo and I are planning something very good.'

'H'm!' Maria gave her half-sister a look compounded of suspicion and amusement. 'Well, say your prayers and get into bed.'

Dutifully, Teresa took her place at the little stool in front of the picture of the Mother and Child. When she had made her act of contrition and reeled off the long list of relatives and friends who must be remembered, she hesitated. Ought she not to tell God that she was on her way? Then she recalled that He already knew. God knew everything, and was for ever and ever and ever and ever–

'Get into bed before you fall asleep on your knees,' Maria ordered.

Teresa, who had been shrinking smaller and smaller under

the weight of imagined eternity, was jolted back to full size again. With hands tightly clasped, she looked for an instant like some inexperienced angel bewildered by its mission. Then she jumped up and bounced into bed, shrieking as her toes met the cold sheets.

'What were you talking about with Mother?' she asked.

Maria, unpinning her fair plaits, flushed a little.

'There's talk of a marriage for me in a few years' time,' she said.

'To Señor Martin de Guzman y Barriento?'

'What do you know about it?' Maria asked, sharply.

'He's always visiting here, and when he's asking after the health of Dona Maria, his voice goes all soft and drawling.'

Teresa lowered her own voice and rolled her large, brown eyes languishingly.

Half-vexed Maria couldn't help smiling.

'Well, I'm in no hurry to wed,' she remarked. 'A wife has to obey her husband, and stay indoors, and have large families.'

'Hernando, Rodrigo, me, Lorenzo, Antonio, Pedro and Jeronimo,' Teresa said, sleepily, thinking of her own pretty mother.

'And it's killing her!' said Maria with a violence so that Teresa was startled into wakefulness again.

The elder girl, seeing the quick, puzzled glance, bit her lip.

'Marriage is a long way ahead for you,' she said, hastily, 'and I'm happy where I am. Now go to sleep.'

Teresa screwed her eyes up tightly, enjoying the coloured shapes that swam through the darkness. Sometimes she tried to make pictures in her mind, but she was never able to manage it, and when she opened her eyes the pretty colours melted away.

The bed sagged under Maria's firm body, and there was the pungent smell of melting wax as Maria leaned over to snuff the candle.

Teresa thought of the journey that lay ahead and felt a prickle of apprehension. To comfort herself, she said in her head some words her mother had once read to her. She had liked them so much she had learned them by heart.

'Said the Lover: O ye that love, if ye will have fire, come light your lanterns at my heart, if water, come to my eyes, whence flow the tears in streams; if thoughts of love, come gather them from my meditations.'

The man who wrote that had been, so Dona Beatriz said, murdered by the Moors in the year thirteen hundred and fifteen. Exactly two hundred years before I was born, Teresa thought, and tried to picture the same longing for heaven stretching between old Ramon Lull and the little daughter of Don Alonzo. Like a silver cord on a party dress, she thought, and fell asleep to the rhythm of her sister's breathing.

She awoke before dawn and slid out of bed, feeling for her clothes in the darkness and heroically repressing a yelp when she stubbed her toe against the bureau. It was hard to dress without assistance, but Rodrigo would help with the bits she had left undone. She took down her cloak from its hook and delved into her little cupboard for the raisins.

It was difficult to slide back the bolt on the garden door, but by dint of using both hands she managed it, and passed out into the orchard which joined and separated the two great houses. Trees and bushes loomed up, and she hesitated, wondering if Rodrigo would come. A moment later, he emerged at her side.

'We'll go through the Adaja gate and then towards the Salamanca bridge,' he said briskly.

'And then down to Africa,' she breathed, squeezing his hand in excitement.

'Are you sure you really want to go?' Rodrigo asked, stopping to peer into her face.

'I want to be a martyr,' Teresa said simply. 'A glorious one. And then we can fly up to heaven, without having to spend our lives doing good works.'

'Perhaps we'd better wait until we're a bit older,' he suggested.

'I want to go now; this minute.' Teresa's mouth set in an obstinate line.

Rodrigo, looking down at her, heaved a sigh. There was no arguing with Teresa in this mood. Instead he gripped her hand more tightly and set off down the narrow, flagged bridge towards the gate in the wall.

The sun was rising in a first promise of splendour as they trudged along the sandy river-road. Behind them, Avila rose in tiers above the rust-red walls, rays of sunshine catching gleams of gold and scarlet hues of the town banners.

The colours blurred in Teresa's tear-filled eyes. She had never been so far from home before, and the beauty of Avila mingled in her mind with the tenderness of her father's face when she noticed him looking at her, and the scent of jasmine in a room where her mother had been. The shores of Africa seemed a very long way away and her feet were already beginning to ache.

'Are you tired? Shall I carry you on my back?' Rodrigo asked.

She shook here head manfully and trudged on, shielding her face against the increasing heat with a corner of her cloak.

It was mid-morning when they neared the bridge and Rodrigo had already had most of the raisins. Teresa had fallen down twice and her face was streaked with dirt. She tried not to weep, but tears insisted on welling into her eyes and rolling down her cheeks. She asked hopefully if they were nearly there, but Rodrigo snapped at her to be quiet, and after that she didn't like to ask again.

Don Francisco de Cepeda, riding back to Avila after an overnight visit to Salamanca, reined in his horse and stared in astonishment at the two small figures, covered in white dust, who approached with dragging feet.

'Teresa? Rodrigo? What in the world are you doing so far from home?' he demanded.

Rodrigo shuffled his feet uncomfortably but Teresa looked trustfully at her big, bearded uncle.

'We're going to Africa,' she said.

'Africa! Why not the Indies or the Kingdom of Cathay?'

'We are going to proclaim ourselves as Christians and have our heads cut off and fly straight up to the glories of heaven,' Teresa explained brightly.

'It was the little one's idea,' Rodrigo said treacherously. 'She made me do it.'

'That's not fair!' the intending martyr said indignantly. 'You wanted to come as much as I did.'

'I think,' said Don Francisco, trying to look stern, 'that you had better take my place in the saddle while I lead you home. By the time we reach Avila your poor parents will imagine some terrible fate has befallen you.'

His prophecy proved correct. Servants were streaming out of the main gate as the odd little procession approached, and Don Alonzo himself, looking so haggard that Teresa began to cry all over again, hurried through the orchard.

'I found these two rascals on their way to Africa to get their heads cut off by the Moors,' Don Francisco explained.

'It was my idea,' said Teresa. 'I wanted to fly straight up to heaven.'

'Your mother was convinced that you had both fallen down

a well,' Don Alonzo said, coldly. 'She has made herself so ill that the physician had to be called. How could you bring yourselves to be so wicked?'

'I wanted to be a martyr,' Teresa said, dolefully.

'If martyrdom is offered we must accept it, but to go seeking it is a great sin,' Don Alonzo said. 'You, Rodrigo, should have known better, and for your thoughtlessness, you will be well beaten. Teresa, you will stay here and I will send Father Vicente out to you. Perhaps he may be able to bring to you some sense of guilt. Brother, will you step in for a tankard of wine? Beatriz has been confined to bed, but Maria will wish to express her gratitude to you.'

They went past her into the house and she was alone, with blistered feet and a desolate heart. Her legs ached so much that she sat down on one of the big rocks bordering the path, and sighed deeply. She had wanted so badly to reach those glories of heaven that Father Vicente was always talking about. Now she would have to wait until she was an old woman, and there were so many sins she might commit in the years ahead.

She had been piling the small stones at her feet into a heap, and now, as she looked down at them, the glimmerings of a new idea arose in her mind.

Father Vicente, entering the long-shadowed orchard in search of his charge, saw her on her knees before a pile of stones, and felt a keen stab of disappointment for he had not thought her so insensitive that she would begin to play within an hour of having her naughtiness discovered. But as he watched, the pile tumbled down and she turned such a woebegone face to him.

'Come, now, it's not the end of the world because your play is spoiled!'

'It isn't play, Father,' Teresa said. 'I am building a little house where I can spend my whole life praying to God.'

'A hermitage? Aren't you a trifle young to be considering such a life?'

'I wanted to be a martyr but I see now, you can't choose that,' Teresa explained. 'So I will become a hermit and then I can go straight up to heaven as soon as I die. Only – ' her lip trembled – 'my hermitage has fallen down and I haven't even got the roof on yet.'

'The stones you used were too small.' Father Vicente hitched up his cassock and knelt beside her. 'A building must have strong foundations, little one, else it will not stand. You cannot build with pebbles, and if you wish to erect a building for God, you need more than stones. You need training in discipline and prayer, and strong faith. Do you understand me, Teresa?'

'Come light your lanterns at my heart,' she murmured, and gave a sudden, sleepy yawn.

'Go in and beg your parents' forgiveness and ask for God's pardon also,' Father Vicente said. 'And do not try to grow up too quickly. Childhood too is a gift from heaven.'

Teresa, rubbing her smudged nose thoughtfully with a dusty finger, gave one last, regretful look at her hermitage and walked slowly towards the house.

CHAPTER TWO

Avila was rousing up from the afternoon siesta. Servants were folding back the sun-repelling shutters and bringing out trays piled with thirst-quenching peaches and slices of dewy melon.

In the market place, women were setting out their goods, chattering to one another over the piles of vegetables and bright-skinned fruit. A few urchins, dirty skin showing in the rents of their tattered garments, sprawled in the patches of shadow, watching with envious eyes as gallants, short cloaks swinging over their shoulders, rode past on gaily caparisoned horses.

In the shade of the great plane tree, two housewives rested their laundry baskets on the ground, and stared with pursed lips at the group of vividly dressed youngsters who flocked across the square. The boys, ear-rings and sword-hilts glinting, walked with all the arrogance of privileged youth. Their voices mingled with the lighter voices of the maidens, who held their skirts above the cobbles and laughed, slant-eyed, through their jewelled masks.

In the centre of the group, one girl, tinier than the others, had taken off her mask as if to dare the sun to do its worst with her delicate white skin. Her dark curls, touched with the red-gold tints of autumn beeches, cascaded below the veil of her mantilla. Her high, infectious laughter drew attention as much as the wide-skirted dress of orange brocade with its narrow pleated ruff of black lace and sleeves cut away at the elbow to reveal cuffs of silver. There were moonstones in her ears, and between her narrow, beringed hands she carried a pomander ball inlaid with mother of pearl.

Her voice floated across the square.

'Come, we'll go into the orchard and practise the algéria. Jeronima will teach us the steps!'

She had run ahead of the others now and was darting through the high arched gate beyond which the walls of a large house rose.

'Who is that?'

One of the gossiping housewives stared after the crowd of youngsters as they streamed after the tiny figure as eagerly as bees flock towards some exotic flower.

'Teresa y Ahumada. You remember Don Alonzo de Cepeda's little girl, don't you?'

'The round-eyed child who used to come to Mass with her older sister?'

'Half-sister,' corrected the other. 'Don Alonzo wed twice. The eldest son was killed in the French wars a couple of years ago. The girl was married last month to Señor Martin de Guzman. High time, for she's past twenty-six and has been betrothed for years, but of course, she was needed at home after her stepmother died.'

'Wasn't that Dona Beatriz y Ahumada?'

'Aye, poor soul.' The woman sighed sentimentally. 'Such a pale, pretty thing she was, and always ailing. Her ninth child killed her.'

'Does Don Alonzo allow his children to roam the streets?' her friend questioned in shocked tones.

'It's my guess he's gone over to Gotarrendura. His wife had property there which she left to her daughter, Teresa. The girl isn't sixteen yet, so can hardly be expected to administer her own estates.'

'If I were Don Alonzo de Cepeda, I'd marry her off as quickly as possible. She looks ripe for it,' the housewife commented, with a lewd nudge.

'She goes about with her brothers and cousins,' said the other. 'I've not heard of any particular suitor. In any event, where's the hurry? Teresa y Ahumada is pretty enough and wealthy enough to marry whom she chooses.'

The object of their conversation had settled herself on a bench in the orchard and was calling imperiously, 'Pedro!

Diego! Come and sit by me, and we will invent some round game while Jeronima and Rodrigo show us the steps.'

'It's too hot to dance,' Rodrigo said lazily, stretching out on the grass at Teresa's feet.

His sister leaned over and tickled his nose with a straw, while twelve-year-old Lorenzo shouted gleefully, 'And this is the great adventurer who wants to go to Peru with Hernando!'

Rodrigo cuffed his younger brother absentmindedly.

'Watch your tongue, youngling, or I'll not send for you when I've made my fortune.'

'I wish I could sail to the Indies,' Pedro grumbled.

'As a cabin boy? I can just see Father allowing it!' Teresa scoffed.

'Do you remember when we tried to run away to North Africa?' Rodrigo exclaimed.

'To become martyrs!' Hernando cried. 'You lost your taste for martyrdom after you'd had a taste of father's belt, didn't you, brother?'

'And Teresa's head is far too lovely to be separated from her shoulders!' Pedro Alvarez said.

'Is it, Pedro? Is it really?' Teresa looked at her cousin with shy eagerness.

'Very lovely,' Pedro said, blowing a strand of hair from the side of her face. Then he leaned forward and kissed her cheek. Her white skin flamed damask, and she looked at him for a moment with all her young heart in her eyes. But Pedro had sprung up and was laughing.

'You blush like a ninny, cousin. I'll wager Jeronima does not change colour when she's saluted in friendly fashion!'

'A test! A test!' cried the others, and Pedro caught his sister by her hands and leaned to kiss her cheek, but Jeronima moved her head and stood pressed mouth to mouth with him.

'Stop it! Stop it!' Teresa cried, and they drew apart, staring at her in amazement for her voice was ugly with pain.

'May I not kiss my own sister?' Pedro demanded.

'And not only his sister!' Jeronima mocked, twisting away and coming over to Teresa. 'Pedro practises his arts in other places too. Did you know – ?'

Her voice dropped to a whisper as she bent, cupping her hand about Teresa's ear and murmuring.

'That's enough, Jeronima. Leave the little one a few illusions about me,' Pedro ordered, and Jeronima straightened up, giggling, and held out her hand to Diego.

'The algéria! We must be perfect at it before the ball,' cried Inés, and they began to form into couples.

'Are you feeling well, Teresa?' Lorenzo whispered, slipping his hand into hers and peering anxiously up into her face.

The white line around her mouth faded and she dimpled at him, showing her pretty teeth.

'Come and dance with me, little brother!' she said, gaily. But they had taken only a few steps when Rodrigo and Pedro caught her between them and whirled her, orange skirts flying, up and down the grass.

At the far end of the orchard, a servant had appeared and stood waiting, with a sly, expectant look.

'It looks as if we were seen leaving the house,' Hernando said, wryly.

'If Father discovers we went to inspect the bulls, he'll be furious,' Rodrigo said, apprehensively.

'Then stop the man's mouth with ducats. You still have some of last month's allowance left,' Hernando suggested.

'Always my purse. Never yours,' Rodrigo grumbled.

'I've better things to do with my money than bribe servants,' Hernando yawned, putting his arm around his cousin Beatriz.

Teresa was dancing again, snapping her fingers and stamping her heels on the flagged path, as she twisted and turned in the intricate flamenco. Inés clapped softly in time to the beat.

Lorenzo, watching, cried proudly, 'My sister is the best dancer in Castile.'

'And deserves the best partner,' Pedro said, beginning to rise again, but she eluded him and went, half-dancing, half-running, down the path, between the tall cypresses to the grove of lemon trees behind the wall.

There was a well here, deep and echoing, protected by a stone rim where a dolphin sprayed water through its ever-open mouth. Teresa pushed up her cuffs and held her hands under the jetting liquid. The drops were cool and sparkling, and in the basin of the fountain tiny pebbles gleamed like jewels. She scooped up a handful but their beauty vanished and the little stones were grey and cold, their rainbow brilliance gone.

There was, she thought, something in water to suit every mood, whether tranquil or stormy, and water lent loveliness to things that were themselves not lovely at all. Or had the beauty been hidden in the pebbles all the time, waiting to be revealed in an unfamiliar setting? She dropped the stones and saw her own hand, caught in a ray of sunshine, so that she seemed for a moment to be wearing golden gloves.

'What are you dreaming about?' Pedro asked, kneeling down behind her.

'I was wondering who I was,' she said slowly.

'Why, you're Dona Teresa Sanchez y Cepeda Davilla y Ahumada,' he began, grandly teasing.

'And who is Teresa?' she asked. 'This hand is part of Teresa but if I were to cut it off, Teresa would still exist. If I had my heart cut out, Teresa would no longer be, I suppose, or would she be changed into something new and strange, like pebbles under the water?'

'I don't know what on earth you're talking about,' her cousin said.

'Nonsense. Just nonsense! My brain is full of moonshine today.' She turned towards him, laughing at her own foolishness.

'Will you dance with me tomorrow?' he demanded.

'Not if you flirt all the time with Juana Suarez,' she warned. 'It was quite shocking, the way you hung about her at the bull-fight last week. I'm sure people were talking about it.'

'As Juana Suarez intends to take the veil in a few months' time, I think I'm fairly safe, hanging about her, as you put it,' Pedro argued.

'I know. Isn't it dreadful?' Teresa looked at him, with pity for her friend all over her face. 'And she actually *wants* to be a nun! She cannot imagine anything better for herself than being shut up for the rest of her life, and never having any fun!'

'And she is very pretty, enough to catch a husband,' Pedro agreed.

'Marriage?' A tiny frown creased her brow.

'Well, it's either that or a nunnery, unless a girl wants to be an old spinster, and have everybody laugh at her,' said Pedro.

'I wish girls could sail to the Indies,' Teresa said wistfully. 'Think of the gold and silver out there, and the unusual fruits, and the Indians all painted and feathered. Wouldn't it be marvellous to see it?'

'Castile is wide enough for me.'

Pedro jumped up and held out his hand, but when she stretched out her own fingers he pulled her so close that their breaths mingled.

'You're very pretty,' he said huskily, and for a moment she felt a great leap of desire within her breast so that her heart somersaulted and her legs became unsteady. For a moment only, and then she had torn herself free, and was running back towards the others so swiftly that she looked as if she were trying to escape from her own shadow.

The orchard was silent and one glance told her why they stood, demurely mute. Don Alonzo had returned from Gotarrendura and faced them gravely, his black mourning suit, which he had refused to brighten even for his daughter's wedding, emphasizing the deeply carven line from his nose to his mouth.

'Pedro, Diego, Beatriz, Jeronima, Inés – have you no home of your own that you must raise such a din in the garden of mine?' he began.

His nephews and nieces began to drift away sheepishly.

'Teresa, my dear.' His voice automatically softened as he turned to his daughter. 'The sun will burn you brown if you expose yourself to it so thoughtlessly. Go to the library and wait for me there. I have something very serious to say to you.'

Her wild gaiety stilled, Teresa went slowly towards the house. As she climbed the stairs to the long, low-ceilinged room where her father spent so many hours, she heard the youngest of the children laughing and chattering in the nursery below. At any other time she might have looked in, to bounce a ball to four-year-old Agustin, or to let three-year-old Juana, named for her dead half-brother, play with her ear-rings. But her father was not accustomed to be kept waiting.

Neither was she kept waiting herself, for scarcely had she entered the library when she heard Don Alonzo's firm tread on the stair behind her, and a moment later they stood face to face.

Don Alonzo, punctiliously well-mannered even with his immediate family, bowed slightly and took his place in a carved chair. Opposite him, Teresa fixed an innocent expression upon her face, and tried not to look as if she was thinking about the visit to the bulls earlier in the afternoon.

'Well, Teresa, have you anything to say to me?' Don Alonzo began.

'Father?'

'Have you anything to say to me?' he repeated.

'About what, Father?'

Don Alonzo banged the palm of his hand against the side of his chair.

'I want you to tell me about it yourself and save me the pain of accusing you,' he said, sternly.

Teresa stared at her father in bewilderment.

'If you're angry because we went to see the bulls,' she hesitated, 'then I beg your pardon, Father, but we all went together, and it's a short distance, and it was such a lovely day.'

'I know nothing about bulls,' Don Alonzo said coldly. 'I am talking about books, Teresa.'

'Books?'

'Aye, filthy Provençal rubbish, smuggled back into this house after I gave orders all such works were to be banned. It was found and brought to me. Apparently you persuaded one of the servants to bring it to you.'

'But it is only romantic poetry,' Teresa said. 'There's no harm in it, Father.'

'No harm? No harm in the tale of a girl seduced and betrayed by a rascally knight?'

'But it's only a story!' she protested. 'Things like that don't happen now.'

'They don't happen because fathers are careful for their daughters' honour and keep such trash away from them!'

'But to read about such things doesn't mean one has to do them,' Teresa argued.

'It is the next step,' her father said. 'And I've heard talk – I pray it is not true – that you and your brother, Rodrigo, have actually tried to write one of these so-called romances yourself.'

'We gave it up,' Teresa said, quickly.

'At least you showed some moral sense,' Don Alonzo began.

'We couldn't find enough rhymes to vary the couplets,' she interrupted, reluctantly honest.

'Teresa, what can I say to you?' He stroked his beard and stared at her with anguish in his eyes.

'I don't think a few little love poems are so harmful. Mother read them,' Teresa said defiantly.

'How dare you!' Don Alonzo's rare rage erupted. 'How dare you compare yourself with your mother? She was the sweetest, most obedient wife a man could have, and would die of shame now if she could know that her one fault had lived on in her daughter and given rise to such sin! Did your dear mother ring her innocent eyes with charcoal or rub rice paper upon her fair skin? Did she walk in the public street with her face uncovered? Did she raise such a noise of dancing and laughter in the garden that I could hear from the front gate?'

'But times are different now,' Teresa sobbed. 'You are old, Father, and don't know the new fashion.'

'And God forbid that I or any of my family should begin to learn it. I have seen the harm that is done when girls are left to amuse themselves as they please, to neglect their prayers and needlework, to show their faces in public, swinging their skirts and letting the world see their feet.'

'I don't neglect my needlework or my prayers,' Teresa said sulkily.

'But you read foolish books, and chatter and laugh too loudly, and now you tell me something about bulls. Did you go out to see the bulls today?'

She nodded, blinking water from her long eyelashes.

'Why cannot you be like your sister, Maria?' he asked, almost pleadingly. 'She was always such a good girl. So gentle and quiet. Why could you not follow her advice and stay secure at home as she did until it was time for her marriage?'

'Because I am not like Maria,' Teresa said, seeking a gleam of understanding.

'No, you are not. There never was any evil in your sister,' Don Alonzo said, so sadly that she was filled suddenly with a wild dread. 'You were such a sweet child. Such a sweet, funny child. You were my favourite of them all, dearer to me than the rest of my children. When you were very little you used to dress up your dolls as nuns and stand before them, wagging your finger and lecturing them on their faults. On the day your mother died, I found you at the feet of our little Madonna, talking softly to her, begging her to take you under her protection.'

'But I haven't done anything bad,' Teresa cried. 'I'm sorry, truly sorry, about reading those books and going out without permission, but I meant no harm. I only wanted a little freedom, Father. Hernando and Rodrigo may go where they please, but I must sit at home as if I were dead and laid away in lavender!'

'Freedom? So that you might unleash the evil in your soul? Don't you know that women are so feeble and full of sin that it is necessary to guard them closely? I cannot believe you are so blind!'

She tried to speak, but her tears were choking her.

'I blame myself,' said Don Alonzo, heavily. 'I blame myself for having neglected you while I tended to my business. It is only by the mercy of God that your reputation is not in shreds, and when a maid loses her good name, her life is ruined. No decent man will wed her; the shadow of her shame touches all her family. And more important than that, Teresa, her very soul is seized by the devil and tossed to and fro in his grappling hooks.'

He rose and put his arm about her shoulders.

'I cannot believe that you have as yet sinned gravely,' he said in a kinder tone. 'But can you truly look into your own heart and tell me there is no evil there?'

There flashed into her mind Jeronima's sniggering, only half-comprehended whisper, mingled with the remembered leap of her heart when Pedro touched her hand. Was that what her father was talking about? Were those half-wild, half-sweet urges of feeling temptations of the horned one? Had Maria ever known such thoughts, bubbling half-formed below the surface of her mind? But Maria was good and gentle and had taken a pure heart to her wedding.

'You cannot answer me,' Don Alonzo said. 'It is as I feared. You are in grave danger and it is fortunate that I have already taken steps to prevent it.'

'Steps?'

'I enrolled you today as a boarder in the convent school of Our Lady of Grace. You leave tonight.'

'A convent! To be locked up and shut away! No, Father, no!'

Horrified, she began to struggle against his restraining arm.

'A school, Teresa. You cannot imagine I would force you to become a nun against your will?' Now it was his turn to plead for understanding. 'You will be happy there, my love. The Augustinian Sisters are kind.'

'They are old hags who have forgotten what it was like to be young!' Teresa cried passionately.

'The headmistress is a saint. When I spoke to her last week –'

'Last week? You have been plotting to send me away since last week?'

'Dona Maria de Briceño has agreed to take you as a pupil for a year,' Don Alonzo said inexorably.

'A year? A whole year?'

'Teresa, don't cry so much. A year is not very long.'

'But you said I was to go tonight? You didn't mean it, did you? You'll let me wait a month or two? You cannot have forgotten that the Empress Isabella is bringing her little prince to Avila to be breeched in a few days' time. You know all the balls and parties that have been arranged? It's the height of the season, Father!'

'I know it well and that is why you leave tonight,' Don Alonzo said grimly. 'If I left you open to any more occasions of sin, who knows what might happen?'

'People will gossip. They will think that I am being sent away because I have been wicked.'

'We will let it be known that your health is too delicate for the strain of the festivities,' Don Alonzo soothed. 'And now that Maria is married, it is not fitting that you should stay here without a duenna.'

'But I will miss all the excitement, all the gaiety!' she wept.

'And that is all you can regret?' Her father looked at her with deep disappointment. 'Have you no word of apology for your disobedience, for your vanity, for your foolishness?'

'I did apologize for all that,' she said, sulkily. 'I'd be so good if you'd let me stay at home, Father. Won't you?'

She let her tone slide into pathos but when he shook his head, the pathos became genuine sorrow and she sank down on the chair vacated by her father and wept bitterly, her hands shielding her trembling mouth.

Her eyelids were still puffy later in the day when she alighted from her pony in the narrow street outside the high-walled convent. There had been no time to bid farewell to her cousins, scarcely time to grip her brothers' hands or kiss Juana. The rest of the family had watched in silent sympathy but not even Rodrigo had dared to protest. Instead they had all tactfully pretended to believe that she was going away because it was felt she was unequal to the strain of the forthcoming celebrations.

It would serve them right, Teresa thought mutinously, if I did fall sick and die. Then they would be sorry for me.

She was so sorry for herself that she managed to squeeze out a few more tears, as she stood waiting for the nail-studded door to open. By her side, Don Alonzo stood immovable, not betraying by the flicker of a muscle what it cost him, for conscience' sake, to take this step. Teresa was his darling but there was in her that undisciplined gaiety he had gently and successfully checked in her mother. Only Dona Beatriz had never openly cried out for freedom. Freedom indeed! What use could any woman have for freedom? It was, Don Alonzo decided, one of those crazy modern ideas against which all right-thinking men must set their faces, and, so deciding, he took a firm grip on his daughter's arm and led her inside as the door opened.

There was a blur of white in the narrow hall and a voice spoke, cool and clipped, out of the shadow.

'Good evening, Don Alonzo de Cepeda. Dona Teresa y Ahumada? Will you wait in there, my daughter?'

'We'll say goodbye now, Teresa. I will come and see you as soon as you are settled. You will be a good child and make me proud of you?'

His tone was almost pleading and because she loved him even though she didn't understand him, she nodded and put up her face to be kissed.

But when the door of the apartment had closed behind her, rebellion surged up in her again. The softly lit room – she thought of it as gloomy – was panelled in dark wood and there was a statue in the corner, placed so that light from the angled windows fell upon the haloed head and the small hands clasped in everlasting acceptance. For a moment, the girl looked at it with reluctant yearning, and then she turned away impatiently and frowned at a delicate carving of two cherubs' heads decorating the opposite wall. When the door behind her opened and closed again, she remained with her back to the voice which drifted, sweet as honey-wine, across the room.

'Teresa, my daughter? It is a great joy to have you here among us.'

She turned, drawn by the sweetness, and looked, with a dying defiance, at the slim figure, all black save for the startling pallor of hands and face and the dull silver of a cross at the narrow waist. She was unaware of the picture she herself made as she waited there with her curls springing impishly from her hood and her gay orange dress challenging the austerity of her surroundings.

She wanted to cry out that it was not a joy for her to be there, that she intended to hate every minute of her enforced stay, and that she did not fully understand what she had done that was so terrible. But because it came naturally to her to please people, she lowered her eyes and submitted to a cool, unscented embrace.

'Dona Maria de Briceño?' she questioned.

'I am in charge of the young ladies here,' the other nodded. 'They are at supper now and in a moment we will join them.

There is great excitement among them at the prospect of a new companion. Do you sing and dance, my child?'

'A little,' Teresa admitted.

'Then you will be an asset at recreation,' the nun said cordially.

Teresa gaped at her in astonishment. 'Surely it was for excessive levity that she had been sent to this place! Yet this woman was apparently encouraging such gaiety. It could only mean that there was no harm in such pursuits for most young girls, but that in Teresa herself there was such a capacity for evil that she must guard herself more carefully than most against the vanities of the world. Guilt and shame mingled in her mind, together with dull, burning resentment, against her father who was so ready to think evil of her, against Pedro who had half-awakened her desires, and most of all against herself, so fair on the outside and so twisted and ugly within.

Dona Maria couldn't help wondering what had led Don Alonzo de Cepeda to describe his weeping daughter as undisciplined and in need of strict correction. The girl was small for her age with a too sensitive lower lip and loving look under the taut misery of her expression, and she had nervous, slender hands twisting the brilliant brocade of her gown.

'As it is so late, perhaps it would be better if you ate your supper in here and met the other girls in the morning,' she said tactfully, taking no further notice of Teresa's sobs. 'We do our needlework and practise our music after Mass, and study languages and the principles of our faith later in the day; but you will soon accustom yourself to our ways.'

Teresa nodded and tried to smile.

If I grow accustomed to such a life, she thought, then you might as well bury me and be done with it, for by then I will be dead, and there will be no more longings for green orchards and freedom to roam where I choose.

CHAPTER THREE

'I always said cousin Teresa would turn into a beauty,' Francisco de Cepeda remarked complacently to his wife.

Maria de Ocampo, secure in her own warm fecundity, nodded without jealousy.

'At twenty-one it is time she settled down with a husband,' Maria remarked.

'She is mistress of my uncle's house. Why should she be in a hurry to exchange it for another?' Francisco asked.

His wife glanced with a hint of complacency over to where three tiny girls played in the orchard.

'I thought your brother, Pedro, admired her,' she said casually.

'Cousins cannot marry,' he reminded her.

'It's not too difficult to obtain a dispensation.' Maria yawned and reached for a grape. 'It's my opinion that your brother will never marry if Teresa won't have him.'

'My sister, Beatriz, told me that Teresa was considering the religious life,' Francisco said.

'Isn't it enough,' Maria asked tartly, 'that Beatriz should persuade Ana and Inés to follow her into the convent?'

'My sister Maria also intends to take the veil,' Francisco said.

'Mad as hatters, all of them.'

His wife, rosy in the fifth month of her fourth pregnancy, laughed with a touch of pity.

'It looks as if only Diego and I will give my father grandchildren,' Francisco said, thoughtfully. 'Jeronima will certainly never wed. No man would put up with her tongue-lashings. And Vicente is too shy to pluck up courage to talk to a lady let alone propose to her.'

'I am glad you had more courage than your brother,' she said softly, and they looked at each other for a moment.

Then Maria returned to her earlier theme, with the slightly peevish air of a happily married and fruitful woman who cannot understand why all her sex do not rush to embrace the same fate.

'Fancy Beatriz imagining that Teresa would ever hide herself behind convent walls! Why, it's your cousin's duty to wed and beget children as lovely as herself. Your uncle would agree with me, I'm sure.'

'I know he would. Beatriz told me that he refused to consider the idea of Teresa's becoming a Carmelite. He thinks the life will be too much for her health.'

'It seems to me that the nuns down at the Incarnation Convent have a very easy time of it,' Maria said. 'Your sisters are forever coming home on visits and the last time I went there I could scarcely get into the parlour for all the young gentlemen who had thronged to gossip.'

'You sound as if you envied them,' Francisco teased.

'I do, except for one thing,' she retorted lovingly. 'They are not married to you!'

'Then tell Teresa that,' Francisco said, 'for here she comes now.'

She came, treading daintily in her thin slippers, through the door that divided the two orchards, and Maria de Ocampo watched, half-envious and half-admiring. Teresa dressed so cleverly, always in colours that reminded one of sunlight – amber, saffron, orange and yellow. Against the buttercup gown she wore today, her white skin looked faintly golden as if she had dusted herself with pollen, and heavy emerald rings dangled from her small ears.

'I brought some lemons over,' she said, putting down a wicker basket on the table between the two stools in the porch. 'The season will soon be gone, with all the trees bare and winter closing us in. You are looking very handsome today, Maria.'

'Because Francisco is with me,' Maria said. 'I never feel remotely good-looking when my husband is absent.'

'Oh, fortunate damsel!' Teresa said, lightly, wondering briefly if she herself would enjoy living in the reflection of a masculine sun.

The three tiny girls had abandoned their play and ran up to Teresa, pulling with small, impatient hands at her skirt and loudly demanding a story.

'Dona Teresa is too busy to be bothered with you now,' Francisco began, but Teresa laughed, shaking her head, and joined the children, taking the youngest on her knee and spreading wide her skirts so that the others could cuddle close to her sides.

'A story! Tell us a story!' demanded Leonor.

'About what, little one?'

'About when you were young,' the little girl said, imperiously.

'That was such a long time ago that I've almost forgotten what it was like,' Teresa said, solemnly.

'Then tell us anything. Just talk,' said Maria, leaning her head against the older girl's arm and preparing to enjoy the sound of the clear voice, rising and falling in gentle cadences.

'Well, there was once a lady,' Teresa said, slowly, 'who had a garden.'

'A big one?' asked Beatriz.

'No, just a small one. But when she saw how thin and dry the soil was and how hard it would be to make flowers and fruit grow there, the garden looked very big indeed. So big that she knew it would take her a very long time every day to water it.'

'But didn't the lady have any servants?' Leonor asked, in astonishment.

'Yes, indeed. But she wanted to tend the garden all by herself, so that it would be completely her own.'

'So what did she do?'

'First of all she drew buckets of water from the well and threw the water over the dry soil; and the soil drank it up thirstily and wanted more. So the poor lady spent hours and hours letting the bucket down into the well and carrying the full buckets into the garden. She had no time left in which to do anything else. No time to cook, or to spin, or to weave –'

'No time to eat!' Maria said, with a horrified look on her small, flowerlike face.

Teresa dimpled at her and went on.

'To save time, the lady had a windlass and a rope fitted, so that she could draw up the water more easily. She saved a little time in that way, but there were still not enough hours in the day to do all the other things she wanted to do. So she had to find a quicker way.'

'What did she do? What did she do?' Beatriz chanted.

'A river ran past the garden, and she diverted its course so that it thrust a number of streams into the heart of the soil.'

'All by herself? She must have been a very large lady!' Leonor exclaimed.

'She told the servants to help her, I suppose,' Teresa conceded, 'and after that the little streams wound their way through the garden and watered it when the river ran high. But sometimes the river ran low and then the soil became dry again.'

'So where did she get the water then?' asked Maria.

'Why, from the sky,' Teresa said gaily. 'Our Lord looked down from heaven and saw how long and hard she had worked, so He sent rain down upon the garden and the fruit and the flowers grew, and the lady was completely happy.'

'That was a pretty story,' said Maria, contentedly.

'I can't see why our Lord didn't send down rain in the first place and save her all that trouble,' Leonor said sceptically.

'Because He expects us to strive for what we need,' Teresa began.

'But strive as we may, we do not always get what we want,' said another voice.

The little girls jumped up at once to greet their uncle who shooed them back to their parents and then held out his hand to assist his cousin to her feet.

'Well, Teresa!' he said.

'Well, Pedro?' She drew away imperceptibly, and smiled brightly at him.

'Is it true that we don't always get what we want?'

'What we may want may not be what we need,' Teresa said, moving back towards the gate.

'I need you, Teresa,' Pedro said.

'Yes, of course. A handsome gallant like yourself needs the admiration of all ladies. My brother, Lorenzo, has the same complaint. He is never happy unless six ladies swoon away when he walks down the street.'

'I don't want six ladies to swoon over me,' Pedro said. 'I want you to love me, Teresa.'

'But I do! I do! I love all my family. You are my dear cousin.'

'Only that? No more than cousin? It's four years since you came back from the convent school and I've been patient and waited, saying nothing. Teresa, is it only as cousin you think of me? Only as that?'

She had known for months that this moment would come, had tried desperately to fend it off, but now she was suddenly unprepared and trembling. She ran her tongue round the inside of her lips and looked at him piteously.

'It's four years,' he repeated. 'I never looked seriously at any girl after you came home.'

'We're cousins, within the degree of forbidden kinship.'

'And dispensation may be obtained in such cases. I asked Father Vicente –'

'You had no right to discuss such matters!' Teresa cried, the ready colour flaming into her face.

'But our marriage would please the whole family,' he coaxed. 'Won't you give me an answer, Teresa? Surely you owe it to us both to make your plans clear, or do you find it amusing to keep me dangling like a fish at the end of a bit of string?

Or maybe –' his voice rose a trifle – 'you think yourself too good for me.'

'Too good? Oh, Pedro, if you only knew.'

If you only knew, her thoughts ran, how great is the capacity for evil in me! If you only knew what it's like to be gnawed day and night by temptations I don't even understand, by impulses tearing at me like wild beasts. And marriage? The idea of marriage fills me – has always filled me – with horror, as if in some small corner of my mind where reason cannot penetrate, I know that my destiny is to be different. But how? If I don't marry then I must either go into a nunnery or stay at home. And if I stay at home, who will help me then to root out the evil in my nature? How can I avoid the hell that is waiting for me unless I punish myself so pitilessly in this life that God holds out some hope of mercy in the next?

'Teresa?' Pedro was asking, alarmed at the bright emptiness of her eyes.

'No, Pedro. No,' she said in a low, hurried voice and went swiftly into her father's orchard, lifting her bright skirts and never turning her head.

There was a tang of autumn in the air and a log fire had been lit in the hall. Teresa paused to warm her hands, for she was as cold as if she had just escaped some great danger.

'Have you time to play with me, Teresa?' Juana said, from the corner of the apartment.

She wanted to be alone, to examine her own heart, to strengthen her half-formed decision; but her sister was pulling coaxingly at her sleeve and this might be the last time she would ever romp with her. Certainly it must be the last time she saw Pedro. If she allowed herself to meet him again, she might allow herself to be drawn into a betrothal that would be a disaster for them both. She knew, and it pained her to know, that her warm affection for Pedro was not enough on which to base a marriage, and yet when he looked at her she could almost persuade herself that she loved him.

And he deserves better than that, she thought fiercely, beginning to put a gown on the little doll that Juana held out. Pedro needs a woman who will love him completely and submit to him absolutely, not one with her eyes fixed on the unseen and her ears attuned to a silent whisper.

The wooden arms of the doll were stiff and resisted her fingers as she tried to thrust them into the armholes of the tiny embroidered dress.

If I stay at home, sooner or later, Father will force me into marriage, she reflected, but if I go into the convent of the Incarnation I can avoid that. I cannot resist the temptations of the world, and so it is best for me to leave the world.

And do you think you will endure such a life? said the mocking voice of Reason. *Your health is delicate, or have you forgotten those headaches and fainting fits that made your last months at school so miserable? And how can you, with your love for your family, endure to leave them?*

My cousins, Maria and Beatriz and Inés are at the convent. So is my best friend, Juana Suarez, she argued silently. And my father will be able to visit me. The nuns have their own rooms furnished as they choose, and they pay long visits to their own relatives to lift the burden on the community.

Ah! you intend to be a half-and-half nun, with one foot in each world and your heart nowhere, Self-knowledge said scornfully. *Precious little use you'll be in either place.*

But I am useless already, she thought miserably. When I was at school I longed to taste freedom, and now that I am at home I fear that same freedom. Souls like mine need to be chained for their own protection otherwise they will sink too low to rise again.

And what, pray, have you done to be ashamed about? Reason inquired. *If it is mortal sin to enjoy pretty clothes and get flattery and cherish one's independence, which of us will get to heaven?*

These things do no harm to other people, her nature cried, but for me they are wrong. I feel they are wrong.

'You're dull today, Teresa,' Juana complained.

'Am I, darling? I'm sorry.'

Teresa laid down the doll and hugged her sister remorsefully. Juana was so little and gentle, in contrast to her brothers, that she was apt to be overlooked.

What will happen to her when I am gone? Teresa thought, in anguish. Who will play with her, and tell her stories, and tuck her up in bed at night?

She remembered her half-sister, Maria, whom she had visited the previous summer. Maria was past thirty now and as placid as ever, but there was no fantasy in her nature. She would not know how to enter into a child's world of terror and romance. For her there were no hobgoblins nor kindly fairies, and when Juana woke crying from a nightmare she would probably recommend a dose of rhubarb physic.

And the boys? Who would restrain Agustin's high spirits, or check Jeronimo's tendency to stuff himself with sweets, or help Pedro with his history lesson, or listen sympathetically when Lorenzo confided the latest boyish infatuation? And Antonio? At sixteen, this brother was the gentlest of them all; so eager to please that the merest breaths of opinion would send him veering from side to side. Who would guard Antonio's interests?

I will have to take him with me, Teresa decided.

As if her thoughts had called him, Antonio, small and thin for his age, with the heavy lidded eyes of a dreamer, came into the hall. Juana had taken her doll over to the straw baskct that served as cradle and was patting it into place.

'I saw cousin Pedro a moment ago, riding across the square as if he were off to war,' Antonio remarked. 'Have you quarrelled with him, Teresa?'

She shook her curly head.

'I have made up my mind never to see him again,' she said, almost absently. But when he said nothing, she asked, 'Was I right, Antonio? Was I right to decide that?'

Her brother looked at her in faint surprise. Surely Teresa knew that every single action she took was perfect in his eyes.

'It's the only thing you could have done,' he said fervently.

'You know how we have talked, Antonio, about entering the religious life,' Teresa whispered.

'Yes. We've often talked of it.'

'The time for talking is over now,' she said. 'It's time for us to leave.'

'To leave!' He started up and then glanced towards Juana who was playing with her doll, oblivious to the conversation of her elders. Nevertheless, he lowered his voice slightly as he repeated, 'Leave? Teresa, you know Father will never give his permission. He has refused to discuss the idea.'

'We cannot wait for permission,' Teresa said tensely. 'We must go together, secretly. We knew, didn't we, that sooner or later we might have to do that.'

'We talked about it,' Antonio said doubtfully. 'But to disobey Father! Teresa, is it right for us to do that?'

'When God calls us to His service, we cannot refuse. His authority exceeds all earthly power, including the rights of a parent. You are still of the same mind, aren't you?'

'Yes, of course,' Antonio said hastily. 'If you intend to enter the Carmelite Order I will enter the Dominican Order. What pleasure could there be in the world for me when you had left it?'

'But it's not solely on my account that you want a monastic life, is it?' she asked anxiously.

'I made up my own mind, after talking to you,' Antonio said, loftily.

'And you didn't want to follow Hernando and Rodrigo to the Indies?'

He closed his mind against a brief, tantalizing picture of white sails spread above a blue sea with a palm-fringed horizon drawing nearer, and shook his head, gazing at his sister with something very like adoration.

'The religious life calls me,' he said firmly. 'I will leave when you leave, Teresa, even if Father doesn't give his permission. And he won't, you know. He will never agree.'

'Then we will not ask,' Teresa said, and her lips closed in a tight line that Rodrigo would have recognized.

There was no evidence of strain in her manner later that night when she stood beside her father to bid the younger members of the family good night. But her heart ached when Juana put up her small arms.

'Will you play with me for a longer time tomorrow?' she whispered.

'Not tomorrow, sweeting,' Don Alonzo put in. 'Tomorrow we are entertaining your cousins to supper. Your sister will need the entire afternoon to choose and discard a dozen gowns before she decides upon the one that will flatter her most.'

He turned a smiling glance upon his elder daughter but her own look was suddenly panic-stricken. To have her cousins in the house, to be forced to talk and laugh with them, perhaps even to dance for them because Don Alonzo was fond of music after supper – she didn't think that she would be able to bear it.

Juana was already asleep, curled into a tight ball with her thumb in her mouth, when Teresa finally sought her bed. Her father's good-night caress and his affectionate, 'Sleep well,' had made her want to weep, but she had restrained her tears. What use were tears when a lifetime of weeping lay ahead?

And I deserve it, she thought fiercely. I am fit for nothing except hell. So I will spend the rest of my life as if I were already there. Unfit for life or death, incapable of love, afraid of marriage, resentful of the cloister! Why was I ever created?

When dawn broke her question was still unanswered, but her resolve had hardened into a stubborn determination. She had not undressed but the morning was cold so she put a heavy cloak over her dress, cast one look at the sleeping child and went softly through the quiet passages to the garden door. Antonio was already waiting in obedience to her hurried whisper of the previous night.

Teresa envied her brother his look of suppressed excitement, and remembered wistfully that other dawn which now seemed so long ago, when she and Rodrigo had set out together to seek martyrdom. There had been more than a spice of mischief in that adventure, she now realized, but the desire to suffer had been genuine. And God had rejected her. Not for Teresa the grace of a quick death and a speedy ascent to the glories of heaven, but, for her, a slow death behind high convent walls, where her soul might in the end discover some measure of safety.

Early as it was, several housewives were already on their way to market. Others, mantillas drawn demurely over their foreheads, stepped briskly to Mass in one or other of the many churches from which bells were already ringing in the new day.

The boy in the grey tunic and the girl in the dark cloak attracted not a second glance. Many youngsters went to church every morning, some to pray, others to make eyes over the tops of their missal at their fancy of the moment while they made plans to linger after the service, perhaps in the hope of receiving a hastily scrawled note or a half-open bloom, to be pressed lovingly between the pages of a book.

When they reached the Convent of the Incarnation, Teresa broke the silence between them.

'Antonio?' she said tremulously.

'I'll go on alone to the monastery,' the boy said, so cheerfully that she felt sick with shame at her own sudden feeling of repulsion as they stood before the grilled door. 'I want to thank you, sister, before we part, for choosing me as the one worthy to be your companion.'

'Antonio, dear Antonio.'

She laid her cheek against his for a brief moment and then, before she could weaken, drew away and pulled the rope hanging down the side of the door. The loud jangling seemed a fitting accompaniment to the confused rush of feelings that brought with them such pain that she knew the sensation of having her heart torn out of her breast.

'Deo Gratias,' a slightly surprised voice answered from behind the grille.

'It is Dona Teresa y Ahumada, Sister,' she said loudly closing her ears to the sound of Antonio's retreating footsteps 'I wish to be admitted into the community.'

If they turn me away, she thought, I will know that I am finally rejected.

Yet the slow drawing back of the bolts brought no joy but only a deepening of her misery.

With a strange dream-like feeling, she passed into the enclosure, seeing for the first time that cool and confined world that shielded its occupants from the temptations of the wider world beyond. Faces in white wimples floated towards her and voices came disjointed out of the surrounding mist.

'Somebody must send word to your father, my dear, for you cannot receive the habit until you have his permission to enter.'

'Two rooms are available for you if you can afford to rent them. The Rule here is not harsh, but you may sleep in the communal dormitory if you wish to mortify yourself.'

'Dona Teresa de Querida is extremely wealthy but she uses the communal dormitory so that she may attain greater sanctity.'

'Dona Juana Suarez is already a close friend of yours, isn't she?'

'So nice for you to be with your cousins!'

'Do you know Dona Quiteria Davila?'

'You must meet Dona Maria Magdalena.'

'Is is true that your brother, Lorenzo, has become one of the handsomest young men in Castile?'

'Have you had word recently from your brothers in the Indies?'

'Such a pretty dress! I'm wild about the colour.'

And out of the confusion, Juana Suarez with her firm hand-clasp and her sensible, friendly voice.

'Come and sit down, Teresa. We are not always as noisy as this, I assure you, but if you will insist on joining us in such a dramatic fashion you must expect to create something of a sensation. Did you come out with no breakfast? I'll get you something.'

'I'm not hungry,' Teresa said, bewildered by the swirling habits and the constant chatter. 'I assumed there would be silence and fasting.'

'Oh, there's fasting, when the supplies run short,' Juana Suarez said dryly. 'This is a large community and a poor one. As for silence, the Grand Silence is kept, naturally, but how can anyone prevent nearly two hundred women from gossiping whenever the Mother Prioress's back is turned?'

'Somebody mentioned private rooms,' Teresa hinted, wondering how on earth she was to achieve silence and solitude in such a place.

'Your father will pay for a cell and an oratory for you, I'm sure,' her friend said, comfortably. 'You know, I never thought you were serious about joining us. I always imagined that you and Pedro – '

'No!' Teresa said sharply. 'I have made up my mind to the religious life.'

'Very well, dear, but there's no need for you to sound so grim about it,' Juana Suarez said, amused.

A sweet-faced nun with a careworn expression interrupted them.

'Welcome to the Incarnation, Dona Teresa y Ahumada. I am your namesake, Dona Teresa de Querida.'

'Teresa? Did I hear you say Teresa?' An old nun, bent over a stick, shuffled across the floor towards them. 'These new-fangled names! Yet I heard that name long ago, before your time, when I was younger.'

'Mother of God, isn't it time that somebody explained to our reverend sister that old age doesn't automatically confer the privilege of boring everybody else to death?' another yawned.

'An old man stopped here one day whilst he was journeying,' the elderly nun said, ignoring the interruption. 'I remember we gave him some food. He told us he was a zahvri – what we would call a diviner for gold. But he'd fallen on hard days and needed charity. I recall his saying, "I wish I could repay you for your kindness," and one of the sisters, oh! she's dead long since but she had quite a sense of humour! said, "What a pity you can't divine a little pot of gold for us!" And the old man laughed and said, "I can't promise you gold, but I can promise you a saint will be professed here one day, and her name will be Teresa." Of course, we all smiled at that for everybody knows there's never been a saint of that name, but he was quite definite about it. I've often wondered since.'

There was an odd little silence and then Dona Maria Magdalena said, 'And now we have two Teresas with us.

Would anybody wager which one of them is destined to be the saint?'

'God grant it may be I,' said Teresa de Querida, with deep and genuine piety.

Teresa realized they were looking at her, waiting for her to say something, but she was too full of shame to speak. She had, she knew, been wondering how she could endure a lifetime among these chattering females, as if she could lay claim to being better than they were, when she knew very well they were infinitely more advanced in true virtue than she could ever be. And now her embarrassed silence must appear even more to them like the worst excess of spiritual pride.

'God grant it may be I!' she said hastily, and dissolved suddenly into genuine amusement at such an unlikely occurrence.

CHAPTER FOUR

Father and daughter sat together in mutual anxiety. It had been a long and tiring journey from Avila to the little hamlet of Becedas and Don Alonzo faced a return journey the following morning. If he left the household for longer than a night, there was no telling in what mischief his sons' idle hands might dabble.

'At least Antonio is safely out of it all,' he said gloomily. 'By now the ship should have berthed, and Hernando and Rodrigo assured me in their last letter that they would meet him at the quayside.'

'They will take care of him, Father. And the climate of the Indies will strengthen him more than the cold winds of Spain.'

'You're such a comfort to me, Maria. Why cannot all my children be like you?'

'They all love you dearly, Father,' Maria said, bending industriously over the stocking she was darning.

'But passionate and headstrong,' he lamented. 'All of them, wanting to go their own ways, arrange their own lives, with or without my consent. Hernando and Rodrigo write so seldom. Who knows what they are doing in that savage country?'

'Making their fortunes,' Maria said, placidly.

'They will need to make them,' her father said irritably. 'My own fortune dwindles year by year as taxes grow larger and harvests become more meagre.'

'They will do well. They will all do well,' she comforted.

'Antonio is not strong,' he fretted.

'The monastic discipline was too severe for his constitution,' Maria said. 'His nature was not suited to it, so it was better for him to find out before he took his vows. And the others will do well when they sail to the Indies, too.'

'They need some occupation to use up their energies,' Don Alonzo said. 'Lorenzo is nineteen now and thinks of nothing but young ladies and how the bulls will run. And the others are wild. Agustin has declared he will run away to sea unless I allow him to go out to the Indies when Lorenzo goes. And he is scarcely eleven!'

'And you are proud of him,' Maria said, with affectionate amusement. 'Why, Father, they are fine boys. I pray that my Diego and Juanito grow up to be as vigorous and handsome. Ah! if you could see your grandchildren now, you would be so pleased.'

'Only two of them,' Don Alonzo muttered. 'From my children, only two grandchildren. If only Teresa –'

He broke off as the door opened and Juana Suarez tiptoed in.

'She is sleeping,' she said, in answer to their inquiring looks. 'I persuaded her to take an egg beaten up in milk, and now she is sleeping.'

'I hope the journey was not too much for her,' Don Alonzo said. 'We came as slowly as we could and stopped at Hortingoza on the way. It's seldom I get the opportunity to see my brother Pedro. Teresa seemed quite cheered when she left, didn't you think so?'

'And she will be even better after a few weeks in this peaceful place,' Maria soothed. 'They say the wisewoman has effected some wonderful cures.'

'If only we knew exactly what was wrong with her!' Don Alonzo burst out, rising to his feet and pacing the small room as if he could no longer bear to sit still. 'The best physicians in Castile have confessed themselves baffled. One of them hinted the severe headaches and constant vomiting were caused by a growth pressing upon the brain; another told me that her stomach pains were a result of a shrinking of the sinews, and now they say she is probably consumptive.'

'She will get well here,' Maria repeated.

'You will send me word of her progress?' he insisted.

'Constantly, Father. Please try not to worry,' Maria entreated.

But he continued to grumble until, reluctantly, he bade them good night and went to snatch a few hours' sleep before he returned home.

'Father is growing older,' Maria said sadly. 'He is close on sixty, you know; and this illness of Teresa's has aged him terribly.'

'It was very generous of you to leave your husband and family in order to nurse her,' Juana Suarez said warmly. 'Your father appreciates it very much.'

'Because it may help Teresa. He always loved her best,' Maria said, without resentment. 'Tell me something.' She bent her head over her mending and refrained from looking at the other. 'In the two years since Teresa went into the convent, has she ever talked to you about her reasons for taking such a step? We all thought she would marry. Rodrigo renounced his own share of the family inheritance in order to provide her with a larger dowry, you know. And now she has renounced her own share in favour of little Juana.'

'She is not happy,' said Juana Suarez. 'Oh, she doesn't talk about it, but I see the shadow in her eyes. She says she is content, but to me she seems to be constantly driving herself forward towards – I don't know what. Dona Maria, I should not tell you this but she disciplines herself far beyond the requirements of the Rule. She has used the nettles and the chain until the walls of her cell are splashed with her own blood. She fasts constantly even though our normal diet is too sparse. There was a nun in the infirmary dying from gangrene. Not one of us could bear the sight or the stench of her, but your sister cared for her right up to the end. She would spend whole nights by her side and then she would stagger into the courtyard and vomit, and then go to her cell and scourge herself for having vomited. And not only that! She appeared one day at recreation with a halter round her neck and a saddle upon her back and made us all load it with stones.'

Maria had laid down her work and the eyes she turned upon the younger woman were wide with foreboding.

'No, Dona Maria.' Juana Suarez went swiftly to her, chafing her hands. 'Teresa is not mad. If she were, it might be simpler. At least we would have some idea of what to do for her, but she does these things to herself with a kind of ferocious sanity. She has some purpose in punishing herself so terribly, but she will not speak of it, perhaps because she is not fully aware of it herself.'

'Rest and quiet is what she needs.' Maria spoke firmly but her hands trembled so violently that her needle fell from its thread to the floor. 'We must make this summer a happy one, and see she submits to the wisewoman's treatment. She will recover quickly, you'll see.'

Becedas was a small and pleasant place, almost entirely surrounded by a twisting river which giggled its way skittishly between moss-covered rocks. From her chair by the window Teresa could look out towards the water glinting between the belt of trees covered already with a faint shimmer of blossom.

A peaceful spot, thought Teresa, and I, of all people, have most need of peace.

She fingered the book on her knee. Her old uncle at Hortingoza had given it to her when they brokc their journey there. She had found it easy to talk to Don Pedro, even to begin to confide to him some hint of her misery because she found it impossible to keep her mind on her prayers for more than a few minutes at a time, even though she punished herself cruelly afterwards for her inattention. He had listened, and as they were lifting her back into the litter, had placed the volume in her hands, telling her to read it when she felt dryness of soul.

Since then she had read it over and over, finding in the *Third Spiritual Alphabet* of Brother Francisco de Osuna a gleam of light as if somebody had opened a door in her mind and allowed her to glimpse treasures of unimaginable richness within.

She had been able to discuss the book, not with her sister or her friend, but with the parish priest of Becedas who had called to pay his respects to the sick Carmelite and stayed to talk with the frail and charming invalid whose brown eyes glowed as she read to him from the treatise on prayer held between her delicate palms.

After that he came every day, his eyes resting with pleasure on her ivory skin stretched over the exquisite framework of bones refined and sharpened by illness. He was lost in admiration for the cheerful courage with which she faced her painful and mystifying disease, and when he rose to leave, he held her hand a little longer than was strictly necessary.

Teresa found him equally charming. It was delightful to be able to talk to a handsome man without a grille separating them, and his conversation was so witty even if it was not quite as profound as she had hoped. Indeed, having begun by consulting him, she found herself beginning to advise him and, if she felt an occasional twinge of uneasiness when his eyes lingered on her face, she reminded herself that they were both protected by their habits.

Maria, entering Teresa's room one afternoon, shortly after the priest had left, was perturbed to find her sister in a considerable state of agitation.

'It isn't true, is it? He doesn't really keep a mistress!' she demanded.

'Our comely clerical friend? Why, Teresa, I assumed you knew. He has been living with a woman these past seven years.'

'That's what he told me,' Teresa said miserably. 'I couldn't believe my ears. Why, he wears a charm around his neck, that she gave to him. An ordained priest, to act in such a fashion!'

'They say down in the village that she has bewitched him by means of that charm you mentioned,' Maria said.

'Then I have to get it away from him,' Teresa said, tensely.

'Why, sister, do you want him for yourself?'

'I want his soul.' Teresa cupped her hands as if a stained and trembling soul rested between them. 'If he does not put away this woman, he will burn in hell. How can we sit by and let that happen?'

'It's no concern of ours if a lustful priest breaks his vow of chastity,' Maria protested. 'Such liaisons are common these days. It's regrettable, but you mustn't take things so seriously.'

'I want his soul,' Teresa repeated, and felt within her suddenly a great hunger. 'Call him back, Maria. Make him come back.'

'So that you can save his soul?'

Maria shook her head in loving exasperation but rose obediently. It was, she considered, a hopeful sign that Teresa should begin to take an interest in somebody else's welfare. At least it might take her mind off the painful remedies inflicted by the wisewoman. Maria doubted if applications of scorpion juice and hot brick dust would strengthen Teresa's health. Perhaps it would do her good to pit herself against the wiles of the priest's concubine, and Teresa had always had a persuasive tongue.

But Teresa's coaxing tongue needed to be exercised almost constantly during the days that followed, for although the priest returned eagerly enough and continued to visit, he still wore the charm about his neck. Maria, too scrupulous to linger outside the door, caught only the urgent hushed tones of her sister's pleading voice, varied by the deeper accents of the man.

Then, one afternoon, she heard him leave more hurriedly than usual, and, going into her sister's room, found Teresa huddled, white-faced and triumphant, upon her chair, her eyes averted from the broken chain of the glittering bauble flung upon the floor.

'He tore it from his neck and threw it down, swearing upon his salvation to make fair provision for the woman and part from her,' Teresa said. 'Take it down to the river, Maria, and drop it into the deepest water.'

'Is it truly bewitched?' Maria asked, looking fearfully at it.

'He thinks that it is.' Teresa's mouth twitched in a weary smile. 'The woman had convinced him of it, and by breaking it from his neck, so he broke away from her. And it was for the love of God that he did it.'

And for your bright eyes and gentle thanks too, Maria thought with a tinge of cynicism, but not for the world would she have belittled her sister's achievement.

'You will get well quickly now,' Maria said.

'I intend to.'

Teresa set her lips in their stubborn line as if she had made up her mind to waste no more energy on trivial ailments.

But she grew steadily worse as spring warmed into summer, and not even the handsome priest, glowing with new-found virtue, could discover anything to admire in the white face and dark-ringed eyes of the young woman who lay in bed, hunched against the pains that tore through her body, vomiting up even the smallest morsel of food, burning with fever at one moment and shaking with cold at the next.

'We must take her back to Avila,' Maria said despairingly. 'Father would never forgive us if she were to die so far from home. This so-called cure has sapped the last remnants of her strength. I cannot accept responsibility for her any longer.'

So they went back to the rust-red town, passing through the Square of St Dominic as dusk was falling. Don Alonzo stood at the main gate, peering anxiously into the gloom as he wondered what on earth had induced the normally docile Maria to leave Becedas with only three servants as escort, and give him barely an hour's warning of her arrival. He knew the reason as soon as he saw his younger daughter, her teeth clenched, her face corpse-green in the light of his flickering torch.

By his side, Lorenzo sobbed suddenly, so loudly that Teresa opened her eyes and lifted a feeble hand in greeting. All around her was bustle and confusion, with her father shouting contrary orders to the servants, Juana Suarez and Maria talking at once, little Juana cowering in the porch as the unfamiliar agitation of her elders beat about her ears. And, holding her hand, the tall young brother whom she had scarcely seen since her profession day, looked down at her and tried to smile.

But he is beautiful, she thought. How is it I never noticed that he is the most beautiful of my brothers?

He was, in fact, the masculine counterpart of herself, but tall and dark with the gay, sparkling look that she had lost. Gossip credited him with several broken hearts among the young girls of the neighbourhood, but there was a steadiness in his mouth and a warmth in his hand that displayed some unconscious strength waiting to emerge with maturity.

She heard her own voice, weak and fretful.

'I want Lorenzo to stay with me.'

And heard him answer, 'For as long as you wish, my sister.'

In the library, Maria was weeping bitterly, pressed down with tiredness and disappointment.

'We did everything for her, Father. Dona Juana will tell you that we neglected nothing that might bring her comfort or ease. But the treatment was too severe. It would have crippled a person in good health and she has grown steadily weaker. She is dying, Father. Teresa is dying.'

'Don't say that! Never say that.' Don Alonzo glared miserably at her. 'Teresa is very sick but she will recover. She has been sick before, and she has recovered before.'

'Father.' Maria clasped her hands and tried to speak calmly. 'She has headaches that blind her for hours at a time; everything she eats is vomited up within a few minutes; her sinews have shrunk so that the faintest touch runs like fire along her nerves; she had two heart attacks on the way home when she gasped and moaned for breath in pitiful fashion; she coughs up blood, as much as a basinful at a time. Nobody can suffer from all these things and live. We must begin to accept the fact, Father.'

'She has asked for the last Rites,' said Dona Juana. 'Would

you like me to fetch Father Vicente, Don Alonzo?'

'No priest enters this house tonight,' said Don Alonzo. 'Teresa is not going to die.'

The two women looked at each other with silent despair, but he had turned away and was pouring wine with a consciously steady hand. Afterwards, Maria was to regard this as the longest night she had ever spent, as hour followed hour in slow monotony, as the candles guttered low, and the servants huddled in the corner, whispering about the tragedy of so early a death.

Dawn was an extension of the night with a chill wind sweeping through the grey corridors. The physician, cloak wrapped tightly against the elements, arrived as the first birds were singing in the leaf-deep orchard and, having conferred with Don Alonzo, entered the bedroom where Lorenzo sat, haggard-faced, by the curtained bed.

A moment's professional bustle, the clattering of pans from the kitchen quarters, a pause heavy with dread, and then the physician's gravely reproving tones.

'You left it too late, Don Alonzo de Cepeda. Your daughter is dead.'

It was Lorenzo who spoke, calling through the half-open door.

'He is wrong, Father. She is still alive.'

'If you would step inside for a moment?' The physician held open the door. 'Your daughter's heart has ceased to beat, sir. When I hold a mirror to her mouth, its surface remains unmisted. I can feel no pulse in wrist, throat or temple. Her skin is cooling and she has ceased to sweat. These are unmistakable signs that life is extinct.'

'Call another physician!' Lorenzo said, half-hysterically. 'Call in somebody else, Father.'

'I will bring two of my colleagues back with me,' the physician said with offended dignity. 'They will confirm my diagnosis.'

They arrived towards the middle of the morning and, with their wide flapping sleeves and pointed hats, formed a sinister trio in the eyes of little Juana who had crept from the schoolroom. She had slept little the previous night, and her dreams had been troubled ones. The servant had been late in waking her and when she laced up Juana's bodice her gnarled hands had trembled and fumbled.

'Teresa is dead,' said Jeronimo, when he saw Juana in the

corridor and she looked at him pitifully for a moment, trying to match her memory of the brightly dressed and laughing elder sister with the present reality of weeping servants and hushed voices.

'She is not dead!' said Lorenzo to his father. 'I promised that I would sit by her for as long as she wished, and she has not yet told me to leave. She would not die when she had not yet released me from my promise.'

'Then stay with her until she awakens,' said Don Alonzo and held up his hand to the protesting doctors.

Juana, her hand to her mouth, crept away from the shadowed room. They had forgotten to give her any breakfast, so she went out into the orchard to search for a few late windfalls. After a while, Agustin joined her and they sat side by side on a fallen log, munching the small, tart fruits and trying not to think of what was happening in the great house.

The day and night passed, and another day and night were endured. Maria, snatching sleep in a chair, tried unsuccessfully to argue with her father but found him as unresponsive as if he too were dead. On the third morning, taking the responsibility once more on her exhausted shoulders, she sent word to the Incarnation that a grave must be dug for Dona Teresa y Ahumada, and leaving Juana Suarez to spoon soup into Lorenzo, prepared the herb-water and linen cloths in which to wash the corpse.

The chanting of priest and acolytes, the weeping of his sons, the scent of incense, all pervaded the house; and Don Alonzo, starting up from a brief doze by the unlit fire, flung wide the door and called out with all his usual authority.

'Sing as many requiems as you please, but I tell you she is not dead!'

'He will not believe it until the smell of corruption fills the house,' Maria said with angry despair.

'And your brother will not leave her side.' Juana Suarez nodded towards the boy, half-hidden by the silk hangings of the bed on which he crouched motionless, his hand locked in the dead hands.

'I sealed the eyelids with warm wax and bound her jaws with crêpe,' Maria whispered. 'And I have set the candles at her head and feet. Father Vicente is arranging for the coffin to be brought. He says that if Father will not give permission for the burial, then I must take it upon myself.'

Lorenzo, who had passed beyond exhaustion to the stage

where dream and reality mix and mingle, heard dimly the slow tolling of the bell, twenty-four sonorous notes, one for each year of her life. His head nodded in the brightness of the candles and his lashes drooped.

The bed curtains, disturbed by his weight, veered towards the steady flame and a trickle of fire zigzagged along the edge of the embroidered silk. The smoke from the candles grew thicker, and Lorenzo, breathing in the stifling fumes, made a half-conscious effort to rise but his legs sagged beneath him and his fingers, groping for the water jug, relaxed like fallen petals.

Hot wax dripped from the bending tapers down to the shroud in which Teresa lay, and little dancing flames skittered and singed the lace-trimmed pillow, and sped down to the rugs laid across the polished floor.

'Lorenzo has not slept for three nights,' Maria worried. 'If he falls sick, too, it will kill Father. Come with me, Dona Juana, and persuade him to rest.'

'There will be no rest for any of us until the funeral is over,' said Juana Suarez.

'I have sent word to my husband,' Maria confided. 'I need Martin's support. Perhaps he will be able to talk to Father. I am sure that I cannot do any more than I have done.'

'Leave your brother and lie down for a while,' her companion advised.

'I will look in on him first.'

Maria rubbed her aching eyes and pushed open the door of the death chamber. A billow of smoke choked her and from behind Juana Suarez, losing her composure for the first time, shrieked.

'They're burning! Mother of God, they're burning!'

'The fire-buckets! Get the fire-buckets!'

Maria reached down for the leather vessels of water that were kept along the upper corridors in case of emergency.

Lorenzo, wandering in a thick mist in search of his sister, who had gone where he could not follow, was aware of stinging pain in his chest, and of loud voices, and rough hands shaking him. He wanted to sink back into sleep, but his father's voice was booming in his ear and Maria, usually so gentle, was slapping his cheek so hard that he wondered vaguely what he had done to offend her.

'No great harm done, but the rugs and curtains are ruined!' Maria was gasping. 'Lorenzo, your arm is burnt. Come with me and I will dress it.'

'Her shroud is charred,' said Juana Suarez, in a frightened whisper.

'And she is still dead!' Whirling, Maria pointed at the motionless figure. 'Teresa is dead, Father! Accept it now, and let her be taken to the Incarnation for burial. Don't deny her the right to a funeral.'

'She needs no funeral. She is alive,' Don Alonzo said, almost absently.

'You must allow us to take her, Don Alonzo,' came Father Vicente's quiet voice. 'It is a sin, against the will of God, to persist in this folly. You have other children to consider.'

'But she is my dearest one,' said Don Alonzo heavily. 'Don't you see? She is the child of my heart, and I, who would cut out that heart to please her, denied her the last thing for which she begged. I would not allow her to receive the last Rites.'

'She is in heaven, I'll swear it, and did not need the grace of a last confession,' Juana Suarez said, earnestly.

'If you had seen how patiently she endured her sufferings at Becedas,' Maria pleaded, 'you would have no doubts.'

'Her sisters are waiting in the cloister to receive her and commit her to the grave,' said Father Vicente. 'She belongs to God now and you do wrong to retain her.'

But Don Alonzo shook his head obstinately and taking Lorenzo's vacant seat clasped Teresa's hand more tightly.

Maria threw back her head and drew a long, quivering breath.

'Father Vicente,' she said, steadily, 'will you have the coffin brought in here? My sister will be placed in it immediately.'

The priest bowed and took one last look at the ruined and blackened bed. She had been, he reflected, such a pretty child and such a lovely young woman. He would have wagered there was greatness in her and now it was all ended. At twenty-four! The girl who had delighted the family with her dancing and the wit of her conversation was silent and still, except for the hand plucking weakly at the burnt edge of the shroud.

The small hand crept up to her sealed eyelids and scrabbled at the wax. Breath, slowly sighing, left her parted lips. Slowly and painfully her eyes opened and a small, puzzled frown creased her brows.

The room was silent, not with the silence of death but with the expectant rush of re-awakening life. Teresa cleared her throat and let her eyes move slowly from one frozen figure to he next. When she spoke her voice was unexpectedly strong.

'I cannot move,' she said. 'What happened to me that now cannot move?'

'We thought you were dead,' Lorenzo sobbed. 'They wanted o bury you.'

'Bury me?' For a moment her eyes were frightened.

'Where were you, Teresa? Teresa, where did you go?' Father Vicente asked urgently.

Her eyes moved to him and the shadow of a rare and lovely smile touched her lips as if at the memory of some unimaginable delight.

'Never believe that I am dead until you see my body covered with cloth-of-gold,' she said.

CHAPTER FIVE

Dona Teresa y Ahumada is wanted in the parlour.'

The voice held a tinge of embarrassment. Every nun at the Incarnation was well aware that Don Francisco de Guzman was waiting eagerly beyond the grille. A charming man, whispered the novices, with such fine eyes and such a musical voice. And so pious and anxious to discuss spiritual matters! Many gentlemen visited the Incarnation to talk through the grille with their spiritual sisters. It was accepted practice for the nuns to lend and borrow books of devotion, to write letters of advice and consolation, to receive poems praising their virtue, to munch the sweetmeats passed in the sliding drawer beneath the grille.

Dona Teresa y Ahumada was one of the most popular nuns in the convent. Certainly she was one of the most attractive, with her dainty figure and bright eyes, swathed so tastefully in the well-cut habit. The other nuns tried to imitate her, but it was impossible to copy her gliding walk, her gurgling laughter, her gaily sparkling conversation. The postulants pointed her out to one another and gossiped about her history.

'She was completely paralysed eight years ago, able to move only one arm.'

'She was in such pain that it took four people to lift her in a sheet when she needed to be turned.'

'For three years she remained in the same condition, and

then she began to crawl about on her hands and knees.'

'And finally she was cured, through the intercession o St Joseph.'

'It was a miracle! Everybody agrees it was a miracle.'

'And she is so modest about it. One would never imagin she was different from anybody else.'

'She has furnished her cell beautifully. Very simple but such a divine harmony of colours! She holds discussion groups there It's quite a privilege to be invited to join.'

So they whispered, and Teresa y Ahumada went serenely past them to the small parlour, where a glowing brazier took the chill from the air.

Don Francisco de Guzman pulled his chair nearer to the grille and asked, solicitously, as the shutters were folded back 'Are you quite well, Dona Teresa?'

'Perfectly well, Don Francisco. And you also?'

'The better for coming here,' he told, her, smiling. 'I look forward all week to my visit with you.'

'Did you read the book?' she asked.

'The letters of St Jerome have been my constant companion since I last saw you,' he reassured her.

'But did you derive profit from them?' she demanded.

'Not as much as I derive from your advice,' he said.

A pleasing pink rose in her cheeks as she said, quickly and half-wistfully, 'Once I had a great desire to save souls.'

'And by your prayers you must do a great deal,' he said warmly. 'I appreciate the fact that you extend your petitions on my behalf. Tell me, are the members of your family well? Your sister, Juana?'

'She is growing into a very comely young woman,' Teresa began with enthusiasm.

'She has the best of models to follow,' he interrupted her

'We have not had news of my brothers for some time,' Teresa said hastily, forcing back another blush. 'They are all in the Indies now, you know. Agustin joined them after my father's death. Four years since I saw any of them!'

'I knew your father slightly,' said Don Francisco. 'Don Alonzo de Cepeda was a highly respected man.'

'He was a deeply spiritual one,' said Teresa. 'We grew very close during his last illness. It was a great comfort that he sent for me to nurse him. When I was a girl, I sometimes resented his strictness but he was right to be concerned about my wildness.'

'Come now, I cannot have that. You were never wild, I'm sure!' he protested.

'On the contrary, I was exceedingly so,' she dimpled. 'I longed for the same freedom my older brothers enjoyed. Once, I sneaked out with them to see how the bulls measured up for the next day's fight. And the perfumes and cosmetics I used! I assure you I spent my allowance as fast as I received it!'

'You have reminded me of the gift I have for you!' He dug in his pouch and pulled out a squat package. 'Orange-flower water is so refreshing in hot weather.'

'Don Francisco, how kind of you!' She delved eagerly into the drawer. 'You could not have brought me anything more welcome for the summer will be here before we know it. Wait! I'll put it up on the shelf and then you can give me your opinion of the book I lent you.'

Stretching up to the shelf behind, she half-turned to smile her further thanks, and surprised his long, considering look at her slender ankles revealed by the raising of her skirt.

'Dona Teresa, permit me to tell you,' he said, daringly, 'that you have the most delectable ankles I've ever seen.'

For a moment, uneasiness shook her composure and then, seized by an imp of mischief, she raised her habit a few inches from the ground.

'Then take a good long look, my cavalier,' she said, flirtatiously, 'for it's the last chance you'll get of seeing them.'

'You are not offended by the compliment?'

'Who could be offended by such a pretty one?' She seated herself again, twinkling at him through the mesh. 'We are close friends and there is no harm in a little joke between friends.'

'No harm in the world,' he agreed, and realized that she was not listening to him any longer but was staring past him, with an expression of disgust on her face.

'It's a toad!' she said and shivered violently. 'It must have come in when you entered, and we never noticed it. *Ugh!* I hate all cold, crawling things.'

'It's certainly a large one. Odd that I never saw it.'

Don Francisco skirted it cautiously and opened the outer door.

The creature stayed where it was for a moment, turning its flattened head and bulbous eyes towards Teresa. She had the sensation for an instant that she stood on the edge of an abyss with wind howling round her and then the toad bounded through the door.

'Are you feeling unwell, Dona Teresa?' Don Francisco said. 'You looked quite sick for a moment.'

'I'm quite well. It is simply that I have a horror of reptiles. I would be quite useless in the Indies for my brothers tell me that there are many lizards and snakes out there.'

'And none of your brothers are married yet?'

Teresa shook her head and looked grave. The last letter from her brothers, Jeronimo and Agustin, had informed her, with a glee that she deplored, that they were both the fathers of healthy illegitimate girls. It was difficult to imagine the two bright-eyed little boys she had played with at home being old enough to father children. Yet it was reprehensible of them to have forgotten their moral training so quickly.

She prayed constantly that their sins of the flesh might be forgiven. She prayed also that the girls they had seduced might find happiness in more loyal arms, and that the two little girls might not suffer unduly for their parents' lust. The world could be cruel to illegitimacy, Teresa knew, but, from the tone of her brothers' letters, it was apparent that standards in the Indies were somewhat lax.

She became aware that Don Francisco was talking again and that she had missed what he was saying.

'I beg your pardon,' she said contritely. 'I was dreaming. What did you say?'

'I was talking about the Italian lady who founded the Ursuline Order,' he said. 'A friend of mine visited Brescia a few months ago and was most impressed by the work the nuns are doing.'

'Ah, yes, Angela Merici. I have read about her, but surely she is dead now.'

'Seven years since, but the Order she founded has endured. She must have been a great woman.'

'A truly great woman,' Teresa agreed, 'but new foundations are all the rage, aren't they? The Society of Jesus is quite firmly established they tell me. Their college here in Avila is flourishing.'

'And old Orders are being reformed,' said Don Francisco eagerly. 'I've heard talk of a Franciscan friar who is trying to bring the Order of St Francis back to its original simplicity. Pedro Garavito, his name is. He's from – Alcantara, I think. Apparently the Holy Office has been looking into his activities.'

Teresa shivered as if some firm, official hand had gripped her shoulder and breathed some warning in her ear. They both were well aware how widely the Inquisition spread its tentacles. Anybody suspected of even the smallest deviation from the doctrines of the Church was liable to arrest, imprisonment, even torture. Some such measures were necessary, Teresa knew, in order to protect the Faith but the power of the Inquisition was so deep and so subtle.

'Ignatius of Loyola was imprisoned by the Holy Office,' she said breathlessly, 'but now the Society of Jesus is recognized by His Holiness, and they plan to send missions out to foreign parts. It is most exciting, is is not? To hear of such things, I mean?'

'There are those who are active in the Faith and those who must be content to pray,' Don Francisco began.

'And if the prayers are fervent, are they not of more use than all the activity in the world?' she demanded.

'I'm sure *your* prayers are!' he exclaimed, gazing admiringly at her heightened colour, but the charm of their conversation had been soured for Teresa, and she rose with a smiling excuse on her lips.

It occurred to her as she listened to his flowery regrets that it might be wiser in future if she brought a duenna with her to the parlour. The novices were always strictly chaperoned, but Teresa observed the Rule so carefully that nobody thought of objecting when she went alone to entertain her constant stream of visitors.

She went back immediately to her cell, for it was her habit after enjoying a gossip with a secular friend to spend a conscience-stricken period in prayer. But today, as so often, she found it incredibly difficult to fix her attention upon the words her lips were shaping.

'Holy Mary, Mother of God – next year I will be the same age as my own mother was when she died. She too was cloistered as I am cloistered. Did my father love her and fail to understand her? Poor father! Such a lonely man, and at the end raised to such a pitch of perfection. It is to him I owe my existence, for without his stubbornness they would have buried me. There was some God-given purpose in his stubbornness. But what purpose? Was I preserved above the ground so that I could end my days in a comfortable mediocrity? Yet what else could I do? I keep the Rule meticulously, never claiming privileges for myself, never exceeding the penances allowed me. I am pointed out as an example of charm and sanctity, and I spend many hours on my knees. How long have

I been kneeling here now? *Pray for us sinners now*. We are all sinners and I am worse than most. I know that I accept that. Once I might have changed it, if I had known how to change myself. There have been times when, kneeling in prayer, I have felt a strange, fugitive sweetness dissolving my bones. I tried to hold on to the feeling but it withered away each time and left me as dry as an unwatered garden. And now I cannot even pray properly, for my words fall back to earth like hailstones and make no impression on my indifferent heart.'

'Teresa, may I speak with you?'

It was Juana, slender and brown-haired, with an anxious expression on her gentle face.

'Come in, little sister. What did you want to see me about?'

She expected a request for a new trinket or a pair of gloves, for Juana at nineteen had a taste for innocent finery, but the girl sat down on the stool in the corner and, turning limpid grey eyes to her elder sister, spoke tragically.

'I cannot bear it, Teresa. I cannot bear it for another day!'

'Bear what? My dear, what is it? Are you ill?' Teresa went to her in concern.

'Worse,' wailed Juana. 'Much worse! My heart is broken, Teresa.'

'Broken? Why, little one, has something terrible happened?'

'It is Señor Juan de Ovalle,' Juana said, miserably.

'The young man who has been calling here so regularly? What of him?'

'He has hinted that he wishes to – to marry me,' Juana said, twisting her hands together.

'To marry you? But why then is your heart broken?' Teresa asked in astonishment. 'I thought that you enjoyed his company.'

'I do, I do,' her sister assured her. 'But Juan is a poor man, Teresa. He will not be able to support a wife for many years yet.'

'And you are not prepared to wait?'

'Yes, of course. I will wait for as long as is necessary; but where? It is four years since Father died and I came to stay with you here at the Incarnation. I cannot stay on for another five or six years until Juan can afford to wed. I would surely be required to take the habit.'

'And you have no desire to enter the religious life?'

Juana shook her head energetically.

'I want to marry,' she said earnestly, 'and rear a family. I don't want to spend the rest of my life in a convent. You're not angry?'

'Angry? My love, why should I be? It is very wrong to enter a convent unless one is entirely committed to the life!' Teresa said.

'But many of the girls here would have preferred to marry,' said Juana naively. 'They didn't have dowries or else nobody asked them.'

Teresa sat back on her heels and stared at her sister. Was that, she wondered, what lay at the root of the laxity and coolness of the Convent of the Incarnation? Was it necessary in order for prayer to flourish for it to be concentrated within a few carefully chosen souls, locked together in a harmony of spiritual endeavour, with nothing to distract them from the love of God?

'Teresa, what shall I do?' Juana was asking. 'Tell me what to do.'

'I think you had better tell the young man to call upon me and discuss his plans,' Teresa said firmly. 'As for leaving here or being forced to take the habit, you may set your mind at rest. This is your home now until you marry, and you have a perfect right to be here, for you pay well for your lodging and you keep the rules far better than many who are vowed to them.'

'And you will speak to Juan, when he comes again?'

'If you are certain of your own mind – '

'I am certain. I shall never love anybody as much as Señor Juan de Ovalle,' the girl said, firmly.

Teresa, looking at her, repressed a sigh. She could have wished for an older, steadier man in whose hands to place her sister's happiness, and what she had seen of Juan de Ovalle disquieted her. He was a young, quick-spoken man with a weakly, handsome face and a petulant mouth. She doubted if her gentle sister had the tact or strength of character to handle him; and he had certainly shown some lack of breeding by leading Juana on to speak of marriage before he had signified his intentions to her sister.

'Why, Teresa, whatever are these?' Juana was exclaiming, pulling a pile of cloaks from under the low bed. 'What are these doing here? They're the lay-sisters' cloaks, aren't they?'

'I was mending them.' Scarlet with embarrassment, Teresa pushed them back into their place. 'I noticed how torn and shabby they were, so I thought I would repair them. The lay sisters have so much to do in caring for our needs that they have no time to look to their own wants.'

'So you supplied them,' Juana said, softly.

'I am so useless,' Teresa said impatiently. 'It is only recently I learned to say the Office properly. I used to open and close my mouth in time with the other sisters and hope that it looked authentic. And all those years when I lay sick! Nothing to do but stare at the ceiling and imagine patterns in the cracks! It is only fair that I should make up a little now for my former idleness.'

'Dona Teresa y Ahumada and Dona Juana y Ahumada are wanted in the Mother Prioress's cell,' a voice said from the doorway.

'A letter!' Juana sprang up, clapping her hands. 'I'll wager it's a letter from the Indies. It's months since we heard anything.'

'We will be sending word of your wedding plans to Hernando soon,' Teresa said, fondly, as they walked down the corridor to the square, panelled room where the Prioress slept.

She was seated at her small, elaborately carved desk by the window which looked out to the pleasant inner courtyard. As the sisters entered and bowed, she looked up from the paper she held and her good-humoured face was sad and serious.

'There is news from the Indies,' she said slowly. 'This letter is from your brother, Don Rodrigo de Cepeda. He writes of a great battle that has taken place at somewhere called – ' she referred to the paper – 'Inaquito. The natives there rose up against the Spanish conquerors, banded together against our brave men.'

'Was Rodrigo hurt?' Teresa asked, shakily.

'He was unscathed, but he writes that your other brothers, Don Hernando and Don Antonio, were both wounded. Don Hernando has since recovered although he was seriously ill for many weeks.'

'Antonio?' It was Juana who asked.

'My dears, I am so sorry, but Don Antonio de Cepeda died of his wounds two days later. Don Rodrigo assures us that he died with all the consolations of our Holy Faith.'

Juana had burst into tears, and it was to the white-faced Teresa that the Prioress spoke, uneasily trying to penetrate the hard mask of controlled grief.

'Your other brothers, Don Lorenzo, Don Pedro, Don Jeronimo and Don Agustin were not at Inaquito. They went on an expedition up-river before the revolt began. Of your seven brothers, six are safe. For that we must give thanks. For Don Antonio, we will pray constantly. Now you will want to be alone. Perhaps you would like to take the letter?'

It was the weeping Juana who took it and guided Teresa through the door. She seemed not to hear the younger girl's bitter sobbing, nor see the anxious faces of her cousins as they hastened into the corridor drawn by some sense of disaster.

At the door of her cell, she thrust away Juana's restraining hand and went in alone to kneel by the cross, starkly black, against the white wall. She was not aware when the others left, for her lips were already moving in their litany of despair.

Why, Lord, why? Of all my brothers, he was the gentlest, the least able to look after himself. Why did it have to be Antonio? He was only twenty-six years old, Lord, and he might have lived for years, married, founded a family. I thought when he left the monastery, that was the destiny You had prepared for him. Was this his true destiny? To be struck down on a foreign battlefield, and die there? What use is such a death? Was it more useful to You than my death would have been? Or was I preserved for some other destiny? But what? *What?*

She looked with a terrible longing at the dark silent wood of the cross. It remained motionless against the wall, its very silence a reproach.

I have no tears for my brother, she inwardly whispered, although I loved him dearly. And You? You shed no tears for me, do You, Lord? And why should You? Teresa y Ahumada has always had more than sufficient tears to shed for herself, for her own forgotten dreams and disappointed aspirations.

She tried to pray for the gift of tears but although she had, in the past, shed many over the chronicles of romantic lovers and the martyrdoms of ancient saints, she could only kneel, dry-eyed, trapped in a searing loneliness of spirit.

Even grief for Antonio is turned into grief for my own unworthiness, she had to confess to herself. Sooner or later, everything turns into sorrow for myself, because I cannot escape from myself. Even here, all my imperfections remain and one of the greatest of them is this habit I have of dwelling on my sins without rooting them out of my being.

She dropped her head in her hands, feeling the pounding of her temples beneath the white coif. The legacy from her illness, of vision-distorting headaches which came at the full of the moon, distressed her even more than the nausea which began at dawn and made it impossible for her to eat a morsel until after noon. She had long since abandoned excessive mortification and tried instead to accept the physical weakness imposed on her by a delicate constitution with cheerfulness. And it was so very little to do. Yet others did less than that. Hard as she tried to close her eyes to the faults of others, she could not help deploring the behaviour of those nuns who crowded into the parlour to gossip with their admirers and who sometimes crept out beyond the enclosure to whisper and fondle in the shadow of the outer walls.

Her guilt was merging with the guilt of others, her vision clouding, her thoughts becoming confused, her grief fragmented. She was a chaos of feeling, and then quite suddenly she was emptied of all feeling, suspended in a blank, bright space between time and time. And in the depths of her being a voice spoke, more clearly and more sadly than any external sound she had ever heard.

Daughter, dost thou not know that everything in thee displeases Me?

'Isn't it wonderful,' said Dona Maria Magdelena, a few weeks later, 'how courageously Dona Teresa y Ahumada has borne the death of her brother! If only we could all achieve the same detachment.'

'For my own part, I have no particular wish to do so,' said another of the sisters indifferently. 'Dona Teresa y Ahumada has always seemed to me to be a cold and unfeeling person. It would have been more natural for her to have wept when she received the news.'

'Teresa does not show her deepest feelings easily,' said Juana Suarez, with cold distaste for the other's gossip. 'But it cut deeply into her heart, this death, even if she says little about it.'

The others, aware of Dona Juana Suarez's fierce loyalty, tactfully changed the subject, but shortly afterwards she rose and went out into the open courtyard where her friend leaned by the well and dabbled her fingers in the water.

'Teresa?'

Juana Suarez hesitated, for dearly as she loved her companion, there were times when the other seemed remote as if some intangible veil hung down between her and the rest of the world.

Today, however, the eyes she lifted to her friend were warmly aware.

'Juana, I was hoping you would come out. Look down here.'

Teresa pointed to the rippling surface of the well where a tiny, long-legged spider was painstakingly constructing a web, like a fine tracery of lace against the dark stone.

'I have been watching it for almost half an hour,' she said, low, 'and it is incredible the number of times the poor little thing has fallen into the water and struggled out to begin its web again.'

'And no doubt you drew a lesson from it,' Juana said, with loving irony.

'Of course! The lesson of perseverance! That tiny soulless creature has a virtue which I lack.'

'Nonsense!' Juana Suarez said roundly. 'You have more strength of character than anybody I've ever known. Haven't I watched you for all these years, fitting your nature to convent life, struggling to move and walk again when the doctors all pronounced you incurably paralyzed.'

'The cure was not of my own doing,' Teresa said, quickly. 'I prayed to the good St Joseph and he answered my prayer.' For a moment her eyes were wistful. 'One day, I would like to do something in thanksgiving for that saint.'

'What?' Juana Suarez asked eagerly, for there were dreams in her friend's gaze.

'What could I possibly do that would be of any use to St Joseph?' Teresa asked lightly, her mood changing like quicksilver.

'Once I thought you might do something wonderful one day,' Juana Suarez said.

'And now I've recognized my limitations,' Teresa said in the same light and evasive tone. 'I've discovered that the most I can achieve is to keep the Rule and offer up a few small prayers.'

'Isn't it strange,' the other mused,' 'to think how every day we kneel down to confess our faults and offer up our petitions? Every day, whispering into the silence.'

'Silence?' Teresa looked at her friend consideringly. 'Is it always silence, Juana? Do you never have the feeling that, out of the silence, something, someone, might – speak?'

'Speak?' Juana Suarez looked at her in astonishment. 'Why, Teresa, what could speak except your own imagination?'

'I suppose not,' Teresa said, doubtfully.

'You haven't imagined that you've heard any voices, have you?' Juana asked, with alarm in her face. 'Oh, Teresa, you haven't? Don't you remember that was how it began with Magdalena of the Cross?'

'The Franciscan prioress who pretended to be a visionary?'

'She started by hearing voices,' Juana said nervously. 'Perhaps she really did hear them in the beginning. But then she claimed that she bore the five wounds of Christ, and that the Sacred Host was brought to her by an angel. And it was all trickery! She'd painted on the wounds and studied the art of conjuring. Teresa, the Inquisition burnt her for blasphemy and fraud.'

'Do you think I'd pretend such things?' Teresa asked, angrily.

'Perhaps Magdalena of the Cross didn't pretend, at first,' Juana whispered. 'She may have truly thought she heard a voice and waited for something else to happen, and when it didn't – why, she *made* it happen!'

'Well, as I am neither a visionary nor a fraud, I don't intend to bother my head about the Inquisition,' Teresa said, cheerfully. 'And if I start to hear things, I assure you I'll resist them with all my might! I like to be able to control my own thoughts, even if they do wander off sometimes. Indeed, my head is so full of nonsense that I doubt if there's room for anything else. Come to my cell and read the new song I've been composing in honour of St Clare. I want you to sing it for us at recreation, for I never could manage to keep in tune.'

As the two nuns walked back across the courtyard, the spider in the well continued to spin its tiny, fragile threads.

PART TWO

THE FIRE

CHAPTER SIX

'Tell me everything you know about this nun,' invited Francisco de Borgia. 'Although I will make up my own mind concerning her, it is useful to hear the opinions of thoughtful men.'

The three to whom he spoke looked pleasantly gratified. This new commissary of the Society of Jesus, charged by Ignatius of Loyola to strengthen the work of the Society in Spain and Portugal, had, like all true aristocrats, an easy and graceful manner and an air of great interest in the views of lesser men. It was possible to forget, in his presence, the fact that he was the great-grandson of that most evil of Popes, Alexander VI, and to remember only that here was a man whose public career as Viceroy of Catalonia had been as incorruptible as his marriage to Eleanor de Castro had been happy and fruitful. The lovely Eleanor had died eight years before, and five years after that, her widower had renounced his titles and possessions, provided for his eight children, and entered the Society of Jesus where his abilities were already appreciated.

As the three men studied him, so he studied them shrewdly from beneath heavy-lidded Borgia eyes. Francisco de Salcedo was, like himself, a widower in his forties, handsome, cultured and intelligent, but showing, Francisco de Borgia suspected, some trace of fearful superstition. Next to him, the wiry Gaspar Daza whose preaching had electrified Castile, looked tense and sour as if his own fervour burned his mouth like wormwood. The third man, Diego de Cetina, was a youthful Jesuit with a plain, and at first glance, stupid face; but Francisco de Borgia had seen at once the quiet eyes and steady mouth, the slow, thoughtful speech.

It was, however, Francisco de Salcedo who answered.

'She comes from one of the finest families in the province. Her father was a hidalgo, a fine and spiritual man. He ruled his family with wisdom and severity.'

'And his daughter?'

'Gay, beautiful and intelligent,' said Francisco de Salcedo promptly. 'She was one of the belles of Avila. It's my impression that several young men were disappointed when she entered the religious life. Then she fell very seriously ill. At one time she was certified as dead and when she recovered she was almost completely paralyzed. She attributes her cure to the intercession of St Joseph.'

'And what is the state of her health now?'

'Delicate. She suffers from fainting fits and spells of vomiting, but she has a great deal of nervous energy. Her conversation is sparkling and she has a warmth of manner that draws one to her.'

'Don Francisco has allowed himself to be carried away by her charm,' Gaspar Daza said, dryly. 'He is also flattered because it was to him she first confided her experiences.'

'You did not find her charming?' inquired Francisco de Borgia.

'She has a sweet, subtle way with her,' Gaspar Daza admitted, 'but there is the danger. We all know what fair forms the devil can take and how often he hides within the body of a woman. I agreed to see her at Don Francisco's request, but my time was limited and what she had to say was so vague and unimpressive that I was not much interested. I didn't grant her the right of making her confession to me.'

'But you were interested enough to send for me,' Francisco de Borgia said.

The preacher looked a trifle uncomfortable.

'I believe she is a fraud,' he said, at last. 'We have all seen it, have we not? A young and beautiful girl enters a convent filled with desire for God, eager for these strange experiences which come to the saints. And, finding none, she invents them for herself. It may begin almost innocently as a means of attracting attention to herself but it ends in devilry.'

'The things she told me are quite incredible,' said Don Francisco de Salcedo. 'If such experiences are occasionally given to men, it is only to the greatest of the saints. And Dona Teresa y Ahumada is, for all her goodness and charm, no saint!'

'You, Don Francisco de Salcedo, are of course qualified to recognize saints?' Diego de Cetina asked.

Francisco de Borgia gave his junior a quelling look, mitigated by a slight tremor of the lips.

'You would defend her, my son?' he inquired.

'Yes, I would. I don't understand half of what she's talking about, but I know what she says is true,' the Jesuit said obstinately.

Gaspar Daza snorted as if to express his contempt for all young, impressionable priests.

'It seems, gentlemen,' said Francisco de Borgia, 'that we ought to set out for the Convent of the Incarnation at once. She is expecting us?'

'Oh, yes indeed,' Don Francisco de Salcedo assured him. 'She is most anxious for our advice.'

The portress at the door led them at once to the small parlour and the inquisitive look in her sharp eyes caused Francisco de Borgia some wry amusement. No doubt every nun in the building would quickly be informed that four eminent gentlemen had called upon Dona Teresa y Ahumada. Then, despite himself, he sighed. The whole world seemed to be swarming with half-crazy fanatics who, declaring themselves inspired by God, acted in the most appalling blasphemous ways, flagellating themselves, displaying marks of the stigmata, even stripping themselves naked and rolling in filth to display their contempt of the earth. Mad and pitiable most of them, he considered, others definitely inspired by the devil, a few fakes seeking notoriety, but once, just once, a genuine servant of God might be found!

The shutters were folded back and a small, slim woman with the pale, translucent complexion of the cloistered, stood behind the mesh. He had been told that Teresa was thirty-nine, but she looked, he judged, at least ten years younger than that. Her dark, rather prominent eyes were fixed hopefully upon his face and as she greeted them he had to steel himself against the charm of her voice.

'Gentlemen, it is so very kind of you to come to see me. I am in such great perplexity of mind.'

'Tell me about yourself, daughter,' invited Francisco de Borgia.

'There is nothing very much to tell,' she said, ruefully. 'For the past fifteen years, I have lived here at the Incarnation. Before that I was forced to leave for a brief period because of my illness. You have heard of that?' At his nod, she went one. 'I strive to keep the Rule and I have tried to make a little progress in the spiritual life.'

'And no doubt succeeded?' commented Gaspar Daza.

Teresa shook her head.

'I climb up a little way and then slip back,' she confessed. 'I cannot begin to meditate until I have a book before me, so that I can concentrate upon the words and prevent my mind from wandering. Up to a year ago, I tried to find some consolations from my prayers. Occasionally, I believed I felt some great spiritual sweetness, but when I tried to hold the feeling, to savour it, I became arid again.'

'Tell the good fathers what happened to you last year,' Francisco de Salcedo encouraged.

'I was in the Oratory,' Teresa said slowly. 'I was merely passing through on my way to recreation. I happened to glance as I went by at the painting of Christ At The Column. I have seen it a hundred times before that and thought it rather a crude representation. But as I looked at it this time, my attention was so caught and held that everything else in the world ceased to exist.'

'You were sentimentally stirred,' said Gaspar Daza.

'No, it was more than that. Much more.' She turned towards Francisco de Borgia as if intuitively sensing some kinship with him. 'I became for a moment that figure, hearing the insults of the crowd, feeling the Roman lash bite into my back, bending under the sins of the world. My sins! And then I wept as if the world had come to an end.'

'And afterwards you began to see visions,' Gaspar Daza said sceptically.

'I see nothing,' Teresa said earnestly. 'With my eyes I see nothing, but into my mind there come the clearest of visions, far more real than anything I have ever known.'

'Many of us build up pictures in our imaginations and dwell upon them,' Francisco de Borgia said gently.

'I do not imagine these things,' Teresa said. 'I have often attempted to compose such pictures but I cannot achieve anything vivid. And these are not pictures, Father. It is as if my mind fills with a living reality so that the reality in which I live becomes an insubstantial dream. And these things are not composed gradually. They flash into me, blocking out everything else, even myself, as if I too had ceased to exist.'

'And what is it that you perceive?' asked Diego de Cetina.

'I saw myself,' she answered, 'standing in a great cone of light and I watched while angels and demons fought a great battle. I found myself in the place reserved for me in hell.

I felt the pain of that unceasing fire that burns and does not consume.'

She stopped, shivering violently as drops of perspiration ran down her face.

'I see devils constantly,' she said, with an effort to compose herself. 'I have seen two of them with their horns locked around the throat of a priest as he elevated the Host. When I sing the Office in choir, a demon with a grinning black face peers into my own face to attract my attention. Satan himself has sat upon my prayer-book, breathing twisted flame from his hideous mouth, and causing me such terror as I cannot describe. If it were not for the consolations I receive, I would go mad.'

'These are the fancies of a sick brain. Do we need to waste our time any further?' Gaspar Daza asked, contemptuously.

But Francisco de Borgia leaned forward. 'What consolations, daughter?' he asked quietly. 'Tell me of these consolations.'

'I have seen Our Lord,' she said.

'Seen Him? How?'

'Not with my eyes, nor my imagination,' Teresa said. 'It is clearer than that, as if one stood by a friend in the dark, and yet, it is not dark, but radiant with a light more powerful than the sun and softer than moonbeams. I am filled with Him, not simply with the love of Him, but with His Person, as if He had crept into my soul and changed the colour of my mind.'

'How tall is He? What colour are His eyes?' Francisco de Salcedo demanded.

'I cannot tell,' she confessed. 'I wanted so much to be able to describe these things to you, but when I try to fix my attention upon some part of the whole, it vanishes and I am back in the world again.'

'Then how do you know it is Our Lord?' asked Gaspar Daza.

'He tells me so.'

'I thought He did not speak to you.'

'Not in words,' she tried to explain, 'but He makes me conscious that it is He. I know it, even more clearly than I know you four gentlemen are seated there now.'

'The Mother Prioress tells me that you have several times been found deep in trance,' Gaspar Daza accused. 'She says your limbs were rigid, your eyes open but unseeing, your ears deaf. You have remained in this condition for anything from a few minutes to half-an-hour. The others sisters cannot rouse you.'

'I cannot help it. These states come upon me with no

warning,' she said unhappily.

'Is it true,' asked Francisco de Borgia suddenly, 'that you have been seen to float above the ground?'

'But how did you know – ?' she began breathlessly, and then her face crumpled and she began to weep helplessly.

'Tell us about that,' said Francisco de Borgia.

'I told the sisters never to speak of it, even to the Mother Prioress,' Teresa sobbed. 'It is the most shameful thing, but I cannot help it. Sometimes, as I am lifted up into rapture, my body also is lifted up. I try to resist, but it is like a strong wind which presses beneath my feet and draws me up above the floor. It has happened only twice. The first time, thank God, I was alone for I thought I was dying. But the second time some of the other nuns saw me though I clung to the wall and begged God not to humiliate me thus. I made them promise to say nothing, for it will cause such a scandal if it becomes known. Everybody will point at me, and whisper about me, and laugh at me.'

There was a long silence. Then Francisco de Borgia said, slowly, 'Do you take precautions against these visions?'

'I told her to resist them,' said Gaspar Daza, with the harshness of a man who has been deeply moved. 'I told her to make the sign against the evil eye whenever this so-called person of Christ appeared.'

'And I have given her an ivory horn set in silver which is a sure remedy against the devil,' Francisco de Salcedo said eagerly.

'It is torture to me,' Teresa said very low, dabbing her streaming eyes, 'to have to insult Our Blessed Lord in this manner. I do it, but I have to apologize even as I do it.'

'And the vision does not go?'

Teresa shook her head. 'When Christ is here, no insult will cause Him to leave and when He decides to leave not all the tears in the world will cause Him to remain.'

'You have heard of Magdalena of the Cross, have you not?' asked Gaspar Daza, with a new and ominous rumble in his tone.

'She was condemned by the Inquisition,' said Francisco de Salcedo.

'You could find yourself in very grave danger,' warned Gaspar Daza.

'If I ever offended in the smallest degree against any doctrine of Holy Church,' Teresa said steadily, 'then I would deserve to be burned a thousand times; but I submit to your judgment, gentlemen. That is why I asked you to come.'

There was another silence and then Francisco de Borgia, rising to his feet, spoke with apparent indifference.

'Despite all you have said, you must feel deeply honoured to have been granted such experiences.'

'It is no great honour,' Teresa said miserably, 'to be singled out for such humiliation. And yet –' her voice shook with intensity – 'such favours can be so sweet one would not lose them even at the price of much suffering.'

'And if these favours, as you call them, come from God and not from the devil, what reason do you think He has for sending them to you?'

'To display His power over one of the lowest of His creatures, I suppose,' she decided, and then, seeing them rise and gather their cloaks around them for departure, she said in sudden panic, 'But have you no advice for me? You cannot leave so abruptly!'

'I would advise you to continue to practise prayer,' said Francisco de Borgia. 'To keep the Rule, and meditate daily upon some aspect of the Passion. I will send you a priest of the Society of Jesus who will guide you, but you must be guided by your own confessor, and you must hold back nothing from him.'

'And nothing more?'

'One thing. Banish fear from your mind. It is possible that God is leading you along a mysterious and magnificent path,' said Francisco de Borgia, and his warmly reassuring smile pierced the mesh between them.

'Father, what is your opinion?' Francisco de Salcedo asked, as they walked away from the convent.

'She is perfectly genuine,' Francisco de Borgia said, quietly. 'She displays none of the craving for attention that an hysteric would show. Every word she uttered proves her to be a simple, innocent woman, marked by genuine humility and piety. She is no Magdalena of the Cross.'

'But the visions?' protested Gaspar Daza. 'How can one see something without the use of one's eyes, or understand something without the employment of one's reason?'

'And how can a solid body be lifted up and suspended in the air?' asked Francisco de Salcedo.

'And how,' asked Francisco de Borgia gently, 'can the Creator of all things be born of a virgin in a stable?'

And at that, even Gaspar Daza could find nothing to say.

In the Convent of the Incarnation, the nuns gathered together at recreation, whispering, their faces alight with curiosity or heavy with displeasure.

'Dona Teresa y Ahumada has consulted fathers of the Society of Jesus.'

'They have told her that her visions come from God.'

'They warn her that her visions are inspired by the devil.'

'She has never had a vision in her life, but she wants to be considered important, now that the fuss about her miraculous cure is dying down.'

'So-called miraculous cure! It's my opinion she'd been recovering for months and said nothing of it until she was strong enough to walk among us again.'

'That is a wicked slander. We all saw that she could barely stir!'

'Ah, you are merely her cousin, Inés Tapia, and blinded by family loyalty!'

'Not so blind that I cannot see the truth!'

'But full of the de Cepeda pride. And what will that be worth when the Holy Office scents word of this and we are all investigated? Who will dare to defend her then?'

'Well, I will, for one!'

'It is of no use talking to *you*, Juana Suarez, for you never could see farther than your own nose!'

In Avila, the citizens drank their good wine and talked in the summer twilights.

'So we have our own saint among us. Is this not an honour?'

'They say she has the power of flying about in mid-air.'

'Is it true that she spends all her time in her cell, lost in raptures?'

'The priests of the Society of Jesus are advising her in the matter. They were the only ones who were not deceived by Magdalena of the Cross, so their judgment is important.'

'But they are only human, and Teresa y Ahumada is very charming. She was so lovely as a girl they used to say she could marry anybody she chose.'

'I always thought she would wed her eldest cousin. Pedro Alvarez could never mention her name without using superlatives.'

'And he has never married, nor does he ever go to the convent, though his own sisters are there.'

'The Bishop should be informed of what is going on. Everybody is talking about it.'

'Everybody will find something else to talk about next week.'

In their modest home at Alba de Tormes, Juan and Juana de Ovalle re-read the letter from Juana's cousin, Ana Tapia.

'I don't like it,' Juan said for the tenth time. 'This posturing of your sister will bring discredit upon your family. What right has Dona Teresa to see things that others don't see? Somebody ought to inform your brothers of the scandal it's causing.'

'Perhaps Señor Martin de Guzman – ' she suggested, timidly.

'Your half-sister's husband is too mild and stupid to tackle such a matter,' Juan said irritably. 'And Maria thinks everything that Dona Teresa does is wonderful! They both dislike me so intensely that they will take the contrary opinion merely to annoy me.'

'Oh, Juan, dear,' Juana protested, 'I'm certain that isn't so! They inquire after you most cordially whenever they write.'

'And they send the smallest piece of silver they could find for a wedding gift.'

'But their circumstances are very modest.'

'A fact they never cease stressing. Is it our fault if your mother divided her property between her two daughters and Dona Teresa signed over her share to you when she entered the convent? It's not as if we were wealthy. The value of money has dropped alarmingly since we were wed.'

'We do seem to spend rather a lot,' Juana hinted.

'But we must be well dressed and keep decent horses, and a good cellar. How can we hold our own in local society if we attire ourselves like paupers? The Duke and Duchess of Alba may invite us to visit them one day, but they are hardly likely to do so if we cannot keep up appearances.'

'But last week you ordered three new doublets and an ivory toothpick, Juan.'

'And didn't I buy my pretty wife two satin gowns and one of the Italian coifs?'

'Yes, dear, and I was very pleased, but we haven't paid the chandler's bill yet, and the fishmonger swears he'll deliver no more mackerel until he's received the money for the last lot. Our credit isn't any good any longer.'

'And will be worse if it gets out there's a crazy woman in the family!'

'Teresa is not crazy!' Juana snapped. 'I am ashamed to hear you say such a thing. You would not dare to even think it if my brothers were here.'

'But they are not, are they?' he gibed. 'They're chasing all over the Indies, making their fortunes and having a splendid time, except for Don Antonio who was fool enough to get in the way of a few native arrows.'

'Oh, don't let us quarrel!' Juana begged, bursting into tears. 'I cannot bear it when you say such things! Please, don't let us quarrel again. It gives me a headache.'

'Then put on your cloak and come down to the stables. There's something there you have to see.'

'Not another horse! Juan, you haven't bought another horse!'

'Cheaply, because of mismarkings on the back. But he's a good mount and a promising breeder, if I've an eye for a valuable animal.'

'You said that last time,' Juana reminded him tearfully, 'and the animal was spayed and vicious too.'

But she put on her cloak and went with him because anything was better than having him slander her beloved Teresa who had always been so kind.

'Teresa, was that Don Francisco de Guzman who visited you in the parlour just now?' asked Dona Ana Tapia.

'It was indeed. Did you wish to see him?'

'No, no.' Ana hesitated at the door of the cell and then burst out, 'It causes talk, cousin, when worldly gentlemen of high rank continually ask for you. They say it is all very well for ordinary nuns to have their admirers, but you are different.'

'No different from anybody else,' Teresa said sharply. 'Surely I am not to be denied innocent friendship in addition to my other humiliations! I never go unchaperoned to meet my "admirers" as you call them, and I assure you that if the conversation wanders from spiritual matters I try to bring it back again.'

'And do you always succeed?' Ana Tapia asked, slyly.

Teresa flushed uncomfortably and bit her lip. It was true that the gossip of the town still amused her, but it was also true that worldly chatter drained her of energy and that it was becoming increasingly difficult to divide her time satisfyingly between cell and parlour.

She looked up to reply to her cousin but Ana Tapia had slipped away. Teresa sighed and nibbled her forefinger. Her cousins loved her, she knew, but they were sometimes inclined to regard her as their own particular piece of miraculous property.

As for Juana Suarez – Teresa's lips curved in a half-tender, half-exasperated smile. There was nobody with whom she felt so much at ease as with her childhood friend, and there was nobody less qualified to understand the experiences that came to Teresa more and more frequently, drawing her out of herself, weakening her feeble efforts at resistance. Juana Suarez, having conquered her fear of some devilish influence at work, had accepted Teresa's raptures with her loving, uncomplicated heart but it was impossible, Teresa thought ruefully, to discuss such matters with her.

It was indeed becoming impossible to discuss them with anybody. Her confessors were still harsh and suspicious, laying upon her injunctions that shrivelled her soul. The fathers from the Society of Jesus were kind and encouraging, but they could not advise her how to deal with matters that were, despite their virtue, unknown to them.

It is You and I alone, Lord, she thought. You have inflicted great miseries upon me and shown me great joy. I have accepted all of it, Lord. Even as I protested, I was willing to accept it. I am resigned to the fact that I have no rights, but if I could ask one question, Lord. If I could ask one question I would say 'Why?' Why have You caused these things to happen to me? For what reason have I been welded and hammered and plunged into the icy waters of nothingness, as the swords of Toledo are said to be fashioned? For what reason have I been fashioned, Lord?

There was no answer beyond the sudden numbing of hands and feet, the fading of consciousness, the sharp fear as the soul was drawn up into the sweetness that pained more than any mortal ache, the brief rebellion as human nature sought to establish its own identity, and then all contact with the earth was lost. And the light swallowed her, shaped her, dazzled her, drowned her. And the Voice spoke, in those tones no ear could perceive.

It is time now, daughter, for thee to speak with angels, not with men.

'Dona Teresa, are you coming to recreation?' Dona Antonia paused hopefully and smiled at the woman who sat, placidly sewing altar clothes, in the tastefully appointed cell.

'Is it time already?' Teresa bit off the end of her thread

and tucked it neatly into the hem. 'I'll come at once, Dona Antonia.'

'Has something happened?' the younger nun inquired. 'I never saw you look so glowing before, as if you had received good news.'

'Good news?' Teresa considered this carefully as she folded up her work with her accustomed neatness. Then she dimpled at her companion and said merrily, 'Why, sister, perhaps good news may come to us in many different ways; and it is for us to recognize it when it comes. Shall we go now to recreation?'

CHAPTER SEVEN

Dona Guiomar del Ulloa collected saints in much the same spirit as other ladies of quality collect jewels. Each new religious was another ornament in the necklace of virtue she had been stringing ever since the death of her husband. Now she had good reason to be pleased, having wheedled to her home two of the most noted visionaries of the day.

They were sitting together in her large, cool living room, their hands busy with their spinning wheels while above the whirring their voices sounded in reflective, friendly conversation. Dona Guiomar would have liked to join them, but she sensed that at this moment they spoke privately of matters only they could comprehend.

It gave her pleasure to stand by the door of her parlour and watch their faces, lit by sunlight streaming through the open window from the courtyard, throwing into relief the broad, flat cheekbones of the woman in the coarse friar's robe, etching the small, aristocratic features of the nun. They were a contrast, she decided, and yet she had always guessed they would be drawn together.

Mariadiaz had been sheltered by Dona Guiomar ever since the evening she had stumbled, weary and half-starved, into the twisting street. They had taken her for a man, for her hair was cropped, her feet calloused, her garments copies of those worn in the Franciscan Order. But the body, marked and seamed by frequent scourgings and the spiked bracelets of penance, was the body of a woman.

A farmer's daughter, she said she was driven by hunger for

God into an existence that would have broken most men. Too poor to enter a recognized religious order, shunned by the people, she found in the fussy, kind-hearted widow a sympathetic protector. And, unlike many of the beatas who wandered the Spanish countryside, Mariadiaz worked hard for her keep, her ugly, country woman's hands forever occupied with some household task, while she talked little, and moved close to the wall, signifying her coming only by the slight rattling of the chains she wore.

Next to her, Dona Teresa y Ahumada looked almost worldly in her graceful habit, with her pale, unlined face belying her forty-four years and her brown eyes sparkling with humour when they were not gentle with thought. It had been a stroke of genius, Dona Guiomar congratulated herself, to place her daughter in the Convent of the Incarnation. Young Antonia had been only too happy to lift the burden on the large, impoverished community by returning home for a few months and bringing with her the nun whose visions and revelations were impossible to hide from a gossiping and scandalized town.

'It was impossible to obtain a moment's privacy,' Teresa was saying. 'By the time I return, it's to be hoped they will all have found something else to talk about.'

'It amazes me that the nuns are allowed to chatter,' said Mariadiaz, in her slow, thick voice. 'Surely the Rule of Carmel calls for silence and solitude.'

'The Rule is almost forgotten now except by the oldest nuns,' Teresa said sadly. 'I have never even seen a copy of the Constitutions.'

'There is great laxity among all religious orders,' Mariadiaz commented. 'Is it to be wondered that people are confused when those who should set the example cause such scandals?'

'None of us can escape blame,' Teresa said. 'When I look into my own heart I am appalled at my own selfishness.'

'But you are the least selfish person I have met,' Mariadiaz said, with deep feeling. 'God is showering favours upon you!'

'And can I accept them and do nothing in return?' Teresa asked anxiously. 'You know I have longed increasingly these past years to offer something to Our Lord. If I could soften one soul on His behalf; bring one sinner to see the truth!'

'There is prayer,' Mariadiaz reminded her.

'And people in the world have so little time to pray. If only there could be small communities of religious dedicated entirely to the practice of prayer,' Teresa said fervently. 'That is what

Carmel was originally meant to be, but all that is changed now. The convents are packed with bored and dissatisfied women who have no guidance beyond the weekly visit of an overworked confessor, and nothing to do for most of the time but chew sweetmeats and gossip in the parlour. I am not the only one who thinks as I do. There are several very fine souls in the community who would like to change things. Not long ago, one of my relatives declared that if all else failed we would have to found a convent of our own!'

'Who was this relative?'

'My cousin, Diego, is married and has two girls who are lay-boarders at the Incarnation. It is another infringement of the rules but the fees for their schooling are invaluable in such a poor community. Maria, the younger girl, is a little ferret-faced creature, too shrewd for her years. But she has some excellent notions, even if she is too young to realize they are impractical.'

She broke off and smiled as Dona Guiomar del Ulloa came into the room.

'Forgive my disturbing you,' the lady of the house said, breathlessly, 'but I have such wonderful news for you both. I have been for so long trying to tempt Pedro Garavito of Alcantara to meet you, and my servants have just come to tell me that he is approaching. You are already acquainted with him, I know, Mariadiaz.'

'And will be overjoyed to see him again,' Mariadiaz said, fervently, and turned enthusiastically towards Teresa. 'He is one of the holiest men who walks upon the earth,' she declared, pressing her rough hands together. 'When he was at the Seminary, he disciplined himself never to raise his eyes above the ground so that he could distinguish his companions only by the sounds of their voices. He eats only once in three days and sleeps for no more than an hour and a half of the twenty-four.'

'He has the power of lifting himself above the ground and flying from place to place,' Dona Guiomar whispered. 'And as he leaves the earth he utters shrill bird-like cries to warn people not to approach too closely. What do you think of that, Dona Teresa?'

'I am not sure,' said Teresa nervously, 'if he and I will have very much to say to each other. He will probably regard me as a very immature, unintellectual person.'

'At least he has agreed to meet you,' said Dona Guiomar.

'Aren't you excited at the thought of talking to such a holy man?'

'Oh yes, indeed,' Teresa assured her, 'and I can never thank you sufficiently for arranging it. But I'm afraid his conversation will be above my head. He will think me very frivolous, I daresay, if I make a joke.'

'My dear, he is a great saint!' protested Dona Guiomar.

'But surely saints may laugh!' Teresa argued. 'I never could abide sullen folk.'

There was a faint buzz of chatter from the servants at the gate, and then, as the thin, white-haired figure plodded across the cobblestones, Teresa, peeping from the window, gave an irrepressible gurgle of amusement.

'His appearance is certainly shabby enough,' she whispered. 'He doesn't look as if he could afford a withered leaf to dress a pilchard on.'

'Dona Teresa, he has no possessions and is very old,' said Mariadiaz, with disapproval.

'Like a bundle of knotted roots!' Teresa commented naughtily. 'Forgive me for laughing, but he has already terrified me out of my wits.'

'Dona Guiomar del Ulloa, my greetings to you and to your daughter.' The voice was deep and harsh, the eyes piercing.

'Mariadiaz, it is good to see you again, my daughter.'

'And a great honour to receive you under my roof, Brother Pedro,' Dona Guiomar was stammering.

'And this is Dona Teresa y Ahumada, whom I have been invited to meet? My time is limited. An hour, if that, is all I can spare, but I am glad to give it to you. Daughters, you will excuse us, if you please.'

'I thought,' stammered Teresa as her two companions fussed out, 'that you never looked at a woman!'

The eyes raking every inch of her person twinkled.

'That was my custom when I was a young man,' said Pedro of Alcantara, 'but now that I am past sixty I believe I may occasionally break my own rule. So you are the Carmelite whom everybody is talking about. What do you want from me? Advice? I'm told your Jesuit and Dominican confessors are all giving you advice.'

'My visions – ' she faltered.

'Ah, yes, visions. These raptures, trances, voices, flights in the air – they will either pass or you will learn to ignore them. Such things are not of great interest, unless you have had some new and startling revelation.'

'I have had a wound in my heart,' she said, slowly.

He raised bushy eyebrows.

'A wound in the heart? Evidently that phrase has some meaning for you. You had better make it clear to me.'

His tone was far from inviting but something in his listening attitude encouraged her to begin, and as she spoke, forgetting her audience, so she seemed again to be back in the Incarnation, re-living that experience.

It had happened to her not once but several times over a period of a few days, and each time it occurred was as if it had never happened before, for she was like a person born over and over again and yet not remembering the previous occasion until she emerged from womb-darkness into day.

With the eyes of her soul, Teresa had seen an angel, small in stature and made all of fire so that she knew it as one of the higher spirits, and this being, standing on her left side, plunged a golden spear tipped with fire down into her heart and through her entrails so that she moaned with pain which was more bliss than any pleasure she had ever imagined.

She was aware that she had finished speaking and that her companion had made no reply. He stood motionless, with his deep-set eyes fixed upon her face and his grotesque rags covering a body so full of dignified and passionate rapture that she crouched by her spinning wheel, waiting patiently until the ecstasy had passed.

'You are marked,' he said at last, 'by the spear of God. There is another great man who lives in Rome. Travellers have told me of this Philip Neri who tramps the streets, talking and singing of heaven. God's fool, he calls himself, but no fool ever loved his monarch with more devotion. This Philip also has a divine wound in his heart which burns with such intensity that he has been known to plunge bare-chested into a snow-drift to gain a moment's relief from such pleasant agony.'

'My rosary,' Teresa ventured to say, 'is also marked. Our Lord took it into His own hands and then returned it to me, and since then the stones of its pendant cross look to me like four great gems, brighter and more blinding than diamonds.'

'You have been favoured,' said Pedro of Alcantara, 'more than you deserve.'

'I know, Brother Pedro.'

'And what,' he asked briskly, 'are you going to do about it, my daughter? You cannot sit back and allow God to shower favours into your lap without doing something for Him in return.'

'But there is nothing I can do, except love Him,' she said, sadly.

'Demonstrate that love in some practical way.'

'I pray constantly and hold myself in readiness for whatever God has in mind for me. That is all I have been able to do for more than twenty years.'

'Then you must continue to be patient,' he said, 'though I'm told this is not a virtue often given to the female sex. I don't believe you will have to wait for very much longer, however, and meanwhile you must continue to strengthen the foundations of your spirit.'

'A building must have strong foundations else it will not stand,' she said, and moved her hands as if pebbles trickled through them.

'You may count upon my advice for what it is worth and upon my friendship,' he told her.

'It is so good of you to bother about me!' she exclaimed impulsively.

'Now you are flattering that bundle of twisted roots,' he retorted, and twinkled again at her shamefaced blush.

'You will take something to eat or drink before you leave?' she begged.

'Dona Guiomar would be hurt if I did not,' he agreed, 'though how I will manage to swallow anything I can't imagine. I had some excellent figs yesterday morning.'

'I cannot understand how you can go for so long without eating,' Teresa said frankly.

'Why, daughter, fasting is no great hardship,' the friar said with amusement. 'Now it is a different matter when it comes to sleep. There was nothing I liked more when I was young than curling up for a good seven or eight hours. It took many years before I could discipline myself to sleep only for ninety minutes every night. Fortunately, as one grows older, one needs less and less rest.'

'I cannot match you in that,' Teresa said. 'I sleep well for five or six hours during the twenty-four; I do not fast beyond the required Rule; I do not even use the discipline as much as some of the other sisters do.'

'Penance and mortification are simply means to an end,' Brother Pedro said. 'Some of us need them more than others. And we must not dwell upon them. Better to enjoy a good meal and a sound sleep than spend one's time regretting the lack of them. Now, daughter, I must go and pay my respects to Dona Guiomar and Mariadiaz. Good women, both of them, with more virtues than either of us possess.'

'I am grateful for your coming,' Teresa said, humbly.

'And I am grateful for having met you,' he returned, and she flushed shyly, knowing that this man would always speak the absolute truth.

'What did you think of him?' demanded Dona Guiomar, later in the day, when the shabby, white-haired figure had plodded through the gate.

'That with all his sanctity he is highly agreeable,' Teresa admitted.

'Did he advise you?' Mariadiaz asked.

'He advised patience,' Teresa remembered.

'Only that?' Dona Guiomar looked a trifle disappointed.

'He gave me his friendship,' said Teresa, 'and that is worth a great deal.'

'But you will always make friends wherever you go,' Mariadiaz said, without envy. 'Is it true that you are to go and see Dona Luisa de la Cerda?'

'I wish I could stay here for a longer time,' Teresa confessed, 'but my sister, Juana, has written begging me to see this lady. Apparently, since her husband's death, she has lain in a darkened room, weeping without pause, finding no comfort or consolation even in her children. They say she is one of the richest ladies in Spain, but she wishes only to die.'

'And she has asked you to visit her?'

'Through my sister, and to please Juana I will go, though what I can do I cannot think,' Teresa said despairingly. 'I feel desperately sorry for the poor lady if she is truly heart-broken, but what can cure such grief beyond acceptance and time? However, Dona Luisa has offered to lodge me in her mansion which pleases me, because Juana and her husband cannot really afford to support any visitors.'

'I will be sorry to see you go,' Mariadiaz said, gruffly. 'It is not often one meets another woman who understands one's troubles and one's hopes.'

She seemed about to say more but pressed Teresa's hand and went away.

'Poor Mariadiaz!' Dona Guiomar sighed, looking after her. 'Not many people are kind to her. My own servants treat her with scorn unless I am there to keep them in order.'

'She is truly a fervent lover of God. If ever a woman worked towards sanctity, that woman is Mariadiaz,' said Teresa.

'But God chooses His saints,' said Dona Guiomar with unusual shrewdness. 'He does not wait for them to knock upon His door.'

'Dear Dona Guiomar! You have more wisdom in one thought than I have in a whole imagination,' Teresa teased, and wished regretfully again that she had not agreed to see the sorrowing widow.

She was sorry to leave the quiet, congenial company of her two friends, and when she reached the white shuttered mansion, within which the widow grieved, her distaste turned to annoyance for the gates were crammed with servants, grooms, clerics and tradesmen who gaped and pointed at her as she stepped from the covered cart.

'There goes the miracle worker! The nun from Avila who talks with the angels.'

'Her sister lives here. That too is an honour for us.'

'She has come to cure Dona Luisa de la Cerda.'

Teresa, drawing her veil over her head, scowled at the floor of the paved courtyard as she stood waiting to be admitted. By her side, Juan de Ovalle preened himself a little. His fear that the talk about Teresa would cause a family disgrace had changed into vicarious pride because she was spoken of by many as a noted beata, capable, it was rumoured, of the most amazing miracles.

A small hand tugged at Teresa's skirt.

'Are you Dona Teresa y Ahumada, please?'

The speaker was a small girl in a richly embroidered gown, with rings dangling from her ears and covering her hands.

'I am indeed, and who may you be, little lady?'

'I am Dona Maria de Salazar,' the child said, eagerly. 'I am maid to Dona Luisa de la Cerda.'

'Maid!' Teresa looked in some surprise at the elaborate dress and sparkling jewels.

'I am being educated with Dona Luisa's children,' Maria de Salazar explained. 'Already I am fluent at Latin and very skilled in music and dancing.'

'Are you indeed? Wouldn't it be better to wait until others told you of your skills?' Teresa asked, dryly.

'But they tell me all the time,' said Maria with beautiful simplicity. 'Dona Luisa says I am the most brilliantly gifted girl of ten she has ever known. She tells everybody I am a prodigy and it's no more than the truth. She entrusts me already with a great deal of responsibility, more than her own son, I assure you. I have given orders for the decoration of your room while you are staying here and you will please let me know at once if anything is not to your liking.'

'But you don't spend all your time learning and supervising, do you? Don't you ever play any games?' Teresa asked.

Something lonely and wistful flashed into the bright, self-confident eyes.

'I used to play with dolls,' the self-confessed prodigy admitted, 'but since Dona Luisa was widowed, somebody has had to arrange things. The slaves are very lazy, you know, and need a firm hand. They might not obey a girl who plays with dolls.'

'You said you could dance?' Teresa reminded her. 'When I have talked with Dona Luisa, would you like to dance for me? I have brought my guitar so we could play some tunes together, if that would please you.'

'Oh, it would! Indeed it would please me!'

The little girl gave a most unsophisticated hop, and then scurried ahead through the opening gates.

Teresa, taking a brief leave of Juan de Ovalle, passed from the bustling courtyard into a heavy silence. Straw deadened the footsteps, heavy carpets hung limply against the walls, the gleam of silver, ivory and gold intruded upon furniture draped in black and purple. Slaves, clad in mourning, moved bare-footed through the gloom and somewhere in the great palace a dog howled dolefully.

The major-domo, who was conducting her through the long corridors, paused before a door hung with black velvet and inclined his head solemnly.

'The apartments of Dona Luisa de la Cerda,' he murmured, and pushed the door ajar. As she entered Teresa's quick ears caught a new sound, that of hopeless, helpless weeping that went on and on, intensifying the silence around.

Maria de Salazar watched the door close behind the small, graceful figure and waited until the major-domo strode bulkily away. Then she pulled up a little stool and sat quietly, with her hands clasped, while she began to invent a poem, in Latin, of course, about nuns with lovely eyes. When it was finished, she would copy it in her best handwriting, with the capital letters all touched in with gold leaf, and present it to Dona Teresa y Ahumada.

The hours passed slowly as day lagged into evening. Slaves lit the tapers and chained the gates; someone fed the howling dog; the scent of baked fish mingled with the mustiness of crêpe and the acrid tang of stale incense. There was no sound from behind the closed door of Dona Luisa's apartments. Maria's neatly-braided head drooped a trifle and then she jerked into wakefulness again with a tinkle of gold earhoops.

Teresa looked tired but contented when she finally emerged into the dim corridor again. She had been battling for hours against a grief that fed upon itself and selfishly denied all other emotion; but Castilian practicality and Christian compassion had, she thought, turned the tide. Dona Luisa would not now weep her life away but would honour the memory of her husband by showing charity to the living.

Maria de Salazar, jerked into a fit of wakefulness by the consciousness that she was no longer alone, stumbled to her feet.

'I will show you to your rooms, Dona Teresa. And I am ready to dance for you whenever you please,' she said valiantly.

'I was detained for longer than I expected,' said Teresa tactfully, 'and it is now rather late for me to appreciate music. Would you be kind enough to dance for me tomorrow instead?'

'Oh, yes, Dona Teresa! And you will play your guitar?'

Teresa nodded and took the child's hand.

'We will spend some time together every day,' she said warmly. 'I know all sorts of exciting games my brothers and I used to play.'

'And Dona Luisa will get better?' The swift, upward glance was anxious.

'She will get better very quickly,' Teresa said confidently. 'You will have time to be a child again. Is this my room?'

She uttered the question in a tone bordering on dismay, for the chamber into which Maria led her was draped in purple and gold and so crowded with valuable ornaments that there was scarcely room to move.

'I arranged it myself,' said Maria, proudly. 'I'll wager the Duchess of Alba hasn't a room finer than this in which to sleep.'

'I'll wager she hasn't,' Teresa agreed, and wondered how in the world she could ever manage to simplify her surroundings without hurting her small friend's feelings.

'I don't really enjoy being a child very much,' Maria confided suddenly. 'I look forward to becoming a grown woman, you know. I am so clever now that, if I continue to learn and to study, when I am fully grown my brain capacity will be truly amazing.'

Teresa took one look at the small, brightly-clad figure and, sitting on the end of the over-decorated bed, gave vent to peal after peal of delighted laughter. Maria glared indignantly for a moment and then, infected by the silvery gurgle, put her hands to her mouth and laughed too, her sleepy eyes brimful of merriment.

'Child, you have given me something more precious than diamonds!' Teresa declared. 'I was hemmed in by weariness and another's grief, but you have lightened my heart. And I thank you for it!'

'I wasn't actually trying to amuse you,' Maria said primly, 'but I'm glad I gave you pleasure. That's why I took off my mourning clothes and put on a green dress, so that it please you. You didn't think it wrong of me?'

'Of course not. Your dress is lovely,' Teresa told her. 'But all those jewels for a little girl! One of them would buy food for us at the Incarnation for a month.'

'You can have them then,' said Maria, promptly.

'No, little one. You will need them later when you come to wed. No doubt they form part of your dowry.'

'I'm never going to marry,' said the child serenely.

'Come now,' Teresa rallied her. 'You have not met any young man yet, so you cannot tell!'

'I have never met a boy who is more intelligent than I am,' said Maria, 'and I would never be able to honour and cherish one who is less intelligent. So I will never marry. I think I would like – I would like to become a nun and come to live with you. Would you have me?'

'Not unless you were much older and much wiser and empty of all conceit,' Teresa said, solemnly. 'But you will forget me, little one. You will find other ambitions and amusements and take your place in the world with other ladies of rank.'

'I will remind you of that when I come to live with you,' Maria said, and yawned.

'Child, go to your bed.' Teresa rose briskly, patting her on the shoulder. 'I will ring for a servant to bring my supper but you must go to your bed now. Goodnight, Maria de Salazar, little slyboots.'

'Goodnight, little mother Teresa,' the child retorted softly and pattered out.

Little mother? Teresa looked thoughtfully round the brilliant room.

Is it to be thus, Lord? I cannot begin until You give me the command. And how much longer must I wait to know Your Will? How much longer, Lord?

CHAPTER EIGHT

'If one more mishap prevents us, I declare I shall lose courage,' Teresa said, dolefully.

'Lose courage? I would like to live long enough to see that day,' laughed Dona Luisa de la Cerda.

'Oh, it has not happened yet,' Teresa said. 'But these difficulties spring up at every turn. As if my hands were not full enough, Juan has started another lawsuit against my half-sister.'

'Another one?' Dona Luisa looked up from her needlework.

'All over that wretched property my mother divided between Juana and me in her will,' Teresa said crossly. 'I gave my share to Juana when I entered the religious life. Maria's husband always felt that she was entitled to something from my mother's estate, so he began a lawsuit against my sister Juana. The suit was nullified when Martin de Guzman died so suddenly, and now Juan de Ovalle is reopening the whole sorry business, though he promised me to settle the matter out of court. My half-sister has not been well since her husband's death, and she needs money with four children for whom to provide dowries. Juan could afford to pay her a reasonable allowance if he gave up some of the luxuries to which he has accustomed himself.'

'I can send something to Dona Maria,' began Dona Luisa impulsively, but Teresa shook her head.

'You are the most generous of friends,' she said warmly, 'but I regard you as something more than a bottomless purse into which I can dip in order to benefit my family.'

'But I owe you more than I can ever repay,' Dona Luisa said. 'When you came here three years ago, I was dying, not simply of grief but of self-pity. And you made me realize my own selfishness. When you went back to the Incarnation, I vowed then that I would do everything in my power to help you in any way you needed.'

'A rash vow!' Teresa chuckled. 'You did not imagine when you made it that you would be called upon to help finance a new convent.'

'I am very wealthy,' said Dona Luisa with a tinge of sadness. 'Money is all that I can give.'

'Nonsense! You have given me your friendship,' Teresa said. 'You have given me a private place where I can stay quietly, away from the gossip.'

'It must have been dreadful for you these past months at the Incarnation,' Dona Luisa said sympathetically.

'It was not easy,' Teresa said quietly.

There had indeed been nothing but trouble since Teresa had received her instructions. And such instructions! They had caused her heart to stand still for a moment and then to race with fear.

It is My Will, that you found a convent, dedicated to St Joseph. Tell this to your confessor and tell him that you are not to be hindered or opposed.

She had waited for so long for her instructions, had half-guessed that when they came they would march with her own desires, and yet she was afraid, even too frightened to tell her confessor. Instead she had written to him and then waited in a fever of indecision until her request had been passed on through the Father Superior to the Father Provincial.

It had all gone so smoothly at first; too smoothly, she realized later. Father Gregario Fernandez had tentatively approved of the idea but asked for more details. It was Dona Guiomar del Ulloa who had agreed to sponsor the plan and had helped Teresa to draft out a simple document.

She had been so careful to make her request a modest one, asking for permission to buy or rent a small house where a limited number of Carmelites might live in strict enclosure, working for their livings, praying constantly for their fellow-men, observing strict silence and mortification.

And the Father Provincial had sent verbal approval. The fathers of the Society of Jesus had brought encouraging messages. Dona Luisa de la Cerda had sent a large contribution.

And then some incautious visitor had chatted too freely in the parlour of the Incarnation, and the storm had begun to rage around Teresa's head.

'So we are not good enough for Dona Teresa y Ahumada. She is not satisfied with the way we keep the Rule, and wishes to separate herself from us.'

'She cannot even keep the Rule herself. Look how often she goes to the parlour without a chaperone!'

'To see Don Francisco de Guzman.'

'And Don Francisco de Salcedo? He is a most worldly man!'

'She thinks herself too fine to remain longer in such a poor community.'

'It isn't enough that she causes such scandal with her visions and raptures.'

'She wishes to be more cloistered, so she says. Why, she cannot stay here for a month without finding some excuse to go off on a visit to one or other of her friends – '

'*Rich* friends! Haven't you noticed that her friends are always wealthy?'

'Naturally! It's dry bread and straw pallets for everybody else, and apricots out of season for Dona Teresa!'

Not all the voices were outraged. She remembered with gratitude that her cousins, Maria, Ana, Beatriz and Inés had loyally supported her. The young daughters of her cousin Francisco were now in the convent too, and Maria, Beatriz and Isobel de Cepeda had all spoken up boldly, declaring they would follow Dona Teresa wherever she led.

'For didn't she play with us and tell us stories when we were very tiny?' demanded Beatriz, imperiously.

'And wasn't it for love of cousin Teresa that we have entered the religious life?' cried sixteen-year-old Isobel.

'For love of God, rather,' corrected her sister, Maria de Cepeda. 'But it was cousin Teresa who pointed the way.'

There were others who had supported her, some defiantly in the midst of the whole community and others timidly plucking her sleeve and whispering encouragement. Teresa de Querida was not, she declared, too old to support her namesake, and gentle Juana of the Holy Spirit, whose excessive fasts were a source of wonder in the community, had stood up at recreation, trembling from head to foot, and announced that she would follow Dona Teresa to the new convent if her friend thought her worthy.

The Incarnation parlour had rattled with gossip; the walls of Avila had throbbed with it.

'Another convent, in a town so packed with churches and monasteries that there isn't room to build any houses for us to live in!'

'We cannot support the religious orders we have here

already. Now this woman speaks of living in complete poverty.'

'Wasn't there some talk of these new nuns earning their own living?'

'The idea of it! Does Dona Teresa y Ahumada think we are too mean or too impoverished to give alms?'

'The de Cepedas used to be extremely wealthy, but two of the daughters married poor men, and with seven sons!'

'One of them is dead, isn't he?'

'Two of them now. The second son, Rodrigo de Cepeda, died in Chile about three years ago. There was a younger one, Antonio, who was killed at Inaquito.'

'Well, one of the five who are left ought to sail back to Spain and use his authority to prevent his sister from making such a fool of herself.'

Seated in Dona Luisa de la Cerda's private sitting-room, Teresa said, wistfully, 'If only my brothers were here! They could go to the Father Provincial and persuade him to give us the written authority.'

'It was intolerable of him to take back his verbal permission,' Dona Luisa said.

'Ah, no! the poor man simply could not stand up to the blows aimed at him,' Teresa said charitably. 'He preferred to retire from the contest.'

'But you bought a house anyway!'

'I had already purchased it when he told me to forget the whole idea,' Teresa reminded her. 'My sister and her husband have been staying there while we wait for permission from Rome.'

'Do you think it will arrive?'

'It *must* arrive!' Teresa clenched her small hands. 'When I consider what I have dared to do, in sending secretly for authorization from the Holy Father, I tremble at my own foolhardiness. But matters have already gone so far! There are four prospective novices for the convent, and Juan tells me the house is already scrubbed and whitewashed with a turn installed. If I go back to Avila, I must go to the new convent to give the nuns their habits and to witness the inauguration ceremony. Once I'm back at the Incarnation it will be difficult for me to obtain permission to leave again. Already they are grumbling that I spend too long outside the cloister, as if I were bent merely on my own pleasure.'

'Did you never wish to travel, to broaden your horizons?' Dona Luisa asked curiously.

'Once when I was small, I set out to run away to North Africa and become a martyr,' Teresa remembered.

'Alone?'

'My brother Rodrigo came with me,' she said, softly.

'He died a few years ago, didn't he? You never speak of him.'

'And I did not weep when I heard the news. There are some pains that hurt too much for the relief of tears. Rodrigo was my favourite brother when we were children.'

'But the others are all well?'

Dona Luisa could have kicked herself for having brought an unhappy memory to her friend's mind.

'Hernando is an alderman of Pastro now,' Teresa said cheerfully. 'I wish he would write to me oftener, but I suppose his duties keep him busy. And Lorenzo sends me all the news. He and Pedro are both married to girls of good Spanish family. And Lorenzo's wife is expecting her third child soon. Francisco is just two years old and Lorencito almost ten months. Oh, I wish I could see them! And Agustin and Jeronimo too! I wish they would settle down and marry, but there! Lorenzo waited until he was thirty-seven before he chose a bride. So there's hope for them both yet!'

'There's a messenger coming through the fountain court,' Dona Luisa observed, glancing through the unshuttered window.

Teresa, aware of the habits of aristocrats, smiled a trifle to herself. It would have taken no more than a few seconds for her hostess to step over the window and intercept the letter, but Dona Luisa would never have thought of such a thing. Instead she waited in her luxurious apartment while the letter passed through a series of hands, until it arrived finally on a golden salver in the hands of one of her waiting women.

'These new girls are so slow. I wish Maria de Salazar were with me, but her relatives would insist on her paying them an extended visit. Oh, but the letter is for you, Dona Teresa.'

Dona Luisa passed over the missive and tactfully busied herself with her embroidery.

'It's from my brother-in-law, Señor Juan de Ovalle,' Teresa said, looking up. 'My sister went back to Alba de Tormes a few days ago because one of the children had a slight fever, and now Juan sends to say that he himself is not well. He is managing alone in the little house at Avila, you see. Poor man, I must go and see what I can do for him.'

'At least you will have an excuse to delay your return to the Incarnation,' Dona Luisa pointed out.

'I hadn't thought of that! You're right, of course, but it seems rather hard on poor Juan. Let us hope,' said Teresa earnestly, 'that his illness is a slight one.'

'And lasts until permission for your convent arrives from Rome,' Dona Luisa added, fervently.

'Even if it never arrives, I shall be truly grateful for your kindness,' Teresa assured her. 'These past months have meant a great deal to me. There is more peace and privacy here at Toledo than in the Convent of the Incarnation.'

'And you have finished your manuscript too,' said Dona Luisa.

A small frown indented Teresa's brows. In the midst of all the turmoil about the proposed new convent, there had come orders from her confessor that she was to write down a full account of her life in order that the Inquisition might examine her beliefs.

'But I am not a writer!' she had protested. 'My education is limited, my powers of expression poor. Cannot I appear before a Tribunal of the Holy Office and answer any questions put to me?'

Her protests had been unavailing. Father Pedro Alvarez and Father Gaspar de Salazar had insisted upon obedience, intimating that she was fortunate to have been given the opportunity of putting her case in her own words. The task had not been to her taste and it irritated her to think of the hours she had spent chewing the tip of her pen and racking her brains as she stared at the blank paper. It was agony to spread herself out in phrases and sentences as if, with each stroke of her pen, another piece of her soul was laid bare. But she had written as honestly as anybody could write, dwelling considerably upon her sins lest it be supposed for an instant that she was deserving of any special consideration. And sometimes her words flowed so freely that she would be astonished when she stopped and saw how much she had written. If only her memory for dates was more reliable; and if only she had a wider training in theology so that she could explain clearly the various stages of prayer through which she had advanced!

Now, however, the first, rough copy had been finished and was ready to be checked, Teresa having grave doubts as to whether her spelling or punctuations were up to the standard of those eminent theologicians who would discuss and analyse her ideas. She had not the smallest doubt that her book was doctrinally correct, and if it were not, she supposed innocently that the Inquisition would point out her mistakes. At all events, nobody would see the book during her lifetime except her superiors, and, after her death, nobody would be very interested in the story of an obscure nun.

'I must go back to Avila,' she said now to Dona Luisa. 'The authorization cannot be long and Brother Pedro of Alcantara has already sent me one of his own disciples to take the habit. His advice is always so encouraging.'

She sighed a little as she spoke for she had seen death written clearly in the friar's face the last time he had visited her. He had been well aware that his days were limited and accepted approaching death with eager curiosity, but Teresa had not yet managed to conquer her natural aversion to the dissolution of soul and body.

The next morning she was on her way back to Avila, pausing only long enough to obtain permission for further leave of absence from the Incarnation, before she alighted at the small, white-washed house where she found her brother-in-law suffering from what she deduced to be an attack of gastritis, but behaving as usual as if he were the only person in the world who was ever indisposed.

With outward patience she set herself to preparing broth and milk jellies and lavishing sympathy on the petulant invalid, while her ears were constantly pricked for the ringing of the doorbell which might announce the arrival of the permission from Rome. Her only visitors were the preacher Gaspar Daza, who had overcome his earlier scruples concerning her and was now a party to the secret, and the prebendary of Avila, Julian de Avila, who had also pledged his support.

Father Julian was a lively, good-natured priest with a taste for gossip and a delight in intrigue that amused Teresa immensely. With him he had brought his young sister Maria, who was to be one of the four novices. In contrast to her volatile brother she was silent and gentle with huge childlike eyes and an engaging simplicity of manner.

Pedro of Alcantara's disciple trudged in a few days later, looking tired after her journey. Antonia of the Holy Spirit was, Teresa judged, another childlike soul who would follow the Rule with great and earnest simplicity. Hard on her heels came Maria of the Cross, a protégée of Dona Guiomar del Ulloa. These three were, Teresa had decided, young enough to be moulded into the pattern of a perfect Carmelite and fervent enough to live up to the ideals they had embraced. Maria de Avila's engaging manner might soften Antonia of the Holy Spirit's Spartan self-discipline and Maria of the Cross was intelligent and well educated.

The fourth, she had chosen herself, not without some misgivings, for Ursula of the Saints was a widow already past forty and a trifle set in her ways. But she had plenty of sound common sense, and with her firm yet pleasant manner would become an excellent Prioress.

It was Ursula of the Saints who had taken one look at the three girls praying together in the tiny, white-washed chapel and suggested they might care to help Dona Teresa to finish making the habits.

'And we must lay in some supplies,' she added, 'for without lay-sisters it will be very difficult to provide for ourselves. We cannot go junketing off to market.'

'Dona Guiomar del Ulloa has promised to come regularly to see what you need,' Teresa assured her, 'and Father Julian is not likely to let his own sister starve. And you will be able to earn what you need when you are fully established. We ought all to have a little independence, so that we can contribute to the community.'

Ursula of the Saints nodded and regarded the neatly stitched habit of brown frieze with approval. Almost of the same age as Teresa, she enjoyed her company immensely and thought all her friend's ideas marvellous.

'Simplicity,' Teresa said, tapping her needle against the stone floor on which they squatted. 'A ruthless pruning of all that distracts us from the love of God. Complete simplicity of line, absolute purity of shape and colour. Perpetual silence except during our two hours of recreation or when we are saying the Office. But gaiety too, Sister, for I cannot abide weepy-wailers. To live and work in a joyous harmony of spirit. That is what I long to see achieved.'

'The permission will surely come soon,' piped up Maria de Avila.

'I hope so. He will be so disappointed if it does not,' Teresa said, and the others knew she was not speaking of any earthly friend.

But three weeks passed before the precious document lay in her hands, signed not only with the Papal Seal but by the Bishop of Avila who had apparently decided to admit this little rebel offshoot of the Carmelite Community under his jurisdiction.

Citizens of Avila, on their way to early market or the first mass of the day, were not inclined to notice amid the clamour of bells from the surrounding churches one more calling peal – somewhat out-of-tune, for the bell purchased by Teresa was secondhand and slightly cracked.

Within the chapel, decorated with fresh flowers, adorned by two carefully clothed statues of the Mother and Child and St Joseph with his lily, a small group of people knelt respectfully before the altar of polished wood where Gaspar Daza offered up the mass and gave a short, triumphant sermon.

Juan and Juana de Ovalle were there, with the richly-dressed Francisco de Salcedo, and good-humoured Father Julian. Three nuns from the Incarnation had also contrived to be present. Juana Suarez was kneeling sedately next to Teresa's cousins, Ana and Inés Tapia. Near Teresa herself, Dona Guiomar del Ulloa, her enthusiasm for collecting saints undiminished, closed her eyes tightly and prayed that all the difficulties were over.

One by one, the four nuns of the new Convent of St Joseph stepped forward to receive from Dona Teresa the rope-soled sandals, the coarse brown habit, the white coif and black veil that they would wear to the end of their days. To each newly garbed nun, Gaspar Daza gave a narrow wedding ring, a rosary, a Breviary and the coiled discipline which would mortify their fleshly desires. Then each veiled figure passed slowly through the grilled arch into her world of high walls and infinite horizons.

Teresa's one dread had been that she might fall into a rapture and distract attention from those to whom the day belonged, but she was fortunate in suffering from no more than satisfaction at a task completed.

As she knelt, her thoughts went back to the orchard where as a small girl she had tried to build her hermitage. Had there been in her even then that desire for contemplation that was the mark of Mary Magdalene?

But I am Martha too, she thought, the bustling little gossip concerned about the welfare of my fellowmen. And in all my Carmelites, Mary and Martha must meet and mingle, for Love is not confined to the chapel and Our Lord enjoys a stroll amid the pots and pans.

'And what are your ambitions now?' Don Francisco de

Salcedo was asking.

'Ambitions?' Teresa looked at him for a moment in genuine surprise and then laughed. 'Why, I don't believe I have any desires left, my friend, except to enclose myself here with my Sisters, away from the glare of the world.'

'First you must return to the Incarnation,' Gaspar Daza warned her. 'By noon, news that Dona Teresa y Ahumada has founded a convent without permission will spread through the town. The Prioress of the Incarnation has not given you leave to abandon it. If you do so without authority you are liable to be expelled from the Order altogether.'

'But I have permission from the Holy See, and am under the protection of Bishop de Mendoza!'

'And because you went over the heads of the Mother Prioress and the Father Provincial, do you imagine they will all rush to approve?' the preacher asked dryly. 'You are bound by your vow of obedience to the Mother Prioress who is the Christ in your community.'

'I have never broken that vow, for the Prioress never actually forbade me to found a convent,' Teresa said earnestly. 'When the Father Provincial withdrew his verbal approval, he did not actually tell me *not* to apply to a higher authority.'

'It is easy to tell that you have Jesuit advisers,' Gaspar Daza said, not without humour. 'And I am beginning to understand why poor Diego de Cetina complained recently that he would rather argue with all the theologians in Christendom than with you!'

'We will support you upon your return,' Juana Suarez said. 'You will not have to stand alone, for many of us approved of what you have done.'

'It is time that some reform of the Order took place,' Ana de Tapia said stoutly, 'and Inés and I will tell them so.'

'You will do nothing of the kind! Heaven help me! but the last thing I need is a flock of chattering friends and cousins all seeing who can bleat the loudest!'

Teresa put her hands to her coif and regarded them with affectionate exasperation.

'The responsibility is mine,' she said firmly. 'The blame, if there is any blame, is mine and if there is punishment that too must be mine.'

'At least you will accept my escort back to the Incarnation,' Julian de Avila said, warmly.

'And that would make a fine beginning!' she retorted, 'to arrive at the convent unchaperoned except by a secular priest. I sometimes think you haven't an atom of worldly sense between the lot of you! No, I will return with my cousins and my friend, and you, Father Julian, will remember that you are now chaplain to four Discalced Carmelites.'

'Shoeless Carmelites?' questioned Dona Guiomar del Ulloa.

'Metaphorically speaking,' Teresa smiled. 'They would go literally barefoot if I did not have more compassion for their poor toes. Now, good Fathers, give me your blessing before I leave.'

'What will she find when she reaches the Incarnation?' Julian de Avila worried.

'A prioress in a rage,' said Gaspar Daza bluntly. 'Our friend is in very great danger of being imprisoned or publicly disciplined.'

'And she faces it alone!' marvelled Francisco de Salcedo.

'Alone? Ah, my worldly friend, what a great deal you have to learn!' exclaimed Gaspar Daza and seemed much amused at his own remark.

Not only the prioress was in a rage. By noon, the Convent of the Incarnation resembled nothing so much as an angrily buzzing hive of bees who have just learned that one of the worker insects has set up a rival hierarchy.

All pretence of work or prayer had ceased, and groups of gesticulating nuns had collected in the passages and recreation room to argue, to condemn, to marvel, to scold, even to weep, for most of them were very fond of Teresa and mortified to learn she had turned out to be so sly and disobedient. The parlour was also crammed for it was amazing how many citizens suddenly felt the need for a little uplifting and spiritual conversation.

The Mother Prioress, flanked by the Sub-Prioress and the Mistress of Novices, sat, grim-lipped, in her chair of office. She had reached the stage when the genuine kindliness she felt for the Ahumada nun was swept away by a torrent of unreasoning passion.

'She entered the religious life in a dramatic, unseemly fashion; she foisted her sister upon us for years; she made us the talk of Castile with her visions and vapours; and now she sets herself up as some divinely appointed foundress,' the Prioress burst out suddenly, and stopped, listening to the silence as if all the threads of conversation had been severed by a knife.

There was a soft patter of feet beyond the room, a discreet tap upon the door, and at the Prioress's shrill 'Deo Gratias', the small, slim woman with the glowing eyes entered and made her reverence.

'So! Dona Teresa Sanchez de Cepeda Davila y Ahumada!' Each name was a stone flung bitterly at the neatly coifed head. 'And what have you to say to me?'

The eyes fixed themselves upon the older nun's implacable face and Teresa answered, modestly and quietly, but with a hint of steel under the gentleness.

'Mother Prioress, I have renounced all my titles. In future, I wish to be known as Teresa of Jesus, Carmelite.'

Anger receded, leaving the Prioress to flounder in the shallows of her own inadequacy. To her astonishment, she heard herself say, 'Tell me about it, daughter,' and knew she was beaten before she had begun.

CHAPTER NINE

'These have been the happiest five years of my life,' Teresa remarked.

The thirteen sisters of the Discalced Community at St Joseph's, Avila, were at recreation and as it was too hot to dance they were devoting their leisure to conversation, interrupted only by the occasional tinkling of the little bell to remind them they were still in the presence of God.

'You speak as if you will never return to us,' said Ana of St John, tears starting to her eyes.

'If it were not God's will I would not be leaving now,' Teresa said, with no shade of reproof. 'Believe me, but I long to spend all my days here with you. One convent was all I ever visualized, but you know Our Lord's little ways. First He caused Brother Alfonso Maldonado to visit us and tell us about his mission to the Indies, inspiring us with such fervent desire to save souls that we were overwhelmed. And then Our Lord said to me: *Wait a little, daughter, and thou shalt see great things.*'

'And then the Father General visited us and approved so

greatly of our way of life that he gave you licence to found more convents wherever you saw fit,' Inés de Tapia said enthusiastically.

'And two for men!' chimed in Ana de Tapia. 'Only to think of it! A woman licensed to establish monasteries!'

'It would have been more to the point,' said Maria Baptist, acidly, 'if he had made some financial contribution. Mother Teresa had about a ducat in the treasury when the licence arrived. How many convents can be founded by Mother Teresa and one ducat?'

'None,' Teresa said merrily, 'but if Mother Teresa has a ducat and God, she may found as many as she pleases!'

'And there was no need for you to spend the one ducat,' said Maria de Avila, 'for when you wrote for advice to the Prior of St Anne's at Medina del Campo, he offered to rent a suitable house there for you.'

'Brother Antonio de Herédia has always written most kindly and helpfully to us,' said Teresa. 'He has spent a lifetime among the Calced but he has great sympathy with the reform. I look forward to meeting him.'

'I hope he has provided us with a decent dwelling,' Maria Baptist said, being evidently determined upon pessimism.

Teresa glanced at her but bit back a sharp retort. Dearly as she loved her cousin's daughter, there was much about the former Maria de Ocampo that irritated and disquieted her. She would never forget that it was Maria who had first remarked, though jestingly, that they ought to establish a convent and there was much in the young woman's quick wit and shrewdness that was admirable, but there was something unpleasing in her character, a kind of subtle insolence that defied analysis.

Yet she kept the Rule rigidly and had never been found wanting in obedience. Teresa had tested this by giving her a rotten cucumber and telling her to plant it in the garden. Maria had merely asked, 'Horizontally or vertically?' and gone quietly out to do as she was bade. And it was Maria who had ordered the reluctant workmen to dig more deeply for water in a spot they declared was dry and betrayed not a sign of conceit when the resulting gush of water was christened the Maria Baptist spring by the grateful nuns.

She will make a good Prioress, Teresa thought. She has a managing streak and the desire to exercise it.

Ana and Inés de Tapia were also going to Medina. Without

the watchful anxiety of her sister, the delicate Ana would work beyond her strength. Two other recruits from the Incarnation, Ana of the Angels and the ascetic Teresa de Querida, would be a steadying influence upon the sixth nun, excitable Isobel Arias.

And when they are settled there, I can return to St Joseph's, Teresa mused. Ursula of the Saints will be Prioress while I am away, and there is an excellent chance of my avoiding re-election upon my return.

'Do you think there will really be trouble from the Augustinian friars?' asked Isobel Arias, who was inclined to be nervous.

'They are only afraid we may attract alms away from their own monastery. Once we are settled, I anticipate very little trouble,' Teresa soothed.

'A two-day journey,' Inés worried. 'I'm glad that Father Julian will be escorting us.'

'He has hired a covered wagon so we can maintain privacy and the rule of enclosure as far as possible,' Teresa said gratefully. 'And he has hired rooms at Arévalo where we make our overnight stop.'

'Even if my brother did not accompany you,' said Maria de Avila, 'you would be safe with Mother Teresa.'

Isobel of St Dominic nodded in agreement. It was she who, going into the kitchen one morning, had found Teresa in deep rapture, her eyes shining upon a sight while in her capable hand a saucepan cradled two merrily frying eggs. Young as she was, Isobel of St Dominic could recognize the exquisite balance between the spiritual and the practical and since then she had trusted the foundress more than she had ever trusted anybody in her life.

They left the next morning, drawing their veils down over their heads under the curious gaze of the muleteers, as they climbed into the large wagon with its black canvas sides. Father Julian, issuing slightly self-important instructions from the back of his mule, was in his element. He had taken immense trouble to bring sufficient provisions and to work out the most comfortable route, and the prospect of a journey excited him so that his good-humoured face flushed and his voice rose higher.

Teresa, seated in the wagon and carrying the carved image of the Holy Child sent by her brother, Lorenzo, hid a grin as she listened to the chaplain. Greatly as she disliked leaving St Joseph's, there rose inside her a small bubble of excitement.

Life was an adventure not only of the spirit but also of the body, and inside the woman of fifty-two there still dwelled a wide-eyed tomboy.

Early as it was, the sun stood high over Avila, and as the day wore on the heat became increasingly hard to endure. The slits in the canvas afforded no more than inadequate ventilation and an occasional glimpse of brown baked landscape; water fresh in the morning was greasily warm by noon, and the constant swaying and jolting as the cart rolled along the rough roads threatened the nuns with sickness and headaches. They all, even Maria Baptist, bore it without complaint and Teresa, fighting back nausea, thought with pride that Juana Suarez had been right when she had nicknamed them 'shock-troops of the Carmelites'.

Dear Juana Suarez! Her oldest and most beloved friend, who had been sensible enough to know from the beginning that the high, heroic path to virtue was not for her and had stayed quietly on the lower slopes at the Incarnation.

They reached the hamlet of Arévalo after dusk and were almost too tired by then to appreciate the luxury of a cool shady room and a daintily cooked supper. Teresa, seeing the abundance of the meal, was half-inclined to scold Julian de Avila, who must have dug deeply into his own pocket to provide it. Then she reflected that there is a grace in receiving as well as in giving, and delighted the chaplain by taking a second helping of the baked quinces.

The next morning, a tall, stout figure in the well-cut habit of the Calced rode up to the door of the inn and dismounting from his horse required that Mother Teresa be good enough to see him. She came down at once and greeted him with pleasure, for Brother Antonio de Herédia had already proved himself a benefactor.

'As Prior of St Anne's,' she informed him brightly, 'you can smooth our path and make it possible for us to dwell in peace side by side. There should not be jealousy between Calced and Discalced, for we are all part of the great Carmelite Order.'

'But I will not be Prior for very much longer,' Brother Antonio told her, 'for it is my intention to join the Discalced and resign my position.'

'Join the – ? But there are no Discalced monasteries for men!'

'Not yet, but you have a licence in your own pocket from

the Father General which authorizes you to found two,' he reminded her.

'At some future date,' she floundered, 'but not yet. These things take time! It will be at least a year before I can think of it, and I must wait until I have recruits.'

'You have one already,' Brother Antonio said. 'And I can recommend another. There is a young man at Medina del Campo who would join me, I believe. His name is Juan de Yepes, of a good family on his father's side but on his mother's of peasant stock. However, she is a good woman so he insists. He joined us three years ago under the name of Juan of St Matthew, but I sent him to study Arts and Theology under Luis de Léon at Salamanca. He has come back to St Andrew's now, and you should see him, I assure you.'

'How old is this young man?'

'Twenty-four, but so highly spiritual that he has already attained the same degree of sanctity as Pedro of Alcantara had when he died.'

'Brother Antonio! How can you possibly measure another's sanctity?' Teresa cried in amazement. 'I will see this young paragon but you will allow me, if you please, to judge him for myself.'

'And you will accept me as your first friar of the Reform?'

Teresa eyed him doubtfully, noting the paunch, the fleshy nose and full, petulant lips, the large, smooth, white hands.

'The life is a hard one,' she said guardedly, 'and you have spent many years among the Calced and are no longer young.'

'Sixty-six,' he informed her, 'and so eager for mortifications that I have already removed my shoes.'

Proudly he thrust a bare and bleeding foot from under the fine habit.

'And what pleasure or profit will it be to God if you are crippled by blisters, at your age?' Teresa demanded. 'Put your sandals back. It would make better sense if you gave up that fine horse on which you arrived and took to a mule for long trips. Even a short walk up the path has cut your toes. What topsy-turvey notions of mortification some folks have!'

For an instant he looked deeply affronted. Then, seeing the twinkle in her brown eyes, he responded with a stiff little smile.

'If I privately follow the Rule of the Discalced for one year, will you then allow me to become the first friar?'

She hesitated and then, remembering his good offices, nodded although she still felt an instinctive doubt.

She was still worrying about it when they climbed back into the wagon on the last stage of their journey. It would be very late when they reached Medina del Campo but that would give them the opportunity of moving in under cover of darkness and delaying the opposition from the Augustinians.

It was, in fact, close on midnight when they rolled into the small town, beneath the walls of the high castle where King Philip's mother, the mighty Isobel of Castile, was buried.

Teresa, dazed with fatigue and dazzled by the torches of the muleteers, walked with her companions into a small room, its walls peeling, its floor littered with scraps of paper. Even by torchlight it was easy to see that the place was in a disreputable state. Julian de Avila was staring round with dismay, and young Isobel Arias was wiping away tears with the corner of her veil. Brother Antonio began to stammer that he had assumed the house would be cleaned before they arrived, but it was obvious from his tone that he had completely neglected to give any order about it.

For a moment Teresa had the childish urge to sit down on the squalid floor and beat her fists and wail. After two days' uncomfortable travelling, it was a rending disappointment to be faced with such a bleak and unwelcoming muddle, and even worse to feel that she had let down those who trusted her.

Then her natural ebullience rose to the surface.

'There is a great deal to do before this will be fit for Our Lord to enter. Brother Antonio, there must be a caretaker here somewhere.'

'There is a steward from whom I obtained the keys,' said the prior. 'He and his wife live farther down the lane.'

'Then rouse them up and ask them to be so kind as to sell us kindling so we may heat a fire for the water. Father Julian, you had best go with them. The muleteers are waiting for payment and the wagon should be pushed under cover. Now, sisters, we must explore further and find brushes and pails. Who is going to be the first to follow me?'

There was a second's pause as the others fought human fatigue. Then Maria Baptist said with cross energy, 'I'll look in all the cupboards,' and Inés de Tapia, ignoring the nagging ache in her back, chimed in with, 'We passed a broom as we came through the door. I'll get it.'

'The walls need washing down,' said Ana of the Angels. 'I only pray there is nothing worse than dust in those cracks.'

'If there is, we will have to sing the song against fleas that Mother Teresa composed for us at St Joseph's,' Isobel Arias said. 'There has not been a single flea there since it was first sung.'

'There is nothing,' said Teresa, taking the broom from Inés de Tapia and wielding it energetically, 'that I detest as much as lice or vermin. I never will be able to understand why these ancient saints of the desert considered it so meritorious to be dirty.'

'The steward is boiling up water himself for us,' said Julian de Avila, reappearing in the doorway. 'I sent two of the muleteers as escort for Brother Antonio back to the monastery. And the steward's wife has given this bedspread as she thought you would need covering for the altar.'

'Blue!' Teresa exclaimed in delight. 'Our Lady's own colour and today is her Assumption day. How truly kind and generous people are.'

It was pale dawn when the little chapel was finished to the nuns' satisfaction. The walls and floor shone in the first feeble ray of sunshine; the artfully draped bedspread covered the wooden table which served as altar, and the sisters, peeping through the cracks in the inner door, flushed with pleasure as groups of citizens, drawn by the ringing of a strange bell, came shyly to the half-open door to see Father Julian, his good-humour merged with simple piety, prepare to offer Mass.

But when the Sacrifice with all its attendant ritual had been offered and accepted, Teresa's glance strayed to the courtyard. She had not seen it properly in the darkness of the previous night but now, stark in the clear light of morning, the broken flagstones and tumbled walls were a dismay to the eye.

'We must find another house,' she said to Father Julian. 'We cannot live here. It will take days to make the place habitable, weeks before a turn and a grille can be installed and the walls repaired. We cannot have an enclosed community living practically in full view of the street!'

'I'm afraid Brother Antonio de Herédia is not very practical,' Father Julian said, uncomfortably.

'You might say that,' she agreed, dryly. 'But it is my fault. I ought to have checked everything before I came, before I allowed others to come with me.'

'I will search the town and find more suitable lodgings,' Father Julian assured her. 'And you must not lose heart or we will all lose heart. Don't you know we depend upon your courage.'

'And I have very little left,' she said, miserably, but seeing Father Julian's fallen face she hastened to add, 'When I have prayed and broken my fast, no doubt God will put a little into my heart again. It is good for us to be discouraged sometimes although, for my part, I can never see it until long after the event!'

This time the discouragement did not last too long. By the end of the week, a wing of a house belonging to a wealthy merchant had been rented as a more suitable convent, and a benefactress appeared in the shape of Dona Helena Quiroga who promptly offered to buy the convent on the nuns' behalf and to do everything in her power to make the property convenient and comfortable.

I do not, thought Teresa, deserve such good fortune. It will be a lesson to me in the future not to plunge headlong into matters without making certain everything is properly prepared.

Then she smiled at her own foolishness, knowing very well that the finer and stronger part of her nature would always hurry to obey the dictates of her conscience; and conscience told her that sometimes it was best to forget practical considerations and follow where God's finger pointed.

At least I will be leaving an excellent Prioress, she decided again, not pausing to reflect why she always found it necessary to add up Maria Baptist's good points in her mind. She has been a tower of strength, working harder than any of us. And she has flung herself into the problem of each new day without a single complaint. Indeed she glories in pitting her wits against every obstacle that arrives.

She drew back her thoughts from wandering along unprofitable lines and turned her attention to the letter that lay before her.

Dona Luisa de la Cerda had written a long and persuasive letter, begging Teresa to found her next convent at Malagon and to allow her to be responsible for the entire cost of it. Teresa was not offended by the slightly peremptory tone which crept into the letter here and there. It was natural for an aristocrat to expect her wishes to be regarded as commands, and Teresa was well aware that the rich Dona Luisa would always be poorer than the youngest novice in the convent, for she would never be able to detach herself completely from her vast possessions.

And if I go to Malagon to establish my next convent there, it will be many months before I can return to St Joseph's for I cannot leave here until everything is settled and secure. And I must make plans for the Discalced monastery, with Brother Antonio de Herédia nagging me daily about his new and excessive mortifications and the licence burning a hole in my pocket – and the Malagon foundation attracts me for another reason too.

Her eyes returned to the beautifully penned letter. Dona Luisa had reminded Teresa of the waiting-maid, Maria de Salazar, who was now almost twenty years old and had set her heart upon entering the Discalced Community.

Teresa had never forgotten the lonely, self-confident little girl in the bright dress and the absurdly numerous jewels, who had prided herself upon her learning and entered with such pathetic eagerness into the games Teresa had invented. It would be worth going to Malagon again for the sheer self-indulgence of seeing her; and there might also be time for Teresa herself to begin to revise the manuscript on which she had been engaged during her years at St Joseph's.

She had not intended, after the strain of writing the story of her life, to put pen to paper. But it had occurred to her, unwillingly, that the time would come when she was no longer there to guide her daughters, to hold the spiritual rein in her own capable hands. One day she would die, or become so old and faltering that she was unable to choose and direct her daughters. And they would forget the rules she had instilled into them or, worse still, would follow them to the letter and forget the spirit of charity and compassion on which they had been formed.

So, with an inward sigh, she began to write a long essay on the way of perfection she wished her nuns to follow; and once she had begun, the essay was stretched into a book, written somtimes with painful concentration and sometimes with such lightning fluency that the words poured out of her as if they were rain and the paper a well waiting to be filled.

The book was imperfect, she knew, as full of mistakes as she was herself. She would need to rewrite it very carefully before she could hand it to her confessors for correction and censorship, but she had tried so hard to advise with wisdom those who would follow her.

She reached for a fresh sheet of paper. An answer must be sent to Dona Luisa informing her that Teresa approved of the plan for a convent at Malagon and would travel there in the spring. Then she must write to the Bishop of Avila whose brother had so kindly invited her to Madrid to discuss plans for a new convent in that city. There was nothing Teresa fancied so little as a winter journey to Madrid, but it would not do to offend the powerful Mendoza clan. She wondered humorously if she were in danger of becoming a lickspittle to the rich, but decided that it did no harm to try to please them a little. The poor things had only money and she had so much more.

'Mother Teresa, Brother Antonio de Herédia is waiting to see you,' Isobel Arias said from the doorway. 'He has another friar with him, young and small.'

Teresa laid down her pen with resignation. It was obviously going to be one of those days when she was not to be allowed five minutes' peace to get on with what she wanted to do.

Drawing her veil down, she picked up the tiny handloom on which she always worked when visitors were present. Its constant whirring had so irritated Don Francisco de Salcedo that he had persuaded her to put it away on condition that she allowed him to pay for the wasted time. Another with more money than sense, she thought, but such a good friend. So many good friends to help and encourage after the lonely years of interior struggle and half-formed ambitions!

It was Brother Antonio who began talking, as usual as soon as she entered the partitioned room which served as parlour. He was anxious to tell her of his spiritual progress and she listened carefully, occasionally interjecting a sympathetic comment, scarcely aware of the boy in the grey habit who stood by his side.

'And now I must introduce my young friend,' Brother Antonio said with an air of patronage. 'This is Brother Juan of St Matthew, of whom I spoke. He is very anxious to meet you.'

If that is true, then he hides it well, Teresa thought, for the boy, who looked nearer fourteen than twenty for so small was he, was gazing at the floor with indifference stamped all over his attitude.

'And what is it you desire, Brother Juan?' she said kindly.

'I desire nothing,' the boy said quietly.

'Not even God?' Teresa was startled into asking.

The young man raised his head and looked at her for the first time. Afterwards, when he was absent, she would never be able to remember his rather commonplace features, but his eyes would haunt her though she would never attempt to describe them. Their colour was grey, she supposed, but then he shifted his glance slightly and they were green, or was it blue? There were a thousand rainbows in each large, slightly prominent iris and behind that – she could not penetrate, for this was a soul too complex, too far advanced beyond her own experience.

'To be nothing in nothing is to know God,' said Brother Juan. 'To walk in a strange path and to arrive at a strange place is to know Him. To cease to exist is to exist at the centre of Existence. To love without hope and to hope without desire is to hold Him.'

She stared at him in perplexity, aware in the core of her being that this insignificant little man had already reached far beyond her most interior experiences.

'And have you found joy in this?' she asked and knew her question to be a foolish one. Brother Juan was consumed in a fire of which she had felt only the outermost flame, and the fire itself had burnt away reality exposing Reality itself.

'I live in darkness,' said Brother Juan. 'And the darkness is clearer than the sun, and the sun itself is lost.'

'Brother Juan is a poet,' said Brother Antonio, uncomfortably. 'He desires to become a hermit.'

'I do not think that he desires anything,' Teresa said, slowly. 'But I will be very happy to bestow upon him the habit of the Discalced, if he will accept it.'

'Then it will be so,' said Brother Juan, and she knew that a contract had been signed and sealed between them.

'And it would be fitting for us to take new names in religion,' said Brother Antonio. 'It would please me if I might be known as Antonio of Jesus.'

'Yes, of course. And Brother Juan shall be –'

She hesitated, knowing that her choice must be a wise one for already she was aware that this boy, desiring only to be nothing, would have that last human impulse rejected and be remembered to the end of time.

'You shall be Brother Juan of the Cross,' she said, at last, and feeling a great kindling of affection towards him began, characteristically, to scold. 'And you must do as Brother Antonio does and, in charity, accept my advice. You do not look strong, my son. It would be wise for you to moderate your fasts, and take sufficient exercise. We have a duty to our bodies for did not St Clare tell us that we are not made of brass?'

She was encouraged by a gleam of amusement in Brother Juan's eyes. He was not yet completely spirit then. It would do him no harm to be called firmly back to the earth of which he seemed to be no more than a fugitive inhabitant.

'We will both be happy to take your advice,' said Brother Antonio, heartily. 'I could not ask for a better companion than Brother Juan.'

And that is how you will be remembered, Teresa thought, with affectionate compassion. When people speak of you, it will be because you once knew a very little man who is very great in the eyes of God.

CHAPTER TEN

The Princess d'Eboli was in a temper, which meant that anybody with a particle of sense found urgent business at a safe distance from the vases and jugs she was apt to fling about in order to give weight to her arguments. Her husband, Ruy de Gomez, whose adoration outweighed his common sense, reclined at ease on a long sofa and watched the performance with keen enjoyment.

Ana d'Eboli was one of those fortunate women who look more beautiful when they are in a tantrum, which possibly explains why she indulged in so many. Tall and slim flanked, with high breasts and exquisite white skin, she aroused her mate's desires whenever he looked at her. Sometimes he found it almost impossible to believe that she had actually agreed to marry him.

He was much older than she, and although considered to be one of the most attractive men in Spain, his post as private secretary to King Philip II had made him more gravely composed than many of his contemporaries. Ruy de Gomez had never attracted and held her. Ana d'Eboli was not a faithful wife for her desires were insatiable and her tastes varied, but that did not prevent her from loving her husband passionately and from thinking of him even when she lay in the arms of some other man.

She made no attempt to hide her infidelities, and Ruy de Gomez, not wishing to give her pain, hid his own and listened tolerantly when some well-meaning friend whispered to him about the latest duke, valet, groom or stableboy who was enjoying the tempestuous Ana's brief and suffocating infatuation.

Today she was not complaining of her latest lover but of her aunt whose letter, torn in two halves, lay on the Persian rug. Ana herself was striding up and down the room, kicking aside her heavy silver skirts as she went and shaking her jewelled fists as her voice rose higher.

'The bitch! The mealy-mouthed, two-faced, jealous bitch! To tell me – *me*, that I would be ill-advised to attempt to impose my will on Teresa of Jesus! She's afraid, of course, that I will do more for the Carmelite than she has done. And that is not much! One paltry little convent at Malagon is all that Dona Luisa de la Cerda has accomplished.'

'She has said the Carmelite will not accept more,' said Ruy de Gomez mildly. 'Apparently Mother Teresa prefers her foundations to be self-supporting and not under active patronage.'

'As if I would ever interfere with the dear creatures once they were established!' Ana cried, indignantly. 'Aunt Luisa is simply determined to be unpleasant. She never has liked me, you know. She had the impudence once to tell me that I'd been badly brought up.'

'And so you were, my love,' Ruy grinned. 'Indeed, I doubt if anybody really bothered to make the attempt.'

'And my aunt need not imagine she can rectify it now,' Ana snapped. 'I tell you, nothing in the world is going to make me change my mind! I am absolutely determined to have a convent here at Pastrana. It will be under my personal patronage and Teresa of Jesus will come here to found it.'

'You have written to her, I suppose?'

'Twice!' Ana cried. 'I put my heart and soul into those appeals. She *has* to come! If she ever needs the ear of the king, are not you His Majesty's private secretary? And she may need royal help if her ideas are not acceptable to the Inquisition. She has received only qualified approval, you know.'

'I hope you did not mention any of these considerations in your letters,' Ruy said, gravely. 'Such a woman is not to be swayed by self-interest.'

'I was sweet!' Ana exclaimed, viciously kicking an inoffensive stool out of her way. 'I was sweet and polite and generous. If she consents to come, she may have the grandest convent that ever was, much better than the ones at Avila and Medina and Malagon and Valladolid and Toledo. I will provision it myself and have habits for the nuns specially tailored and the hangings will all be of silk.'

Ruy de Gomez opened his mouth to speak and then changed his mind. If Ana thought of her proposed convent and nuns as a glorified dolls' house full of puppets, then he would leave it to Mother Teresa to dissuade her.

'I intend to have a Priory too,' his wife declared, her rage against Dona Luisa dying as new projects filled her over-excited brain.

'My love, surely a convent will content you,' he was moved to protest.

One dark eye flashed dangerously. The other, injured years before during a fencing bout with her page, was hidden beneath a velvet patch.

'I want a Priory!' Ana shrieked. 'That first little Priory she founded has been moved to larger premises at Manchera, and Don Luis of the Five Manors has given the Brothers a Flemish Madonna. Well, I will give them two Madonnas and throw in a Christ Child for good measure. And Brother Juan of the Cross must be Prior here. They say he is one of the most spiritual people on earth and you know how attracted I am by spiritual people.'

Taking her husband's look of amazement for one of agreement, she rushed on, pulling loose the curling strands of her black hair as she paced.

'There will be a convent and a priory here at Pastrana! I see it all, in my mind. Blessings will flow upon us and people will flock here from all over Spain to see such holiness. And I shall be remembered as its benefactor. Ah, I have such plans, Ruy. Such great plans!'

She flung herself on him abruptly, kissing him passionately between sentences while her hair fell over his face.

'They will remember Teresa and Brother Juan because I shall be the one who helped and encouraged them more than anybody else! Teresa is going to be my best friend – my only friend! – for all other women are jealous of me. And if there is any difficulty, you will speak to the king, won't you? You have such influence with His Majesty.'

Because I give him my loyalty, he thought, with a touch of sad irony, and you give him your body occasionally, causing him afterwards such bitter anguish at his own betrayal that he is ready to grant me some new request.

'I will speak to the king, if ever it becomes necessary,' he promised, and she kissed him again, and sprang to the window, whistling shrilly through her fingers to the slave who kept two horses always saddled lest the princess wish to enjoy a gallop.

'I am going to ride over the estate beyond the village,' she cried, 'and pick out a site for the convent. We will build it of marble brought from Italy and sink a fountain guarded by silver dolphins!'

She laughed again and ran out, thin-waisted, avid-eyed, her hair streaming down her back. Just before the door slammed he heard her screaming for her maid. Then the room was empty of her tormenting presence and he was cold because he loved her so much he feared for her so greatly.

While the princess of Eboli rode over the countryside, her aunt sat in very different mood, embroidery in her placid hands and laughter in her eyes as Teresa recounted the story of Brother Antonio for the tenth time.

'He assured me that he would buy everything necessary for the little house at Duruelo, so I left him to do so. And when I asked him how he was progressing, he showed me what he had bought. Five hourglasses! *Five*! For fear that four of them would break, I suppose! I laughed until my sides ached, and poor Brother Antonio stood there, saying over and over, "But Mother Teresa, now we will always be sure of the t-time".'

'And yet they managed to settle in beautifully, didn't they?' Dona Luisa remarked.

'If only you could have seen that little Bethlehem!' Teresa cried with enthusiasm. 'I went out of my way to visit them and it was worth every step. I arrived without warning and found Brother Antonio sweeping out the chapel. I called out to him, "Why, what has happened to your dignity?" and he answered me, laughing, "Why, I curse the days when I ever had any!" Oh, Dona Luisa, you cannot imagine how happy I was to hear those words. He and Brother Juan showed me the tiny place, so poor they had no statues or pictures, so Brother Juan had cut out a little crayon drawing of Our Lord and pinned it up. And it moved me, that drawing, more than the greatest work of art I ever saw. It was simple, and crude, and full of such love that it lit up the world.'

'But aren't all your foundations like that? Candles in a dark world?'

'And the flames stretching up to heaven, burning out sin and corruption,' Teresa said. Then she looked across at her friend and laughed. 'And each time a fresh candle is lit, poor Teresa has to take another journey. When I remember those long years at the Incarnation, how I regret the time I wasted. The irony is that when I had the time I could not begin to contemplate, and now I am a contemplative I don't have the time. I meant to return to Avila when I had seen the foundation at Medina del Campo established; but I was persuaded to go on that fruitless journey to Madrid. The city is not ready yet for the Reformed Order. And then Father Domingo Banez ordered me to Alcalá de Henarés to talk over *The Way of Perfection* with him; and from there I went to Malagon.'

'At my request,' Dona Luisa said, guiltily.

'And it was a beautiful one,' Teresa said, warmly. 'It bound us even closer in friendship than we were before. But I could not return to Avila until the summer and then I was at home for barely a month before I had to go to Valladolid. The house there was so damp that I could not, in all conscience, leave my daughters until we had found a healthier building. Now there has been this business of founding a convent at Toledo, for I declare the promise was less than the performance. The house left to us was quite useless, and I was at my wits' end until the splendid Andrada, without two ducats to rub together, found us a new one for a reasonable rent.'

It was no wonder you fell ill,' Dona Luisa said.

'A touch of fever. It quickly passed.' Teresa shrugged off her ailment.

'I wish you could rest here for a longer time,' Dona Luisa said.

'So do I,' Teresa assured her, 'but your niece has made that impossible.'

'Ana d'Eboli *is* impossible!' Dona Luisa exclaimed irritably. 'A spoilt, hysterical young woman, full of fads and fancies, the latest of which is to have a convent of her own.'

'I think you misjudge her,' Teresa said, gently. 'She is as you say, young, and young women are often very foolish. I can speak from experience, for as a girl I was incredibly vain and wicked.'

'Oh, come now! There's no comparison,' Dona Luisa protested. 'You never did half the things that Ana d'Eboli has done.'

'Only because I lacked the opportunity,' Teresa said, serenely. 'Your niece may be feeling the first impulse towards a better life. She shall have her convent at Pastrana. I intend to take Isobel of St Dominic with me as Prioress. She and Maria Baptist don't pull well together at all, so it is better for Isobel to have her own house. My cousin's daughter, Isobel of St Paul, will be Sub-Prioress. It will take a weight off my mind if I know they will begin the work at Pastrana.'

'When the Duchess of Alba hears that Ana d'Eboli has a convent, she will want you to found one in her district,' Dona Luisa warned.

'At Alba de Tormes? I know. My sister Juana has already written to me about it. Well, why not? These rich aristocrats must be helped to spend their money in some way that will enable them to get to heaven. I except you and Dona Guiomar del Ulloa from that comment, for you are well on the way to eternity already.'

'I must write to Maria of St Joseph and tell her of the Pastrana scheme,' said Dona Luisa, 'or did you wish to tell her yourself?'

'No, no. Just give her my love. I have family letters to write.'

Teresa's face brightened as she thought of the former Maria de Salazar who had developed from the quaintly self-confident child into a slender and highly accomplished young woman, still certain of her own genius, and still betraying beneath her surface sophistication the craving for affection Teresa had sensed.

A little later she excused herself and went in to write her family letters. She must send condolences first to her half-sister's children, Juanito and Magdalena. At the beginning of the year, placid, kind-hearted Maria de Guzman had slipped away quietly in her sleep. She had spent, Teresa knew, less than a week in purgatory and she could not wish her back, for Maria's life had been a hard one. Her eldest son, Diego, was married to Teresa's cousin, the sharp-tongued, acid-faced Jeronima. News of the wedding had brought back too many memories of the past to unsettle the present, as if the ghosts of those youngsters dancing in the long ago orchard crept back to mock the people they had become. So Jeronima, whispering obscenity into an innocent ear, now snatched in middle age at her last chance of love with a youth young enough to be her son.

Francisco and Diego had made happy and fruitful marriages. Francisco's little girls, to whom the young Teresa had told stories, were women now; Maria back at the Incarnation as her health was too feeble for the Reform, Beatriz at Malagon, Isobel preparing to set out for the proposed foundation at Pastrana. And Diego's daughters were also professed; Leonor still at the Incarnation and Maria Baptist ruling shrewdly as Prioress at Medina del Campo.

Teresa loved this younger generation of cousins but her deep affection was still reserved for the de Cepeda girls, for the efficient Maria of St Jerome, for lively Beatriz and the faithful Ana and Inés de Tapia.

To talk with these was to become again the laughing girl in the orange dress who had once thought it the worst fate in the world to be confined in a convent! Thinking of herself when young, Teresa laughed again and smoothed her patched habit feeling for an instant the softness of velvet under her shapely hands.

Of Pedro Alvarez she did not think, having schooled herself carefully against the little pain that still tugged at her heart when she remembered that he had never married. For her, that first gossamer love had been only a prelude to Love itself, but Pedro Alvarez had not been granted the joy that made her long ago sacrifice no sacrifice at all.

She shook herself from memories and wrote briskly to congratulate her nephew upon his entry into the Franciscan Order, to assure him of her prayers for his sister, dead in childbirth scarcely three months after her mother's tranquil end; to send her warm regards to young Magdalena.

Then she turned her attention to her immediate relatives, writing first to assure her younger sister – she still thought of forty-one year old Juana as a giddy girl – that she would be happy to oblige the Duchess of Alba by establishing a convent of the Reform at Alba de Tormes; then brief notes to Agustin and Jeronimo who were still chasing rainbows in Peru; a slightly longer letter to Pedro whose wife had not yet managed to bear a living child; and finally the longest and most gossipy missive to dear Lorenzo widowed two years previously and still, in Teresa's opinion, bewailing his loss with more sentimentality than sense. After all, he and his wife had enjoyed eleven happy years together and there were the four surviving children to consider. Francisco was nine now, and Lorencito seven, Esteban six, and Teresita nearly three. Lorenzo ought to come home, Teresa decided, for the climate and conditions could not be suitable for the little ones. But she would not hint at such a thing for it would be gross imperfection for her to urge something that would contribute to her own happiness so greatly. Yet she could not hide the slight moisture in her eyes as she sealed the letter for it was nearly thirty years since her handsome brother had set sail for the New World.

Less than a week later, Teresa was off on her own travels again, rattling over the unmade roads in the covered wagon with the two lively Isobels to make light of the discomforts. They stopped at Madrid where, for once, comfortable accommodation was provided, not in a small, overheated tavern but in an exquisitely clean and simple convent of Franciscan nuns, who received their Carmelite guests with beaming smiles of welcome and the hospitality of those who have wed Lady Poverty and found the match a delightful one.

When she resumed her journey her party had been increased by two, both friars eager to enter the second priory of the Reform. Brother Juan of Misery and his companion, Mariano de San Benito, were, she knew, of very different stamp from Brother Antonio of Jesus and Brother Juan of the Cross. They had already prevailed upon Ruy de Gomez to grant them a house at Pastrana before applying to Teresa for the licence she held. But it was good, she reflected, to find men of initiative willing to act upon their own authority, and Brother Mariano was full of Italian charm. Teresa, who saw no reason why a holy man should not also be well mannered and amusing, found his company delightful and resolved that Brother Antonio should be persuaded to help this newest community to settle down.

Her spirits sank when they entered Pastrana, for the princess met them upon the steps of the palace and her effusive welcome, so different from her aunt's quiet handshake, was somewhat overwhelming.

'You cannot imagine how much I have longed for this day! I have been pining away as I waited, haven't I, Ruy?'

Flushed with health, she whirled in a blur of scarlet and gold to the tall gentleman in the green doublet who stepped forward to speak with less vigour but more sincerity than his wife.

'We are both glad to welcome you all to Pastrana. Rooms

have been prepared for you in the north wing, for the building of the convent is not yet completed.'

'I wanted a new building,' Ana said, 'but Ruy says it would take six months to build and I cannot wait that long for a convent. So we are using the existing foundations of one of our guest houses, only it's far too small so I had some of the walls knocked down, and a new well is to be sunk, and I have sent to Seville for new hangings, and to Toledo for steel for the grilles – or would you prefer gold? Ruy says that would be ostentatious but gold sparkles so prettily and increases in value.'

Teresa, slightly dizzy under the barrage of words, said hastily that steel would be perfect.

'Ruy said you would say that.' Ana sounded a trifle peevish. 'But everything must be just as you wish it to be, dear Dona Teresa.'

It was so long since anybody had used Teresa's worldly title that she was taken aback for an instant. When she replied it was with a shade of coldness she could not disguise.

'You are overwhelmingly kind, Your Highness, but we of the religious life do not use terms such as Dona. I am plain Teresa of Jesus.'

'How charming! How truly magnificent to give up all! How I envy you!'

Ana, who would as soon have thought of cutting off her beautiful head as dispensing with a single one of her own titles, clasped her hands in rapture.

'And how is dear Aunt Luisa?' she rattled on. 'It is so long since I saw her, but then she lives so quietly and Ruy and I spend so much time at court. My husband is quite indispensable to His Majesty, and the dear king often wishes for my presence too. I cannot imagine why, for I am a sadly scatter-brained creature!'

About as scatter-brained as an army on the march, Teresa thought grimly, looking after the scarlet figure as her hostess ran ahead of them.

She felt a light touch on her sleeve and looked up into her host's embarrassed eyes.

'Ana is young and heedless, but she is truly pleased that you have come,' he said unhappily.

'And I am truly pleased to be here.'

Teresa, who could never cure herself of the desire to mother every living being who seemed to need it, held out her hand cordially, deciding that if her presence brought some good, then there would be no need to inflict the discipline upon herself for putting charity before truth.

It was the outspoken Isobel of St Dominic who broke the silence when the door of their allotted rooms had closed behind them.

'Oh, the poor man! To be saddled with such a wife!' she exclaimed. 'Why, she never stopped talking from the moment we arrived until the prince practically pulled her away from the door! And all that about its being her convent! Not once did she acknowledge it as yours!'

'All our convents belong to God,' Teresa said sharply. 'We are merely caretakers for Him. Have you not even learned that much while you have been a nun? It is not for you or for me to criticize the Princess d'Eboli, for her ways are not our ways. And her husband is a noble gentleman who would hardly appreciate being regarded as a fool by an ignorant woman!'

Isobel of St Dominic flushed scarlet at the rebuke, and Isobel of St Paul said with quick and kindly tact, 'Our quarters are certainly charming. Don't you think so, Mother Teresa?'

'I do indeed, and they are not as luxurious as I feared they might be. The mosaic is particularly fine. Would you agree with me, daughter? You have excellent taste in such matters.'

She addressed herself to Isobel of St Dominic for, having scolded a nun, it was not Teresa's way to prolong her displeasure.

'The colours are beautiful,' Isobel of St Dominic said, with a swift, grateful look. 'But it will be difficult for us to remain enclosed, don't you think? Obviously these are guest rooms, not intended for contemplatives.'

'Then we must manage as best we can,' Teresa said briskly. 'It can only be a matter of weeks before the new convent is repaired, so until then we will keep silence and solitude as well as we can, short of giving offence.'

In fact they were delayed at Pastrana for three months, and long before the time was over Teresa had learnt that silence and solitude were two words unknown in the princess's vocabulary; and that, tread as delicately as they might, it was impossible to avoid giving offence.

From early in the morning until late at night, Ana's harsh, high voice echoed through the palace. She seemed incapable of carrying on the simplest conversation without screaming out her opinions or of expressing an opinion without raising clenched fists to heaven and shouting everybody else down. She considered that she had a perfect right to break in upon the nuns a dozen times a day, usually to scold them violently for staying dull and quiet within doors when they might be luxuriating in the sunshine of her presence. The only time they could be reasonably certain of a few hours' peace was when she strode out, dressed in doublet and breeches, to ride one of her horses across her estates.

And yet she meant to be kind. When she learned of Teresa's morning vomiting, nothing contented her until she had called in her own physician. She brought unwanted gifts of fruit and flowers, declared Isobel of St Paul was too delicate and insisted upon her swallowing nauseous concoctions of honey and vinegar, and, basking in reflected religious glory, referred loudly to 'my dear friend, Mother Teresa of Jesus'.

Teresa bore it as patiently as she could, although there were many occasions when her fingers itched to turn the high-spirited lady over her knee and give her a thorough spanking. Only once did she almost give way to her anger.

The princess rushed in to announce the arrival of some fashionable friends.

'They are all wild to see you and longing to have you fly up into one of your raptures while you are here; so do hurry down and meet them.'

She had stopped then, aware for the first time in her insensitive life that she had intruded upon ground where she had no right to tread. The face the older woman turned to her was white and still but the brown eyes blazed with contempt.

'I thank Your Highness,' said Teresa icily, 'but I have other things to do.'

The princess blushed to the roots of her black hair and involuntarily took a step backwards. Then she curtsied with none of her usual grace and went out with her head hanging. A few moments later the screams of a slave echoed through the courtyard as Ana's pearl-handled whip rose and fell, and rose and fell again.

Afterwards Teresa would declare that she would have given up the project altogether, had it not been for the kindness of the prince. Ruy de Gomez, like the true aristocrat he was, treated his guests with gentle, unobtrusive courtesy. The nuns seldom saw him but they were aware of him, always in the background, never interfering with his wife's vagaries, and yet, at the precise moment when Teresa felt that if called upon to endure any more she would run screaming back to Avila, Ruy de Gomez would step forward and put things to rights.

It was he who persuaded the workmen to stay when the princess ordered them to tear down the south wall for the third time. It was he who sent back the brocade hangings the princess had bought and presented Teresa instead with sheets and blankets of linen and frieze.

And it was Ruy de Gomez who, sensing the doubts Teresa was too kind to put into words, said as he bade her farewell, 'You need not fear that anybody will interfere with the convent. While I live, your daughters will be free to follow the Rule.'

'I thank Your Highness.' Her words were formal, but their tone was warm.

'It has not been easy, I know,' he said.

She followed the direction of his gaze to where the princess stood, issuing a thousand different directions to the muleteers. As they watched, she flung back her head and laughed, clear and mocking and soulless as a bird.

'She is very lovely,' said Teresa gently.

'The loveliest thing I possess,' said Ruy de Gomez. 'And I do not possess her at all, really. I merely hold out my hand so that when the butterfly's wings are tired, it may rest for a moment. And I do not dare to close my fingers lest they bruise it beyond repair.'

'I will pray for you,' Teresa said, and gripped the edge of her veil as a high wind skittered down the street and set the bells on the mules jangling.

There was no time for more. A final bow and the prince was ushering her into the wagon, having tactfully refrained from pressing the offer of his own carriage upon her. As he stepped back, holding his wife's hand, Teresa had a brief glimpse of them together, smiling and at ease as she had never seen them.

She knew then that she would not meet the prince again and fear mingled with her sadness. He had promised protection to her daughters while he lived, but afterwards? What then?

PART THREE

THE FURNACE

CHAPTER ELEVEN

'If she dares to come here, I swear I will risk excommunication and leave the convent without permission!'

The nun's voice and face were tense with a fury reflected in the faces around her. She was hardly allowed to complete her sentence before a babble of voices interrupted.

'By what right does Teresa y Ahumada impose herself upon us as Prioress?'

'Teresa of Jesus! She links herself in vulgar fashion with Our Blessed Lord.'

'If the Father Provincial thinks we are grown so lax, why does he not let us choose a nun from among ourselves to rectify matters?'

'She will force the Rule of the Discalced upon us.'

'And use our meagre revenue for the benefits of the convents she had founded.'

'She has seven of them already. Why cannot she go to one of them as Prioress?'

'I thought we had seen the last of her eight years ago!'

In the tumult, the quieter voices of Juana Suarez and the Cepeda cousins, Mary and Leonor, went unheeded. As friend and relatives of Teresa, they were not considered worthy of a hearing nor capable of an unprejudiced viewpoint.

One nun summed up the feelings even of the most moderate when she spoke with an obvious effort to be scrupulously fair.

'For my own part, I am ready to believe she is a great beata. But we are all quite comfortable as we are and I certainly don't intend to co-operate. She will find the nuns of the Incarnation a very different proposition from those impressionable young girls flocking to her own convents.'

'One week of us and she will be begging the Father Provincial to let her return to Medina del Campo.'

'They elected her Prioress there so let them keep her.'

But Teresa had already, and with infinite reluctance, left Medina, and was, at that moment, eating a hastily prepared meal in the refectory of St Joseph's. She had left behind her a group of bitterly disappointed young women who, having elected her as Prioress, were now forced to accept as substitute the harshly unbending Alberta Baptist. True, she was a great servant of God but they would not easily forget how she had interrupted a gay recreation with a severe, 'Surely we enter the contemplative life in order to pray, not indulge in childish games.'

Teresa, shaking with laughter as she watched one of the novices attempt to extricate her fingers from a game of cats cradle that had become tangled in the middle, had answered gaily sarcastic, 'Very well then, Sister. You go off and contemplate and we'll stay here and enjoy ourselves!'

It would not be easy to find another Prioress who not only encouraged merriment but instigated it, enjoying the sound of laughter and the clear voices rising and falling in harmony as they practised one of the little songs she had invented, or acted out some hastily composed playlet, in which, to her great delight, she was often imitated or caricatured with great glee by some of her livelier daughters.

Now at St Joseph's, Teresa tried to forget the unhappiness the nuns had not been able to hide and turned her attention to the baked egg and stewed figs laid before her. Knowing she had little time to spare, she had summoned the Sisters to her while she ate, for their concerns were very near to her heart. Two newcomers attracted her attention at once, and she wished she could spend a few days talking to them and discovering their characters. The elder of the two was one of the most beautiful young women Teresa had ever seen. Carrying herself as proudly as an Amazon, her fine eyes sparkling with humour and intelligence, it was easy to understand why her companions had nicknamed Ana of Jesus 'queen of the world'. It was not so easy to remember that she had been professed only the year before. She already bore herself as if she had spent all her life following the Rule, and possessed, Teresa decided, the qualities of leadership and sympathy that would make her an ideal mistress of novices.

Yet the younger newcomer was equally interesting. Little Ana of St Bartholomew had the stunted figure and broad, sallow face of a typical peasant but there was something in her candid eyes and slow, comfortable smile that drew Teresa to her. She was a lay sister without the smallest ambition to don the white veil of a choir nun; but her conversation, if sparse, was saltily humorous. The infirmary which was in her charge was spotless and smelled of new pounded herbs; and the meal she had cooked was one of the most delicious the older nun had tasted.

As always, it interested her greatly to learn the reasons for their entry into the religious life. Ana of Jesus gave her own account in characteristically decisive terms.

'I was bored with my beauty, irritated by my wealth, and out of patience with all my suitors. I decided to go to church to pray for guidance. On the way there I gave alms to a beggar in the street. There was something about his face – he had wonderful eyes – so I turned round to ask his name, but he had gone, though I looked up and down for several minutes. However, I went on to the church and knelt down beneath the crucifix. When I looked up at it, the face of that hanging figure was the face of the beggar I had seen, and I knew that to possess what had been promised in those eyes, I must enter the religious life.'

'And Ana of St Bartholomew?'

'I always wanted to be a nun,' the lay sister said. 'Even when I was a small child I wanted to be one, but I didn't know which Order was best for me to join. Then I began to dream, the same dream over and over. I was in a tiny convent and nuns in coarse habits held out wooden bowls of water to me. But when I drank the water it tasted like wine and when the nuns put back their veils their faces shone. I told the parish priest of it and he said I had described the convent of St Joseph's at Avila where he had once visited. I had never heard of the place, but he brought me here, and it was exactly as I remembered it from the dream.'

These two were the only ones who did not waste breath on exclamations of sympathy and horror over Teresa's enforced return to the Incarnation. Ana of Jesus remarked, eyes shining, 'What a splendid challenge!' and Ana of St Bartholomew fixed clear eyes upon her superior and remarked in her matter-of-fact way, 'I believe the Community there is in very bad financial difficulties, so you will let us know if there is any way to help.'

Then they encouraged her, between mouthfuls, to amuse them with the story that had already filtered along the grapevine of her arrival at Salamanca.

'I was very doubtful about making a foundation there at all, especially after all the troubles we had endured at Pastrana. But the house had been requisitioned from some university students for us, so I thought I would risk it; only taking one companion with me in order to spy out the land, as it were.'

'And you took Maria of the Sacrament,' prompted Maria of St Jerome.

'I did indeed, for she proved her worth as Prioress of Malagon and I considered she would be the most suitable person to leave in charge at Salamanca; but when we reached the house, we found it a warren of a place, full of tiny rooms, and twisting stairs, and passages that didn't lead anywhere. The students had left it in an appalling mess, with the most shocking remarks scrawled over the walls. I wanted to explore the place and set to work to clean it, but it was past dark and we both feared some of the students might have hidden themselves away somewhere in the building and be planning to give us a fright. So we found a room with a bolt on it and some straw inside and locked ourselves in there. And then Maria of the Sacrament had to remember it was All Souls' night when earthbound spirits are said to walk. I said I hoped that, if there were any ghosts about, the locked door would discourage them, and then, if you please – ' Teresa stopped to control her merriment. 'She said, "Oh, Mother, whatever will you do if I die in the night?" At any other time I'd have thought the question very comical for she's never had a day's illness in her life; but in that great, groaning, shadowy place I didn't feel in the least like laughing. Anyway, I retorted that I'd think what to do when it happened and wrapped myself in my blanket and went to sleep.'

'And Maria of the Sacrament?'

'Terrified herself so greatly with her lurid imagination that she stayed awake until dawn, listening in case my breathing should suddenly stop!'

'It won't be very gay for you at the Incarnation,' said Maria of St Jerome. 'They are saying there that they don't intend to obey you.'

'Well, there is obedience *and* obedience,' Teresa reminded her. 'I can usually deal with a little rebelliousness, but I tell you there are some souls whose obedience is worse than downright defiance. There was one sister – I won't mention her name – who drove me frantic with her constant niggling requests for things for which she needed no permission. When he'd come to me for the tenth time for permission to e-thread her needle, I lost my temper and snapped, "Go jump n the river!" and bless my soul, but a moment later there was an almighty splash, and the silly creature was dripping from head to foot.'

'And the worm? You told me in your letter but the others haven't heard it.'

'Oh, yes! One of the novices was gardening and picked up a large worm saying, "What shall I do with this?" and joking, I said, "Fry it for supper."'

'And she didn't!'

'Indeed she did. The lay sisters rushed out of the kitchen in panic for they thought she'd lost her wits, and when I went in, there was the dear little soul trying to stop the worm from crawling out of the frying-pan!'

Laughter rippled through them, and under cover of it, Isobel of the Cross said, 'You told us those stories to make us forget about your own troubles, didn't you? I wish we could do something for you.'

'But indeed you can. I shall need all your prayers,' Teresa said warmly. 'And you, Sister, can help me in a particular way. I am taking you with me as Sub-Prioress to the Incarnation.'

'I cannot,' Isobel said miserably. 'I am quite unworthy to give you the support you will need.'

'You began your religious life, as I did, at the Incarnation,' Teresa reminded her. 'You were always well liked there. Now you have your experience as Prioress of Valladolid behind you, to strengthen your character and give you the tact we will need to deal with these Calced nuns. But I will not order you to come. We all know, in our own hearts, how much we can endure.'

There was a brief pause, and then Isobel of the Cross, drawing reassurance from Teresa's friendly smile, said, 'Then I will be very proud to accompany you.'

She felt less proud when they reached the courtyard of the Convent of the Incarnation. The great outer door was barred and bolted and from within there came the steady drumming of feet as the indignant nuns drowned out the pleas of those few who wished to allow their new prioress to enter.

'Do you think they are preparing the boiling oil?' Isobel of the Cross whispered, with a nervous giggle, but Teresa's probable answer was interrupted by the Father Provincial.

Father Angel de Salazar, although himself of the Calced, had already determined that this Discalced Foundress, whom he considered to be a saint, should be allowed to bring the community of the Incarnation back to some semblance of order. The locked door was an insult, not only to him and his companions but to the letters patent he carried from the Apostolic Delegate.

'Sisters of the Incarnation,' he cried, in a thunderous voice, 'open this door immediately for your new Prioress to enter.'

A tiny window was thrust open above his head and a shrill voice called down, 'She is not our Prioress but yours, so take her back to her own convents!'

'We will have to call the constables,' Angel de Salazar said angrily. 'Even if they opened the door, I could not be responsible for your safety. I know these women and they are in a mood to gouge out your eyes rather than accept you.'

'It will cause such a terrible scandal,' poor Isobel sobbed. 'The Prioress breaking into her own convent!'

'We have no other choice, unless you are ready to employ a battering ram by yourself,' Teresa said briskly. 'This is no time for sweet words and promises, for my voice won't carry through stone walls.'

'You will never be able to tame them,' Isobel shuddered, as they stood listening to the shouts and cries. 'It sounds to me as if they were all devil-possessed.'

'Possessed by fear and spite more likely,' Teresa said calmly, shifting the little statue of St Joseph which she was carrying from one arm to another. 'Most of these who were shocked at the laxity in the Incarnation have joined the Discalced anyway. Those who are left here either personally dislike me and fear my rule, or have never known me and are being encouraged to rebel by the older sisters.'

'But how will you begin?'

'By allowing the constables to break down the door,' Teresa said, with a spice of mischief. 'Anything I do after that will seem mild by comparison! Hark at the noise. Anybody would think they were Christian martyrs and we were the invading Moors.'

To the drumming of feet and the screeching of voices was added the splintering of wood as the newly arrived constables, under the direction of the excited Father Provincial, began to employ their axes against the bolted door. Those within had also evidently heard it for there was a sudden cessation of the tumult and then a slow, reluctant drawing back of bolts.

The next moment it broke out with renewed vigour as the constables entered, forcing a pathway through the screaming, hysterical women down which the small but disorderly procession marched. The Father Provincial had begun to read aloud the articles of induction immediately but his sonorous voice could scarcely be heard above the hisses and catcalls.

One group of burly lay sisters blocked the way to the choir. Two of the more timid sisters had swooned away quietly and been dragged unceremoniously into a vacant corner. Several of the younger and prettier nuns were clinging hysterically to the embarrassed constables, begging to be saved. In the midst of it all, a few struggled forward to try to greet Teresa. She had a glimpse of Juana Suarez. Then somebody caught her old friend a sharp blow across the face, and, in another moment, combatants were scratching and biting, and tearing at one another's habits as they rolled over the floor.

Mass hysteria, Teresa thought, clutching her statue. Let us hope they will all be thoroughly ashamed of themselves afterwards.

Protected by the constables she inched forward, the loudly truculent declaiming of Angel de Salazar pounding in her head beneath the surrounding yells. She became aware that by some means they had reached the choir, that Angel de Salazar was handing her the keys of office, that some intrepid supporter had raised a thin cheer and that the whole disorderly, distasteful ceremony was finished.

The noise was still so great that it was several minutes before anybody else realized the fact, and then those who had been thrust to the back of the crowd surged forward, demanding of one another if it was true that Father Provincial had actually dared to carry out the official installation against their wishes.

Taking advantage of the comparative silence, Angel de Salazar faced the crowd and cried, dramatically, 'This is your new Prioress. Are you for her or against her?'

From the back of the nuns a tall, thin woman, who had observed her more war-like sisters with a calm, amused look, raised her hand.

'For my part,' she said, 'I am willing to accept what authority has decreed.'

Her reedy, nasal voice sounded completely indifferent but some of those nearby nodded and made vague efforts to tidy their coifs.

It is time for me to speak, Teresa thought, but what can

I say to them? What can anybody say in the face of such opposition?

She stepped forward, her hands damp around the image of her patron, her eyes scanning the dishevelled and hostile community. They were so thin, these untidy and hysterical women. Easy to tell the poverty of these poor creatures, and yet many of the younger ones wore bangles and brooches: beneath the defiance their eyes were frightened.

'Ladies.' Her voice was clear and pleasant, interrupted by nothing more than an occasional hiss. 'I have been imposed upon you as Prioress against your will and against my own will too, but it is our duty to obey our superiors and so, for that reason and for charity's sake, I am come among you. Some of you knew me when I was a daughter of this house and others know of me only by reputation. I am here to serve you and to make things as pleasant as I can. Don't be afraid of the Rule of the Discalced for it is not my intention to force it upon you; only to serve Our Lord in sweetness. And with His grace you will help me to do this.'

As she finished an uneasy shuffling of feet and a low muttering broke out again. Many of the nuns were looking sheepish, one or two were weeping, but it would take more than soft words to change the hard-eyed majority who waited in sullen silence, their fingers talon-curved.

'I will see you in Chapter,' Teresa said, and motioning Isobel of the Cross to follow, she stepped down into the midst of them and walked steadily towards the Prioress's cell. Slowly and reluctantly the nuns parted to make way for the two of them, but the door of the cell had scarcely closed behind them when the shouting broke out again with renewed violence.

Teresa sank down on the wooden bench and clasped her hands tightly together to still their trembling. Then, seeing Isobel's white face, she forced herself to speak calmly and cheerfully.

'The situation is worse than I feared, but not hopeless. These poor souls have had no adequate guidance for years. They have forgotten how to follow even the Mitigated Rule! And how could one expect them to remember it when all their attention is obviously taken up with keeping themselves from starving?'

'Then what are we to do?'

'Write to everyone who could possibly spare anything,'

Teresa said briskly. 'Don Francisco de Salcedo, Dona Guiomar del Ulloa, Dona Luisa de la Cerda, my sister Juana – oh, there are many who could send something. You will have the task of spending money as I will have the task of begging for it. It is of no use to expect a higher spiritual standard from these nuns until we have improved their physical conditions.'

'If they allow us to remain here for that long –' Isobel began, and jumped violently as a tap sounded on the door.

It was Juana Suarez, her cheek darkened by a bruise, her eyes troubled.

'I wish I could welcome you with a quiet heart,' she began, 'and indeed for my own part I have prayed for your coming. But I cannot see how you are going to be able to achieve anything, for the hatred against you is intense.'

'And will burn itself out quickly for it arises from hurt pride and ignorance. Dear Juana Suarez, it is good to see you again!'

Teresa embraced her warmly and drew her down to the bench.

'The tall, thin sister who spoke out at the end – who is she?' Teresa inquired.

'Catalina of Christ. She is very ascetic, rather cool when one tries to make friends, and completely uneducated.'

'Oh?' Teresa looked at her in some surprise.

'Apparently her father was so afraid she might be tainted with heresy that he would never allow her to learn how to read or write, nor allow her to leave the house except to go to church,' Juana Suarez explained. 'She is intelligent though and very devout.'

'I would like her for the Reform,' Teresa said, thoughtfully. 'Good sense is one of the most important attributes of a Discalced Carmelite.'

'Devotion too, surely?' Isobel of the Cross protested.

'We can instill devotion into a soul, but we cannot fill up an empty head with common sense,' Teresa said. 'I will send for the Catalina of Christ and see if my initial impression of her was correct. But I intend to see all the nuns during the next few days. They all have grievances, real or imagined. Juana dear, after Chapter, I want to go to the infirmary. Is Leonor still there? Is there no improvement?'

'Leonor is dying,' Juana said bluntly. 'And she is dying like an angel, with no regrets beyond the thought that she will be leaving her sister.'

'Poor Maria Baptist! It is always hard to lose one's sister, even if one is certain she is bound for heaven. But we will try to keep Leonor with us for a few months longer. I want the sick nuns to have the best possible attention.'

'I'll speak to the infirmarian at once,' Juana Suarez said. 'Is there anything else I can do?'

'Yes. Stop worrying!' her friend teased. 'I know what women are like. They will rage and storm and kick up their heels and declare they are ill-used and cannot endure it, but they will subside into a grumble when they grow hoarse with shouting. So keep up your spirits. Isobel and I will tend to the physical needs of this community, and I intend to bring a new confessor here to guide us all in the spiritual life.'

'Brother Juan of the Cross?' Isobel breathed.

'But I've heard of him.' A small frown creased Juana's brow. 'He is a friar of great holiness, isn't he? Won't his standards be too high?'

'Let me tell you about my little Seneca, for I declare he has, young as he is, the wisdom of the ancients.' Teresa leaned forward enthusiastically. 'His standards for himself *are* high – impossibly so – and I have had to remonstrate with him about it. Upon one occasion, after fasting for two days he felt so ill that he asked Brother Antonio if he might take a bit of bread before supper was prepared. When he had eaten the bread he was so ashamed of having given in to his weakness that he took a length of chain and scourged himself unconscious. But he does not expect or desire such severe mortification from anybody else. He is at the Pastrana Priory now, trying to undo the mischief caused by a Master of Novices who has been inflicting the most horrible penances upon the poor Brothers, in the belief it would please God. Brother Juan has been there, advising gentleness and moderation. He knows very well how much each soul can bear.'

'You think a great deal of him,' Juana Suarez commented.

'So much more than I can express to you or to him! I wish I could spend a lifetime listening to him, but whenever I meet him there is always so much business to discuss, and I spend our time together trying to drum some practical advice into his head. I am,' said Teresa, ruefully, 'always apt to talk too much when I get the opportunity.'

'I hope he takes your advice,' said Isobel, 'for I never heard you say a single word that was not full of good sense!'

'And that is one of the silliest things I ever heard *you* say!'

Teresa cried, laughing.

The brief conversation had revived and calmed her, and it was with a bright face that she dismissed them and went into the oratory next to the cell where she knelt, with hands pressed together tight as a candle flame and lips still, for she seldom needed the tools and trappings of speech when she held conversation with Love.

When she entered the choir, she paused for a moment, her eyes flicking down the serried ranks of white-coifed nuns. They were all reasonably tidy again though some cheeks still bore the marks of fingernails. Eyelids were lowered, but here and there glinted a sullen iris and the atmosphere was thick with resentment.

This is not the homecoming I might have expected, Teresa thought sadly, feeling the waves of hostility flow towards her.

She made her way to the place in which she had knelt for more than twenty years. It was worn smooth by the pressure of her knees and she slid into the accustomed groove as if she had never been away. She raised her eyes slightly, glancing obliquely towards the farther end of the choir where a carved chair waited for the Prioress.

The Prioress? But, dear Lord, I *am* the Prioress!

For a moment she thought she had exclaimed aloud. She had certainly risen with her hand clapped in dismay over her mouth and a deep blush of embarrassment suffusing her cheeks. The atmosphere had changed and lightened, its sullenness dispersed by amused curiosity. She stepped out of her old place, wishing the floor would swallow her up for surely no such breach of etiquette had ever occurred before, and was suddenly overcome by amusement at her wool-gathering wits.

The nuns, watching closely, saw their new Prioress make an expressive gesture of self-contempt with her eloquent little hands, and then a low, warm ripple of laughter escaped her as she shook her head at her own stupidity. The laughter spread, decorous and friendly, for they were amused with her and not at her; and eyelid after eyelid lifted to reveal the stirrings of a new and delightful kinship.

Teresa, excusing herself silently with a neat little bow, left the choir, prepared, so they thought, to enter again with more consciousness of her position. But when she returned she was carrying a dainty statue of the Blessed Virgin, clothed in a silk dress and veil. She had brought it, wrapped in linen, from the convent at Medina, as a gift to her new daughters.

Burdened with the figure, she walked to the empty chair and placed the image upon it.

'Daughters, here is your Prioress.' Her voice still quavered with merriment. 'She will be a better one than I, for she is called Mary of Mercy.'

And placing her bundle of keys in the choir at the tiny carven feet, she sat down on the steps. There was silence for a moment, and then, from among the rows of kneeling figures a young, clear voice rose thin and pure in the 'Salve Regina'. It was joined by another voice, and then another, as the emotion from which the song had sprung drew all of them together in a harmony of praise.

Teresa heard the singing faintly as if from a great distance. Externals did not matter because her eyes were blind, her extremities heavy as lead, her conscious mind suspended, while in the vision that lies beyond vision, a tiny, white-clad girl with the sun as her mantle floated down into the choir of the Incarnation, surrounded by beings of fire and air, bringing with her the fragrance of lilies and roses.

Gravely and serenely, the little Mother of God examined her replica and then bowed with infinite grace towards her Son's brides.

CHAPTER TWELVE

Ruy de Gomez, Prince of Eboli, was dead, and the palace was filled with the sound of his widow's mourning. Those who clicked their tongues and accused the princess of parading a grief she did not feel did her an injustice, for Ana was desolated by the loss of the one who had been both friend and husband. It was Ruy alone who had gently curbed her excesses of feeling, her senseless extravagance, and bouts of cruelty. His death removed the one safe, unchanging relationship in her life, and Ana, knowing this dimly, wept without pause.

Her rooms were draped in black, her garments rent, her hair uncombed, for she could express her deepest feelings only in terms of the crudest melodrama. In this setting, she posed as the tragedy queen she believed herself to be, refusing to receive consolatory visitors, picking indifferently at the delicacies prepared by her servants, speaking, between bouts of weeping, about the love she had begun to idealise.

'He was the kindest, truest man who ever lived! He never spoke a cross word to me nor gave me the least cause for unhappiness. And I did not appreciate it. I did not appreciate *him*! I was a bad wife, faithless, and disloyal, and evil-tempered!'

Casting herself down on the luxurious rugs, she cried bitterly, for like most shallow, selfish people she was capable of excessive, unreasonable and temporary remorse.

'A bad wife!' she repeated vehemently, though none of her ladies had contradicted her. 'And now I am punished for it by his death, for he is in heaven and I am too wicked ever to go there! I will never see him again in this life or the next! Oh, how could he do such a terrible thing to me? How could he leave me like this? Selfish, selfish man to escape the world and leave me alone!'

She began to pound the floor as if it were the unfortunate Ruy de Gomez, as her genuine grief dwindled into hot indignation at her husband's lack of consideration in dying before her. Then the memory of his quizzical smile rose in her mind and she bit her wrist fiercely, watching the blood trickle over the white skin and seeing it as her heart's blood draining out as swiftly as her husband's life.

'There is nothing left for me,' she moaned, 'except to make my peace with God and wait for death. And I will do that, not in this great house that was once happy because *he* was here, but in a convent! Yes! That is what I will do! I will enter the convent here at Pastrana. Who has a better right? Was it not I who inspired its foundation even if the nuns do not appreciate the fact?'

She sat up abruptly, sucking the blood from her wrist and glaring round her circle of attendants, for it was not Ana's intention to waste her display of sorrow upon an empty room. When she thought of the Pastrana foundations she could not help feeling resentful.

The Priory had been, she considered, a model for all other priories. How saintly of the Brothers to flog one another publicly in order to bring down rain! And how horrid that little Juan of the Cross had been, to dismiss the novice master and inform the Brothers they were acting like fools! And he had shown not the slightest pleasure in her company though she had put on her most becoming dress. Instead he had talked business with Ruy and seemed not to notice that a beautiful and intelligent noblewoman was longing for spiritual consolation.

As for the nuns! They had been so ungrateful, so lacking in courtesy! When she visited the parlour they would not allow her past the grille even though she yearned for a peep into the enclosure. And yet she had forgiven them, had even secured for them a miracle-working statue at great personal risk!

Her uncovered eye gleamed with excitement when she remembered her nocturnal visit to the Castle of Zorita at Extremadura. In the chapel there was the famous Virgin of the Underground Passage, visited by the faithful from all over Spain because of the cures it had effected. She had waited until the church was empty and then lifted the statue from its niche, wrapping it in a white cloth and stuffing it into a leather bag, and riding back through the darkness.

And the ingratitude of the nuns when they had received the statue! They had immediately returned it to the chapel of Zorita, with as many apologies as if they had taken it themselves; and Teresa of Jesus had written a stinging letter to Ana that made her ears burn whenever she thought of it.

'I'll enter the convent,' the princess repeated, grief and anger struggling for mastery in her troubled nature. 'It'll serve the nuns right for refusing to allow me among them before, and pay out Teresa of Jesus for her nasty letter, and Ruy for dying when I needed him most, and Aunt Luisa for giving herself airs, and the king – '

She was not sure why she wanted to be revenged on the king, except that his letter of condolence had not been fulsome enough.

'He went on and on about Ruy's sufferings and hardly a word about mine,' she muttered, and began to weep again because, now that Ruy was dead, nobody would ever love her again.

The Mother Prioress of the Discalced Community at Pastrana was sleeping deeply and dreamlessly when she was awoken by the Sub-Prioress.

'Mother Isobel, please, please get up. Please wake up!'

The whisper was urgent, the nun's face white in the light of the candle.

'What is it?' Isobel of St Dominic sat up in alarm, wondering what in the world could have induced the scrupulous

Isobel of St Paul to break the Grand Silence.

'The Princess d'Eboli is here, demanding to be admitted immediately as a member of the community,' said Isobel of St Paul, in much the same tone as she might have announced the arrival of the succubus, Lilith, had that legendary lady taken it into her head to become a Carmelite.

'The Princess a nun? Then this convent is doomed!'

Isobel of St Dominic flung up her arms in despair as she scrambled from her pallet.

'You're not going to admit her?' the other questioned.

'Hush! I'm trying to think what Mother Teresa would do.'

'She would allow her to enter,' said Isobel of St Paul gloomily. 'She would forget all the trouble the princess has caused and remember only that she has been bereaved and is in need of friendship.'

'Then we cannot do less.' The Prioress nodded her head briskly as she made her decision. 'Admit the princess, and if she is of the same mind in the morning, I will see her and allow her into the novitiate.'

'Then may the Good Lord alter her determination,' Isobel of St Paul muttered.

But the princess was obviously set upon becoming a Carmelite. Unhappily the convent in which she could live had not yet been founded, for the idea of conforming to the Rule never occurred to her.

The new novice was, so she gave them to understand, a broken-hearted widow in such a sensitive condition of mind that she must never be scolded or made to do anything against her own inclination. She was delicate and so must be permitted to eat meat. She was used to congenial society and so must be allowed to receive visitors at any hour, and, being addicted to violent exercise, she felt the need for air, the new novice could stroll out into the world she had just rejected.

Those were Ana's conditions before she would consent to don the habit she had demanded, and the nuns at Pastrana, mindful of Teresa's precept that charity was the foundation of their Rule, tried desperately to please their unwelcome guest. They could not, even in charity, think of her as a member of the Order, for she made not the slightest effort to integrate herself as a nun among nuns.

Had she been pleasant in her manner, they could have overlooked her eccentricities, but as her very real sorrow ebbed away it was replaced by her more habitual frame of mind.

Confined with women whom she considered to be her social inferiors, the princess lost no opportunity in impressing upon them her superior rank. She insisted upon bended knee, and the Prioress, finding one of the youngest and most timid of her daughters weeping because the princess had struck her, had clenched her fists and gritted her teeth in silence, wishing with all her heart that Mother Teresa was there.

But Teresa was at Segovia, founding her ninth convent in the midst of even more turmoil than usual. The licence for the foundation had been granted only by the word of the local ecclesiastical authority, the Blessed Sacrament was removed and the nuns allowed to remain only on sufferance until the written permission arrived. Meanwhile, there were three law-suits to contend with concerning the building they had rented, for three monasteries in the district claimed possession of it.

'Nobody looks twice at a building until the Discalced Carmelites move in and then it suddenly becomes the most desirable residence in the neighbourhood,' she grumbled to young Isobel of Jesus.

'Shall I cheer you up with a song, Mother?' the girl asked.

'Gracious, no, child! Your sweet voice would send all thoughts of business out of my head.'

Teresa patted her affectionately on the shoulder, remembering how the simple refrain chanted by Isobel of Jesus during a recreation at Salamanca had sent her into so deep a rapture that it was almost half an hour before the nuns could revive her.

Then she sighed, for embarrassing as raptures and trances could be, they were preferable to the aridity that had descended upon her during the past weeks. It had become impossible to fix her mind upon her prayers, or to derive the smallest satisfaction from meditation. It was due, she supposed, partly to her low state of health. The winter had been a hard one and she had suffered from a series of feverish colds. She had done her best to follow the physician's advice, but it was difficult to get sufficient rest when she was so busy during the day that she had only the night hours in which to write down the account of her foundations that had been ordered by her confessors.

Crouched on the stone floor with the broad window-ledge to serve as desk, she had written steadily, sometimes until a grey dawn made her solitary candle unnecessary, pausing only to blow on her fingers numbed by the icy draughts whistling around the edges of the shutters.

There had been not only the new book to compose, but *The Way of Perfection* to rewrite, and her *Exclamation Of The Soul To God* to revise, not to mention the *Conceptions Of The Love of God upon Certain Words of the 'Song of Solomon'*. This last had been a disappointment, for although she had found joy in the writing of it, the Holy Office had suppressed the book, having found it unthinkable that a female should venture to comment upon the words of the Old Testament.

And it served me right for thinking that I had anything valuable to say, Teresa thought, rubbing her eyes wearily and holding the letter from the Indies close to the light.

'Lorenzo writes smaller than he used to!' she complained.

Isabel of Jesus handed over the spectacles which the physician had prescribed, and hid a smile as Teresa fitted them gingerly on the end of her nose.

'I wish I knew,' the Foundress remarked a moment later, 'why two circles of glass in front of one's eyes cause everything to look so much sharper and clearer. I am so interested in the properties of things!'

She put down the letter with reluctance and glanced up at her companion with something of her usual sprightliness.

'My brothers are thinking of returning home,' she said. 'They have been thinking of it for the past ten years, but this time Lorenzo sounds almost positive that he will soon be seeing me. It will be good to talk over old times again.'

'Your brother is quite an elderly gentleman by now, I suppose?' Isabel of Jesus asked, with the bright tactlessness of an eighteen-year-old.

'Four years younger than I am!' Teresa began indignantly, and then laughed. 'And I will be fifty-nine next week! I'm an old woman, my dear.'

But she said it without conviction, for despite weakening eyesight, and decaying back teeth, and aridity of soul, she could never bring herself to believe that she was no longer young.

'There is a letter from Pastrana,' said Isabel, hastily.

'I have already seen it and sent an answer. It is all I can do, for I cannot spare the time to travel there myself.'

Her depression descended again as she thought of what the nuns were enduring. Isobel of St Dominic had written in an almost despairing fashion quite unlike her usual style begging for advice as to whether the Princess d'Eboli should be allowed to make her final profession when the time came. Teresa had told her that as Prioress she must make her own decisions, but she had added that whatever decision Isobel of St Dominic took would meet with her approval.

For where is the sense in establishing prioresses and not allowing them to act upon their own responsibility? she mused. The princess would certainly seek revenge upon the Pastrana nuns if she were not allowed to make her final vows, which was another excellent reason for getting the affairs at Segovia straightened out so that Isobel of St Dominic and the community might have some refuge.

'I wrote to Brother Juan of the Cross for advice,' she said aloud. 'He told me that the new novice-master at the Pastrana priory would support the nuns against the princess. Apparently Brother Hieronimo Gracian has great ability and a moderation of temper that pleased Brother Juan very much.'

'There is one more letter to be answered, Mother.'

'From little Casilda of Padilla? I know.' Teresa pushed her spectacles up to the bridge of her nose again. 'Poor child!' she exclaimed a moment later. 'Why cannot her wretched family realize that she is destined for the convent? They married her off to her own uncle when she was twelve, and she has held out for almost a year against its consummation. Why, the uncle himself is willing to let her go, but her parents are afraid lest she give her inheritance to the convent. I would take her without dowry, but she declares she will not enter unless she can contribute something.'

She broke off as another Sister tapped upon the door to inform her that Don Antonio Gayton was in the parlour.

'With his little daughter, I hope! That Mariana pesters the life out of me but she has the merriest smile.'

Thankfully relinquishing the letters, Teresa went down to greet her guests, finding a few moments' relaxation in the conversation of the wealthy widower who was helping the nuns to fight their three lawsuits, and even greater delight in the prattle of six-year-old Mariana who informed her every time they met that she was longing to grow up quickly so that she too could enter the Carmelite Order.

But when she was alone again, she prayed for her daughters at Pastrana and for Casilda of Padilla. She prayed with her lips, using the debased coinage of vocal speech, because she had lost the ability to raise up her thoughts and her interior joys had vanished as if they had never been.

She recalled what she herself had written about such matters, warning her daughters to beware of false visions sent by the devil to lure them away from their prayers. Yet her own visions had been such a source of comfort, shining into the dark disappointments of those long, troubled years at the Incarnation when her human weakness dragged her down from the summits her soul had glimpsed.

Brother Juan of the Cross considered all visions highly suspect and could be extremely sarcastic about over-imaginative females. He disapproved of Teresa's own experiences, having himself moved far beyond the need of such things.

But he is a saint, Teresa cried silently. I am a weak woman attempting to perform tasks beyond my strength.

She tried to empty herself of the desire for God even while she concentrated every fibre of her being upon the loving of Him, but she could do neither for a strong wind was rushing beneath her feet, and her body was drawn up from the floor, and her soul drawn out of her body into the nothingness of self.

A nun, with a face white as parchment with fear, was staring at her as if rooted to the ground from which Teresa had just been lifted. She noticed her vaguely through the confusion of feeling that always followed the painful reshackling of soul to body, but it was several minutes before Teresa, sinking back to earth, could organize her senses sufficiently to ask her companion's name.

'Sister Anna of the Incarnation, Mother.' The voice was young, trembling and astonished.

'Yes, of course.' Teresa passed a sweat-damped hand across her brow, as the nun's face swam into focus. Then her voice sharpened. 'How long have you been here, child?'

'All the time, Mother.'

'And you will not speak of this until after my death.'

It was not a question but a simple statement of authority, and Sister Anna knelt mutely in recognition of that command.

After that aridity flooded Teresa again, mingled with the embarrassment and shame of knowing that her rapture had been witnessed. With difficulty she pushed such thoughts away from her and concentrated upon the business matters awaiting attention.

At Pastrana, the princess was screaming for attention in a

loud and angry voice that shattered the peace of the cloister.

'How much longer must I wait before my summons is heard? Are all the nuns grown deaf that they ignore me?'

'She wants some dinner,' said Isobel of St Paul wearily. 'She would not eat when we ate because she declared her head was aching.'

'Would not, will not, cannot!' Isobel of St Dominic laid down her pen with a snap. 'It is impossible for us to carry on in this fashion. The princess must be made to understand that she must either conform to the Rule or return to the world. It is obvious she has no vocation.'

'And who will dare to tell her?'

'I will go to her now, in charity, and inform her of my decision.'

Isobel of St Dominic rose and went firmly towards the door, although the screaming voice would have frayed the steadiest nerves. Isobel of St Paul, not to be outdone in valour, followed at her heels.

The rest of the small community was aware that the princess had stopped, but there was scarcely time to offer up thanks for the cessation of noise when it began again, more violently than before, mingled with sobs and the crashing of wood as Ana d'Eboli flung about the contents of her expensively furnished cell. In language more suited to a muleteer than a daughter of Carmel, the princess announced her opinion of the Prioress, the Sub-Prioress, the Sisters, and all their ancestors. In the midst of the storm, the two spare, coifed figures stood like tranquil rocks while the thunder and lightning of Ana's wrath hurled itself against them.

Afterwards both Isobels were pleased to remember that neither of them had raised their voices nor lost their tempers. And the princess, growing weary of such an unresponsive audience and certain that she had a genuine grievance which must be trumpeted to the world at large, screamed out a final imprecation and whirled through the door, calling her terrified servants to gather her belongings together.

'May God forgive me, but I would not be human if I didn't rejoice at her leaving,' Isobel of St Dominic said unsteadily.

'Do you think we have seen the last of her, Mother Prioress?' Isobel of St Paul whispered.

'I doubt it.' The young prioress tried to smile. 'Women of strong and fleeting passions veer from love to hatred very quickly – and very noisily,' she added, listening to the bumping and banging as Ana d'Eboli's possessions were carried into the street.

'It may be uncomfortable for us here,' she went on, 'now that we have offended the princess.'

Her words proved only too prophetic. Before the day was out, Ana had given evidence of her displeasure by sending word that any person who brought alms to the convent would suffer for it by the reversal of their royal lady's favour. She then proceeded to withdraw her own revenue, leaving the nuns in a virtual state of siege. Had it not been for a few intrepid citizens of Pastrana who came by night to leave fruit and vegetables at the turn, and the friars who shared their own bread, the Community would have been reduced to famine within a week. As it was, an uneasy silence menaced the convent, unlike the usual tranquillity in which the daughters of Carmel moved.

Then, very late one night, the silence was disturbed by the soft padding of feet along the cloisters. Wrapped in their shabby cloaks and carrying only what they had originally brought with them, the nuns crept out of the enclosure to the street where Julian de Avila and Antonio Gaytan waited.

The town slept peacefully in the shadow of the hills, with only the faint shine of stars to guide the fugitives over the cobbles. Their shadows, veiled and narrow, curved up against the walls of the houses. In her imagination each nun pictured a larger, more menacing figure, one-eyed, passionate and spiteful.

Five covered carts waited beyond the walls. Julian de Avila, who would not have missed an instant of the nocturnal adventure, helped the Sisters to climb up into the swaying vehicles. Antonio Gaytan issued low-voiced orders to the muleteers who nodded, cracking their long whips over the backs of the mules and drawing their hats down more firmly in preparation for the jolting, river-washed ride to Segovia.

It was a homecoming to rival all homecomings! Teresa, whose heart had been alternately in her mouth and somewhere near her sandals as she waited for news, shed ten years when she beheld Isobel of St Dominic.

Loving all her spiritual daughters with what she hoped was equal impartiality, her favourites of the moment were always those who were sick and suffering. At the moment she held none of her prioresses in such esteem as Isobel of St Dominic who had proved her courage when she refused to allow the formidable Ana d'Eboli to make her profession.

'She has great influence with the king,' Isobel of St Paul fretted as they recounted the story of their escape.

'His Majesty is a just ruler and will not condemn us unheard,' Teresa comforted. 'I have written to him, entreating his protection for our Reformed Order.'

'Protection from the princess?'

'From her and from those who murmur against us.' Teresa cupped her chin in her hands and looked doubtfully at the others, wondering if it was the time to confide her worries. A reaction was beginning to set in against her foundations. And it came, she thought ruefully, when matters at the Incarnation had never gone more smoothly. The large, disorderly community had settled under firm and tactful rule into a close-knit, affectionate family, keeping the Calced Rule without stint or excess.

'Are the murmurings loud?' Isobel of St Dominic asked.

Her tone was light but her fingers pleated the coarse frieze of her habit and there were lines of strain round her eyes.

'Nothing we need bother to hear,' Teresa reassured, deciding that the Pastrana prioress must not be burdened with new fears.

'We will not be able to avoid hearing the princess,' Isobel of St Paul said gloomily.

'Those who shout loudest often say the least,' another observed with an air of great originality.

'And words never hurt anybody,' said Isobel of St Dominic.

But the princess did not, in this instance, shout empty phrases. There was a brief interval of peace while the fugitive nuns settled into their refuge and Teresa wound up the three lawsuits. Then the angry widow moved, not in useless protests to the king but with the cold decision of a soured and vindictive nature.

Teresa, hearing the news from an overwrought and panic-stricken Julian de Avila, paid her daughters the compliment of telling them the worst.

'The Princess Ana d'Eboli has denounced my writings to the Inquisition.'

She made the announcement in a calm, unemotional tone designed to prevent any unseemly outbursts of dismay, but no amount of self-control could possibly prevent the colour ebbing from the lips and cheeks of her listeners. Every Spaniard, layman or priest or nun, knew that every word written or spoken in public, or whispered in private, might be the subject of an inquiry by the Holy Office. Its powers had been limited by Pope Paul IV, but after his death the Grand Inquisitor himself had been invested with the triple tiara, and although Pope Pius V had been dead for two years, the powers of revitalised Inquisition spread more widely and deeply than ever. To be denounced to the Inquisition, and by so powerful a woman as Ana d'Eboli, was to stand in the gravest peril.

'It is my own fault,' Teresa said quickly. 'The prince was so kind when we established our foundation at Pastrana that I allowed him to persuade me to show him my book. It was a stupid thing to do, for I ought to have known no good comes out of parading one's own work. I should have known the princess would read it and misunderstand it.'

'But your work has already been examined!' one of the Sisters exclaimed.

'And will now be examined again. It is the duty of the Inquisition to investigate every denunciation, even if the motive is malicious.'

'Mother Teresa, what are you going to do?' asked Anna of the Incarnation.

'Do? Carry on with my spinning, for it is almost the end of recreation.'

Teresa smiled at them, drawing strength from their weakness and infusing into them a returning confidence.

'I have done nothing deliberately to place myself in danger,' she said. 'If I am in error then they will tell me.'

'Or burn you?' whispered Isobel of St Paul.

'If they do, I will go with you to the stake,' Isobel of St Dominic said.

'And I, Mother!'

'And I!'

One after another the nuns expressed their willingness to die until Teresa, half-laughing, half-moved by their childish gallantry, held up her hand.

'We will not all rush towards martyrdom,' she declared. 'Let us go back to our work now.'

'And recite the little song you composed for us,' said Isobel of St Paul, on a note of rising hope.

'Song? Which one?' asked another.

Isobel clasped her hands, cleared her throat, and recited

the jingle, thrown off in a moment of joy and remembered now at first with hesitation, and then with a clear, bell-like confidence.

'Let nothing confuse thee, nothing affright thee;
Everything passeth, God never changeth;
Patience gains all.
He who clingeth to God needeth nought,
God alone sufficeth.'

CHAPTER THIRTEEN

The little girl was in such a fever of excitement that she found it quite impossible to sit still but bounced about in the already jolting carriage as it shuddered across the cobblestones. She would have liked to sit on both sides of the vehicle at once so that her round black eyes wouldn't miss a thing. As it was, she had darted from one end of the seat to the next, falling over her brother's feet as she went, and, ordered finally to keep her place, she kept up an incessant buzz of chatter.

She was a pretty child with curly black hair and rosy cheeks that not even the long sea voyage had whitened. It was hard to see the exact colour of her dress for it was richly embroidered and decorated all over with little sparkling stones. Although she wore a mantilla, there was something wild and foreign in her gestures and quick-changing expressions as if her exuberant nature could not be contained within Spanish formality. The same air was apparent in her brothers, boys of fifteen and thirteen, who sat next to her and whose velvet doublets and high ruffs concealed passionate beings carried now into a more tranquil environment than they had ever known.

Opposite the youngsters, their father and uncle sat side by side, both showing the effects of long years in the tropics by yellowed skin and fever-bright eyes. The younger of the two had an air of settled melancholy due in part to his recent widowhood. The elder and handsomer had still the bright, eager look of a boy come home.

'Is Aunt Teresa really like me?' the little girl demanded for the tenth time.

'She used to be, but I haven't seen her for forty-five years.' He narrowed his eyes and stared at his daughter as if he were trying to bring another face into focus.

'She will be very old!' exclaimed the child.

'Older than when I saw her, Teresita,' her father admitted.

'They say she has become a saint,' Uncle Pedro remarked, screwing up his mouth doubtfully, as if he were not sure such a thing was quite respectable to have in the family.

Francisco and Lorencito glanced at each other warily as if they were inclined to agree with their uncle, but Lorenzo, looking out of the window, said in a voice as excited as his daughter's, 'We're here at the Incarnation.'

Lifted down from the high step by Francisco, Teresita looked up at cool white walls and felt the first stab of apprehension. Somewhere behind the high gate, now being unlocked by an elderly lay sister, dwelt Aunt Teresa who had been held up as a model of virtue for as long as Teresita could remember. Aunt Teresa had been gay and beautiful and had suffered the most terrible illnesses without complaint. She talked to angels and fell into trances and was sometimes carried up into the air. She had founded new convents where nuns led lives of incredible penance, and she had written books at God's dictation. She was so good that all the rich people wished to claim her friendship and so powerful that poor people flocked to the gates of the convent to beg for her prayers.

It had all sounded romantic and exciting when Father told it, but now Teresita was not certain if she really wanted to meet this fabulous relative. It was too late to voice her fears, however, for they were making their way along echoing corridors into a small, red-tiled room with a spiked grille set in the wall. For the first time in her life, Teresita neglected to push herself forward, but shrank back towards the door.

There was a Latin invocation, the rattle of shutters, and then a warm sweet voice, greeting them; and the answering voices of her father and uncle.

'But you are not all here!' exclaimed the first voice. 'Where is Jeronimo? And Esteban? And your wife, Pedro? I have looked forward to meeting her.'

'Dead,' said Lorenzo heavily. 'It grieves me to have to bring you this news, sister. Pedro's wife died a month before we left. Jeronimo was taken ill at Nombre de Dios as we were waiting to embark. It was what the sailors call yellow fever, and he died very quickly.'

'And your son.'

'Esteban was not well when we went aboard, but we had been several days at sea before the symptoms of fever appeared. We buried him at sea.'

'May God have mercy on their dear souls,' Teresa said quietly, and there was a moment's pause. Then she spoke again, cheerfully, 'But you were spared to return to me, brothers. And Agustin is well?'

'He will never settle down, that one!' said Pedro disapprovingly. 'He has some wild idea of finding the city of El Dorado and helping himself to some of its rumoured gold. Fifty-three years old and he still acts like a moonstruck schoolboy!'

'Pedro has not been well,' said Lorenzo, as if to excuse the carping note in his brother's voice.

'It is my digestion,' Pedro complained. 'I have a very delicate stomach, and the food on board ship was appalling.'

He sighed heavily, regretting his dead wife who had cherished and cosseted him like the children they had never had.

'And Lorenzo too looks sickly. You must both consult a good physician. That is not advice I need to give your sons, I think. They are fine, well-grown lads! But where is your little girl? Above everything I have wanted to see my namesake.'

Lorenzo, turning round to where Teresita pressed herself into the corner between wall and door, beckoned her forward. She came reluctantly to stand before the grille, raising apprehensive eyes to the figure beyond.

Her first feeling was of disappointment mingled with relief for the legendary Teresa of Jesus was merely a dumpy little woman in a darned and patched habit. She leaned upon a stick and her eyes were bright and black. Staring into those eyes, Teresita felt completely safe and warm as if someone had just laid a cloak around her shoulders enfolding her in an affectionate embrace. Her mother had died when she was a baby, and she had always been her father's favourite, but now she knew exactly what it was like to have another woman who cared for her. All her shyness vanished as she gripped the spikes of the grille with small, jewelled hands.

'Oh, please let me stay here with you, Aunt Teresa! Please!'

'Child, this is a convent, not a school!' Pedro snapped. 'Your place is with your father.'

'And where will that be?' Teresa asked. 'Have you decided where you are going to live, Lorenzo?'

'I thought I would look around and buy a small property,' Lorenzo said grandly.

'And while you are looking around, who will care for Teresita?'

'It would be convenient,' Lorenzo admitted, 'if I could leave her here with you. But would it be permitted?'

'There is nothing in the Rule to forbid it.' Teresa smiled warmly at the vivid little face on the other side of the grille. 'Indeed I have already agreed to take another child. You have not met Hieronimo Gracian yet, but there is his little sister, Isabelita.'

'Gracian?' Lorenzo glanced curiously at his sister, wondering what had caused the lilt in her voice as she pronounced the name.

'I met him at Beas de Sequira when I went there to make a foundation in February,' Teresa explained. 'I had received good reports of him from Brother Juan of the Cross who appointed him novice master at Pastrana, but I did not have the pleasure of meeting him until I went to Beas.'

'You sound as if it was indeed a pleasure,' Pedro commented.

'Oh, you cannot imagine how highly I regard him!' Teresa's face glowed like a girl's. 'He comes of a noble family. His mother is the daughter of a former Polish ambassador and his father is the king's personal armourer. There are nineteen of them already in the family – two of his brothers are private secretaries to the king, and he has several sisters. He himself is highly gifted and exceedingly amusing, with a grasp of spiritual matters that is rare in one so young for he is scarcely thirty.'

'Is his sister the same age as me?' Teresita, who was not used to be being ignored, strove to divert her aunt's attention back to herself.

'A year or so older, my pet, for you are not quite nine; but she will be good company for you,' Teresa said.

'And may I wear a dress like yours?'

'You are a trifle young to think of taking the habit officially,' said Teresa, treating the child's question with a solemnity that further won Teresita's heart. 'But I see no reason why you should not wear it, if you wish. We would have to cut one down for you.'

'But your own dresses are so pretty,' Lorenzo said, in a slightly hurt tone. 'They cost a great deal of money.'

'They itch,' Teresita said flatly, rubbing her sparkling bodice with an expression of disgust on her face.

Teresa burst out laughing.

'My darling, you may wear the habit if Brother Juan and Brother Gracian think it suitable,' she declared. 'But you and your brothers must leave us to talk awhile now. Sister Ana of St Bartholomew has a meal prepared for you in the visitors' refectory. Afterwards you will come back here, for I have so much to say to you, and I want to hear all about your adventures in the Indies.'

'You will spoil her,' Pedro said as the three youngsters went out.

'I will love her,' Teresa said. 'Love never marred anything.'

'They are fine children, are they not?' Lorenzo was eager for praise and received it in abundance.

'You have done wonders!' Teresa cried generously. 'Francisco and Lorencito are young men already, and I shall be so happy to have Teresita here with me until you are settled. If you find any property that interests you, let me know of it and I will do everything I can to help. I am becoming,' she said with a touch of innocent pride, 'quite a good business woman.'

'But you have had troubles,' Lorenzo said.

'Such troubles!' Teresa clapped her hand to her brow in half-comical fashion. 'I tell you, brothers, no sooner do I deal with one problem than another arises! It was Gracian who ordered me to leave Beas and found a convent in Seville. It was hard to obey for I have little liking for the Andalusians, but I went. And, of course, the licence did not arrive in time, and the house we intended to buy was only up for rent, and half the nuns did not come. Oh, it was, as usual, a difficult business. But when all that was settled, there came the news of the General Chapter!'

'What was that?'

'A General Chapter of the Order was held at Piacenza in May, at the very time that I was in Seville. They decreed that no more convents were to be founded in Andalusia. It was an open threat to the Reform.'

'What did you do?'

'I appealed to the king,' Teresa said. 'The king has never hindered the Reform. I put our case before him, asking that the Calced and Discalced communities be separated. It is pure common sense, for while we remain under the jurisdiction of the Calced, how can we keep the Rule?'

'But you are Prioress of a Calced convent yourself,' Lorenzo pointed out. 'Yet the nuns here are apparently content.'

'Because I respect their beliefs,' Teresa said. 'I don't force them to obey the Rule of the Discalced, for they have chosen a different way. But many of the Calced who are in authority over us display neither tolerance nor understanding. They hate us, my brothers. In the beginning they took no notice, perhaps because they thought that one or two poor little convents and friaries would do no harm. But they underestimated the spiritual hunger that is in our land. Now there are eleven Discalced convents and Gracian wishes another to be established at Caravaca. More and more young women are seeking to enter the Reformed Order. So now the opposition against us grows.'

'Fanned by the hatred of the Princess d'Eboli?' Pedro recalled his sister's letter.

'Poor, poor woman!' Teresa exclaimed, a shadow blotting out the indignation on her face. 'The princess is driven by devils, I believe, to perform her acts of malice. She has the officers of the Inquisition poring over every word I have written in the hope of finding some heresy.'

The shadow lifted to reveal a smile of pure amusement but Lorenzo and Pedro exchanged swift glances of alarm. Even in the Indies they had heard tales of the power of the Inquisition.

'Has the king not moved to answer your pleas?' Pedro asked.

'He has confirmed Brother Gracian's appointment as Father Provincial of Andalusia and as Apostolic Commissary for the Reform in Castile,' Teresa said gloomily. 'It was kindly meant, but it has made matters worse. How can *we* protest at being under the Calced if districts of the Calced are placed under Gracian who is dedicated to the cause of the Reform? They have already sent delegates to Rome to protest at the appointment, but the Holy See will not hasten in these matters; and meanwhile Gracian must begin his visitations in Andalusia. It is an intolerable position for him to be in, for they will not obey him. Indeed, I am sometimes afraid that active harm might come to him down there. I don't trust the Andalusians, and Brother Juan of the Cross agrees with me for he cannot abide them.'

'I see convent life has not damped your fires of indignation!' Lorenzo said, half laughing.

'I may be getting old,' she retaliated, 'but my desires are

as fierce as ever! Before I die, I must see the Reform securely established. It is sound within because I have never begun a foundation until I was quite certain that it had the best possible chance of establishing itself. I've not always been proved right – Pastrana was a disaster! – but when a mistake has occurred, I have done everything in my power to rectify matters. When forces beyond my control seek to destroy us, then I am helpless.'

'You say that!' Pedro exclaimed.

'Surely you have only to pray,' said Lorenzo.

'But we cannot always expect to receive the answer our own will desires,' Teresa said, earnestly. 'Our Lord sends trials to test our strength. He told me Himself that that is the way He treats His friends.'

'And how did you reply?' Lorenzo asked, bewildered.

'Why, I told Him that if that was the case it's no wonder He has so few friends,' Teresa said, with the rich chuckle that made her seem like a girl. 'And then He said, "I have heard you, Teresa: now let Me alone."'

Her brothers, nonplussed at this brief glimpse into a supernatural intimacy of which they had no experience, cleared their throats uncomfortably. Teresa, with quick tact, changed the subject.

'You have not asked after our sister, Juana. She is on her way here and should arrive within a few days. You will like her, Lorenzo, for she is as gentle and pretty as she was in childhood.'

'And her husband?'

Teresa hesitated between discretion and truth, and compromised.

'Señor Juan de Ovalle suffers from poor health. It makes the poor man a little testy at times. And then there are the two children. Beatriz is already attracting suitors, and Gonzalo is driving his parents wild for leave to go off to the Italian wars. I have promised Juana that I will use my influence with the Duke of Alba to have Gonzalo accepted as a page in his household. It is little enough to do for Juana. Although her own circumstances are strait, she has sent whatever she could possibly spare to aid our community.'

'There is no need for you to go abegging any longer!' Lorenzo said. 'I am a reasonably wealthy man now, my sister. Any help I can give your convents will be given gladly.'

'You have sent money home all these years,' Teresa said.

'All these long years whenever I needed help, my thoughts flew across the sea to the Indies. And always help came to me.'

'You are my sister,' said Lorenzo simply. 'It is only fair that I should be able to do something for the Cause.'

Her eyes kindled as she looked at him, her affection stripping the fever-yellowed skin and lean, jutting cheekbones from the man to reveal the beautiful youth who had sat by her long years before, refusing to believe in her death. Yet in that romantic boy had been the undeveloped strength and fledgling compassion of the man, as the promise of the rose is implicit in the tight-folded bud.

By Lorenzo's side, Pedro said loudly and jealously, 'I cannot afford to help you as much as I would wish. My affairs have not prospered as much as I hoped they might and my health is not good. The climate of the Indies has ruined my constitution. I have been near to death more than once.'

'Then you must take things very quietly for a while and be sure to see a physician,' Teresa repeated, wondering what disappointments and frustrations had caused her brother's mouth to tighten and his voice to raise itself into a querulous whine.

There was, to her, something infinitely sad about the two richly dressed men with their coldly sparkling jewels. Their vitality had been sucked out of them by the poison-laden winds of the Indies, and Lorenzo's hard-earned gold weighed down his heart as well as his pockets.

Afraid that her thoughts might show on her face she began to talk hastily about their cousins.

'Ana Tapia is Prioress at Salamanca, of course. She is still working too hard, but Inés Tapia tries to make her keep within bounds. Maria and Beatriz are at St Joseph's here. You know that Diego's elder daughter, Leonor, died here three years ago? She was a little saint, that one. The younger girl, Maria Baptist, is proving a very capable Prioress at Valladolid. Oh, and cousin Francisco's wife is very ill. You must try to make the time to visit them for they always inquire most kindly after you.'

'We will try to see all our relatives,' Lorenzo said promptly. 'Indeed, I have already written to Pedro Alvarez, suggesting he might tutor my sons until I can enter them into a good college.'

It was the first time for years that she had heard the name mentioned. Yet, instead of the expected pain, Teresa felt only a gentle nostalgia. She could look back now half-humorously to the girl in the orange dress who had fancied herself in love for a brief summer and yet had shrank from marriage, as if her nature was already craving something that lay beyond human affection and would never be satisfied with less.

'I shall return to St Joseph's as soon as my term of office here expires,' she said, briskly. 'I am sending one of my best nuns, Ana of St Albert, to make the foundation there. It is a tranquil little place and the people are eager for us to arrive, so she will find no difficulties.'

She smiled, remembering that she had originally intended Maria of St Joseph to make the foundation, but Luisa de la Cerda's former maid of honour had declared there was no challenge in such an undertaking and had begged to be allowed to go to the new convent at Seville. Teresa, who loved a fighting spirit, had consented and the brilliantly intelligent young woman was now establishing the Rule in a new convent, filled with over-zealous novices, and surrounded my inimical Calced friars. Gracian was helping them to settle in, and Maria of St Joseph's latest letter indicated that she was beginning to share Teresa's own affection for the golden-hearted friar. Previously she had been rather cool towards him, but then Maria was apt to take a long look at people before admitting them to her friendship. Her initial impulse of love and loyalty towards Teresa had been clouded after her entry into Carmel by an almost suspicious reserve. But her letters these days were always frank and friendly, even if she did embellish them with elaborate Latin quotations. Teresa, who read Latin with the utmost difficulty and spelt it according to her own eccentric notions, had little patience with such intellectual displays, and had commanded her spiritual daughter to write in good, plain Castilian. Nevertheless the occasional Latin tag still crept in.

She became aware that Pedro was grumbling again about his health, that one of the lay sisters had entered with refreshments for the gentlemen, and that in the excitement of greeting her relatives she had forgotten to bring her spinning.

Which only goes to show, she thought with a flash of self-mockery, that I am still unable to discipline my mind. Gravely and sympathetically she set herself to listen to a detailed account of her brother's ailments, shifting her weight surreptitiously from one leg to the other as she was in the grip of an agonising attack of rheumatism.

Teresita, having eaten and drunk heartily, for she had an excellent digestion, had left her older brothers to their own devices, had followed the lay sister into the kitchen and was chattering gaily as she swung to and fro on the half-door.

'At Quito, we had slaves to wash the dishes, and to cook the meals, too. I used to think that it would be great fun to help them. I went down to the kitchen once and the cook let me bake some cakes. When I'm here, will you let me bake some cakes for you?'

'You can make churros,' said Ana of St Bartholomew, referring to the rings of batter deep-fried and dipped in sugar that were eaten before Lent began. 'And honey cakes too,' she added, remembering Teresa's predilection for the tiny balls of egg and marzipan rolled in syrup.

'I'm going to be a Carmelite,' Teresita went on. 'I'm not allowed to take any vows yet but I shall take them as soon as I'm allowed. Perhaps I shall found convents one day like Aunt Teresa. After all, everybody says that I'm very much like her when she was a child.'

'I think she was probably better-looking,' the lay sister said.

'Oh!' Teresita, unused to such frankness, gaped slightly, but heartened by the suspicion of a twinkle in Sister Ana's eye, rallied and remarked optimistically, 'Well, no doubt I'll improve as I get older. And beauty isn't important, Uncle Pedro says.'

'He's quite right, but it's nice to have a little.' Ana, who had deliberately frightened away her first suitor by wrapping a towel round her head and daubing mud on her face, gave the dishtowel a final shake and hung it up neatly.

Everything in the kitchen was, Teresita noticed, spotlessly clean. It would have been quite possible to sit down and eat one's meal off the floor. She thought of the big, smoky, untidy room at the back of their Quito home, where larger slaves had bullied the smaller ones, and the crackling of fat had been mingled with sleepy or quarrelsome Indian voices.

'Once,' she said aloud, 'one of our houseboys got drunk and chased his wife all around the house with a machete. It was very exciting!'

'Heaven preserve us, child! Weren't you afraid?'

'Oh, not in the least,' Teresita began, amending to, 'Well, just a little. He did no harm, for Father took the machete away from him, and then he fell fast asleep under the table. Alcohol isn't good for the Indians, you know. It flies straight to their brains and makes them very savage; but most of the time they're very peaceful and friendly. I don't suppose things like that happen here.'

'Not in the last week or two,' Ana of St Bartholomew said.

'They had feasts too,' said Teresita. 'The drums would sound, calling people; and then the young men and the maidens would dance round in a circle. They wore blossom in their hair and they stamped slowly, and then faster and faster, whirling round and round, while the drums grew louder and louder.'

'And what happened then?'

'I don't know,' said Teresita, 'for Father always made me come away before the end.'

'Praise be for that at least,' Sister Ana said, devoutly. 'But you'll find Avila dull, after so much excitement.'

Teresita shook her head, impelled not only by stubborn politeness but by some dark buried memory of a forgotten fear. Their house had been large, cool and sprawling, surrounded by cultivated land, but always within sight had been the green wall of the jungle, remorselessly hacked down and with equal tenacity creeping back to repossess the ploughed and planted land. Buried deep in those jungles had been the great cities of Cuzco and Corichancha, with their jewelled gardens of emeralds and silver and the tombs where the Inca kings lay, black and mummified, waiting for their savage gods. By day the little silvery bell on the whitewashed church had called the faithful to worship, but at night the drums had sounded from valley to valley, throbbing through fever-laden air, and the Christianised slaves had padded past her window, bare-breasted and flaunting, to the call of the moon.

'There is nothing dangerous here,' she said, awkward and shy again. 'It is so safe, so peaceful.'

Ana of St Bartholomew was not able to fathom the little girl's primeval fear, but she recognized the voice of loneliness, and stooping, hugged the stiff, brocaded figure.

'And you will have good times here,' she promised, 'for Mother Teresa is the kindest soul in the world. She still dances for us at recreation and plays her guitar, and we have all kinds of games and riddles. Why, it's no fun at all if she isn't there! And, when you have learned your lessons for the day, you will help me to make cakes and I will give you a little plot in the garden where you can grow what you please. You'll like that, won't you?'

Teresita nodded and said, with apparent inconsequence, 'My mother died when I was a baby. Father says he was very pleased to have a daughter.'

'And well he might be, for little girls are very precious!' cried Sister Ana, 'and you are lucky too, for here you will have nearly two hundred mothers to care for you; think of that!'

'But my Aunt Teresa – she is the first,' the child said.

Ana of St Bartholomew rose, adjusted her coif which had undergone a trifle of dishevelment during the embrace, and taking the small, jewelled fingers in her own work-hardened palm, said, eyes glowing in her strong, plain face, 'Your aunt, Teresita, is one of the most remarkable people on this earth. I tell you, child, that to be near her is to be very near heaven.'

'You like her very much, don't you?'

'Like her?' Sister Ana screwed up her face in a vain effort to find adequate expression for her feelings but was forced to repeat, 'Child, your aunt is one of the most remarkable women in the world.'

CHAPTER FOURTEEN

'Sometimes I think the good Lord made me stupid so that others would pity me and come forward to help,' Teresa said with doleful humour. 'Why I ever decided upon a convent in the middle of the city I will never know! I should have realized the noise and stench would have been intolerable. But this new house is perfect. The patio looks like frosted sugar.'

'And it was Don Lorenzo who helped us,' said Maria of St Joseph.

'He leaves Seville in a few days in order to negotiate for the property at La Serna,' Teresa said. 'I have persuaded him to let me keep Teresita with me. He is still not completely well, and of course, Pedro has never ceased to ail since they returned. And Teresita enlivens the place.'

'A trifle too much occasionally,' Maria of St Joseph said tartly, remembering how Teresita's shrieks had punctuated a highly edifying playlet about the early martyrs.

'She is a bonny little love,' Teresa said indulgently. 'And if I am to obey Father Tostado and enclose myself in some Castilian convent, she will make life very bearable.'

'Father Tostado has no sympathy for the Cause,' Maria said, indignantly. 'But what else can one expect from a Portuguese?'

'At least we have Father Gracian to stand up for us,' said Teresa.

'I suppose so.' Maria bit her lip and then burst out

impatiently, 'Mother Teresa, you know I don't question Father Gracian's motives. I believe him to be the best intentioned of men, but by accepting the post as Visitor to the Calced, he has gone against the express orders of the Father General.'

'He could not refuse to obey the king,' Teresa excused. 'I personally hold Brother Mariano responsible. He has a training in diplomacy which he ought to have put to better use. As it is, we are torn between temporal and spiritual rulers, and cannot make a move without offending somebody!'

'But at least we have our new house, and our licence is finally ratified,' Maria said, unwilling to argue further.

'That's true! And you have some excellent novices. There is good material for you to shape here, Mother Prioress.'

'And I will shape them to the pattern you have moulded,' said Maria.

'No, no. Shape each one as it pleases God to fashion her,' Teresa said earnestly. 'Go gently with the timid ones, but don't fear to be firm when the occasion demands. And if you must scold, sweeten it with a little honey.'

'As you do?' Maria asked slyly.

'Ah! you've had many a rare roasting from me,' Teresa smiled, 'but I think so highly of you that I would like you to be quite perfect.'

'Excuse me, Mother Prioress, but you and Mother Teresa are wanted in the parlour.'

A very tiny nun, with a sweetly piping voice, hesitated in the doorway.

Maria of St Joseph rose, waiting for her companion, but Teresa, who insisted upon paying scrupulous respect to the position of the Prioress in whichever convent she was staying, motioned the younger to precede her. She herself lingered for a moment.

'And how is Gabriella today?'

The tiny Leonor of St Gabriel dimpled at the Mother Foundress.

'Extremely angry,' she said, 'for I have learned you had a headache yesterday and never came to me for the bromide I had prepared.'

'Daughter, if I ran to you every time I had a little pain, I would be perpetually knocking on the door of the infirmary,' Teresa said gaily. 'Run away now and pound your herbs and mix up your physics, and become a grave and learned infirmarian.'

'Yes, Mother Teresa.'

Leonor knelt briefly, and set off down the corridor on legs that were still more inclined to skip than to glide decorously.

In the parlour, Father Gracian and Lorenzo waited on the other side of the grille, with faces almost as dark as the brown cloaks they wore. It was Lorenzo who spoke first, omitting the usual courtesies.

'Sister! Unless you have more funds than I imagine, I am liable to be thrown into prison at any moment,' he exclaimed.

'We have just discovered that this house is subject to the alcabala tax,' Father Gracian said gloomily. 'As the property was bought in Don Lorenzo's name, he is liable to pay it within a month or else go to prison for debt.'

'This community can barely support itself yet,' said Maria of St Joseph.

'But I fail to see the difficulty.' Teresa looked from her brother to the handsome, balding friar. 'You are a wealthy man, Lorenzo. Cannot you simply pay the tax now and avoid trouble with the authorities and then engage a lawyer to examine the title deeds and find out if it's possible to claim exemption in the future?'

'I'm wealthy on paper,' Lorenzo groaned, 'but the money from my Indian plantation won't be here for at least three months. I put down all my ready silver against the estate at La Serna. Apart from a few ducats for travelling expenses, there's nothing left.'

'But isn't your credit good?'

'In Seville? Mother Teresa, the city is swarming with men returned from the Indies who claim to be expecting money from their estates,' said Gracian. 'The moneylenders are charging the highest rates of interest ever known.'

'Then sell something,' Teresa said briskly. 'You glint with jewels like some pagan idol.'

'So does every other returned traveller,' Lorenzo retorted. 'The country is so flooded with gold and silver that both have lost their value.'

'Cannot you write to one of your friends?' hinted Maria of St Joseph.

'No, I cannot!' Teresa snapped. 'I seem to have spent the last few years of my life writing begging letters, which is strange occupation for one vowed to poverty. Lorenzo!' She turned to her brother. 'It is clear we must wait until the ship docks from Peru. Meanwhile, you will have to disappear.'

'Disappear?' Lorenzo repeated.

'Father Gracian can house you in his cell at the Los Remedios priory. He is Visitor in Seville and has the perfect right to lodge a guest. The civil authorities will not be able to touch you; even if they discover your whereabouts you will be beyond secular jurisdiction. And we will engage a lawyer immediately, for I am quite certain the deeds should have exempted you from payment of the tax.'

'You have such an excellent head for business,' Lorenzo said, with a faint stiffness that reminded her of their father.

'Well, I do not take pride in it,' she retorted, 'for it is surely abominable that a cloistered nun should spend so much time haggling over money.'

Even after the two men had left, a frown of displeasure lingered on her brow. It seemed as if ill-fortune was dogging this foundation in Seville. The disapproval of the Father General over Gracian's appointment, the dangers and suspicions from the Calced friars, the unexpected tax demand – all seemed to pile up on her shoulders like a load of logs. Then she smiled at her own foolishness, because there were often times when, embarrassed by the spiritual favours descending upon her, she had begged for secular trials to test her mettle.

She was returning to her cell when one of the novices glided out of a shadow and tugged her sleeve gently.

'What is it, child?'

Recognizing Sister Beatriz of the Mother of God, Teresa stopped at once. The girl had been presented at the convent by Father Mariano, who had given the Foundress a graphic account of her tragic childhood.

'She spent her early years with an aunt who intended to make Beatriz her heir, but the old lady's servants were afraid that they might lose their own bequests. So they began to put small doses of poison into their mistress's food and then accused Beatriz of having done it. They so played upon the woman's nerves that she sent Beatriz back to her home. Her parents decided next to marry her to a wealthy man – three times her age and of vicious habits. When she refused, she was locked up and her father threatened to hang her. It was then that the mother seems to have felt some sense of remorse for she assisted her daughter to escape and the girl's parish priest brought her to me.'

Teresa's ready sympathy had gone out to the thin, pale girl with the dark, burning gaze and the bitter mouth. Beatriz was quiet and controlled in her manner but Teresa counted on the sweetness and good-humour of the Sisters to eradicate those tragic memories.

'Has Father Gracian left yet, Mother Teresa?' Beatriz asked.

'Yes, daughter. Did you wish to see him?'

'To make my confession,' Beatriz muttered.

'But it isn't Father Gracian's day for hearing confessions, is it?' Teresa inquired.

'I wished to consult him about the state of my soul,' Beatriz said.

'But Mother Prioress is always ready to guide and advise you,' Teresa said. 'You cannot expect poor Father Gracian to run over here every five minutes.'

'Mother Prioress is always busy,' the girl said resentfully.

'But while I am here, I would be glad to help,' Teresa began, but Beatriz ducked her head and sidled away.

It was not Teresa's way to force confidences and Beatriz's nature had been, she knew, twisted by circumstances into reserve and suspicion but she stared after the novice for a few moments with a troubled expression. In small, enclosed communities a single hysterical or over-emotional novice could infect and unsettle the others. Sickness within was far worse than troubles without. In recent weeks they had been forced to dismiss a noted beata, considered by the citizens of Seville to be a saint, and agreeing in her own estimation with that opinion. Teresa, who had known and loved the holy hermit-woman, Mariadiaz, had not been impressed by the woman's excessive tears of devotion nor her frequent raptures combined as they were with every possible infringement of the Rule. The woman had gone with more than disappointment marring her face, and Teresa, in charity, prayed for her ardently.

When she reached her cell, it was to find a small cup of tisane on the window-ledge, placed there, she guessed, by her anxious little infirmarian. She gazed doubtfully at the syrupy liquid, resisted the temptation to dispose of it out of the window, and gulped it down. Then she lowered herself to the stone floor and reached for pen and paper. She had to snatch half an hour before Vespers in order to work on the account of the foundations she had made. Her confessor, Father Ripalda, had ordered her to write the book and dear Father Gracian had added his voice. Teresa, privately considering the occupation a waste of time, was nevertheless pleased at the opportunity it afforded her of paying tribute to the friends who had helped her, and of including several edifying and amusing stories about her dear spiritual daughters. Her pen scratched rapidly over the paper, pausing occasionally to hover, and then racing on. When the bell rang, the pen stopped in the middle of a word and was laid down. Teresa, obeying the Rule, rose and went quietly to join her Sisters in the choir.

The tranquillity of the convent was shattered a few weeks later by the rumbling of black-covered carts, the clashing of steel and the jangling of harness. Those of Seville who had risen early for Mass or the market place, hearing the commotion, came out to peer curiously, whispering among themselves, as a tall figure in the black robes of a Dominican alighted from his horse and knocked thunderously at the door. It was five-thirty in the morning and the nuns were in their separate cells, meditating in the silence of dawn.

Teresa, who had slept badly, was battling with a severe headache as she knelt upright before the crucifix on the white-washed walls of the cell she occupied. Her efforts to concentrate were slowly gaining ground over her bodily indisposition when she was jolted back to full awareness by the tramping of feet along the corridors and by a frightened whisper from the doorway.

'The Inquisition,' moaned Maria of St Joseph. 'We have all been denounced to the Inquisition and the officers are here with a search warrant.'

For a split second, fear ran down her spine like cold water while her flesh shrank from the anticipated flames that would crackle without pause until her body was consumed. Then the consciousness of her entire innocence banished fear.

'In that case we must not hinder them.'

The nuns, in stages of dismay ranging from mild anxiety to near-hysteria, were bunched together in the recreation room, guarded by two rather sheepish-looking men with long staves in their hands. As Teresa entered, the tall Dominican stopped her with a brief jerk of the head.

'You and your community have been denounced as heretics. It is my duty to tell you, Teresa of Jesus, that we will examine every inch of this convent and you would be well advised not to hinder us.'

He had said the same thing many times before and been answered by cold defiance, by tearful pleas for mercy, by attempted bribes, sometimes by a gentle and reproachful silence. This elderly nun, in her patched habit, had the unmistakable air of good breeding and he expected haughtiness, but the eyes she turned upon him glinted with pure amusement.

'If you find any trace of heresy in me or my daughters, I will help you to carry the faggots to the stake myself,' she assured him calmly. 'Have we permission to talk together quietly while your men conduct the search?'

'I ought not to tell you this,' he said, dropping his hectoring tone, 'but you were denounced by the beata named – '

'In charity, we will not speak her name now or in the future,' Teresa interrupted, holding up her hand. 'Let the Sisters note for all time that the one who treated us thus will not be remembered.'

She spoke solemnly and for a moment there was a respectful silence as if some prophecy had been uttered. Then she turned again to the priest.

'We have been denounced before and were not molested then. Would it be improper of me to inquire what is different this time?'

'Opposition to the Discalced Carmelites is growing rapidly,' the priest said in an undertone. 'Here in Andalusia, novelty is frowned upon for it implies the shadow of heresy and where there is shadow there must be substance. We are bound to examine all denunciations.'

Teresa bowed, still looking amused. The attempts of officials to separate their private opinions from their public duty generally tickled her fancy. She wished she could inspire her nuns with a little of her own detachment, for although they had drawn down their veils and stood quietly, she could hear the nervous rattling of rosary beads, and a stifled sob from the half-comprehending Teresita. Kind little Leonor of St Gabriel put her arm about the child and, pulling a thread down from her veil, began a subdued game of cats' cradles.

'There are carts in the street outside,' whispered Maria of St Joseph. 'They will take us all to prison if they find a single scrap of paper.'

'Only think,' Teresa whispered in return, 'if they take us to prison, we won't have to pay the alcabala tax!'

'A fine way you have of cheering me up!' the Prioress retorted, but she smiled in spite of herself.

Imperceptibly the tension was slackening. Although a nun occasionally jumped nervously as a heavy footfall sounded beyond the door, the community had settled into quiet conversation. It was not, Teresa decided, a time to insist upon silence, so she left them unrebuked and talked herself, moving among them with such a cheerful look that even the most timid among them were emboldened to hope that they might not end the day in some foetid dungeon.

'Mother Teresa.' It was the tall Dominican with a decided change in voice and manner. 'My officials tell me that nothing of a heretical nature has been found here, but there are some manuscript writings in your own cell.'

'An account of my convents which I am writing by order of my confessor. He has already undertaken to submit the completed work to the Holy Office.'

'Then I will bid you good day.'

The priest frowned as if to remind her that those who fell under suspicion of heresy would be remembered, restrained himself from a sudden irrational desire to kneel to her, and went out of the enclosure he and his men had so unceremoniously entered.

The crowd outside the convent had melted away, for few cared to linger within the vicinity of the Inquisition carts. As the officials emerged without prisoners, a round, frightened face peered around the corner of the nearest building and as quickly withdrew. Father Julian de Avila, newly arrived in Seville to inform the Mother Foundress that her arrival at Toledo was expected daily, leaned against the wall, his knees sagging, while he mouthed prayers to every saint he had ever heard of.

He confessed as much to Teresa when he saw her later in the day and was not in the least hurt when she threw back her head and laughed heartily at his cowardice. In his present ecstasy of relief, the good-hearted cleric would willingly have lain down and allowed the Mother Foundress to trample all over him if it would have afforded her an instant's pleasure.

Teresa had other things upon her mind, however.

'On our way to Toledo,' she said briskly, 'I intend to stop at Malagon. News has reached me that the Mother Prioress there has introduced a most scandalous form of penance. She has ordered the Sisters to practise humility by slapping and pinching one another! I tell you, Father, such things as that were sometimes done at the Incarnation years ago. They cry out against the very spirit of our Order.'

'I am selfish enough to wish you would stay here,' said Maria of St Joseph.

It was a generous admission from the independent, high-spirited Prioress, and Teresa, recognizing it as such, forgot her irritation with the Malagon Prioress and bowed, half-mocking, half-loving.

'Your brother's money is expected within a day or two. Then he intends to escort you to Toledo in a coach,' Father Gracian said.

'A coach? Is that suitable for one vowed to poverty?' she wondered.

'In the heat of summer, one need not look for more discomfort,' Julian de Avilla began.

'You would not subject little Teresita to a closed cart, would you?' Gracian exclaimed.

'I had forgotten Teresita will be with us,' she admitted. 'Of course, we must make the journey comfortable for the dear child. And you will send Isabelita to Toledo, won't you? It would give me such joy to care for your little sister.'

'Isabelita will be with you,' Gracian promised. 'My mother intends to visit you as soon as she has recovered from this latest birth.'

'And she must bring baby Juliana,' Teresa insisted. 'There must be something very special about the twentieth child in a family.'

'We are all special, in my mother's eyes,' Gracian smiled.

'And you are very special in mine!' Teresa cried. 'Don't you think, Father Julian, that God was very good to send Father Gracian to us here? I can think of nobody better fitted to walk the tightrope between the eagles and butterflies!'

'The – what?'

'Eagles and butterflies,' she repeated gaily. 'We, the Discalced, are butterflies, spreading our wings and dancing for the love of God with no fear for the morrow. The Calced are eagles, tearing and snatching at their prey.'

'Is it truly as bad as that?' Maria of St Joseph asked.

'We will survive if we don't lose heart,' Teresa said, cheerfully.

But when Father Julian had left and Maria of St Joseph had excused herself in order to take her share of the daily cleaning, Teresa leaned forward and spoke low and anxiously.

'There is no point in alarming ourselves unnecessarily, but neither can we ignore the truth. Matters are serious, Father Gracian. This search by the officers of the Inquisition is but a symptom, for I have often been under suspicion before and always been fairly treated. But matters are growing worse, as if some poison were spreading from within, threatening the whole Order. I fear for you, my friend. You still sleep among the Calced, eat with the Calced. Your life is not secure in such company.'

'You cannot think they would seek to murder me!' he exclaimed, profoundly shocked.

'You are so honest yourself that you cannot imagine treachery in others!' she cried. 'I am not suggesting they will murder you in your bed or when you walk the streets, but there are poisons that sap the vitality, eat through the heart and spleen, give the appearance of a slow and natural death. I would like you to take your meals here, in the parlour. Eat nothing at Los Remedios except an occasional egg, boiled in its shell, mark! Do this for me even if it's merely to relieve my mind while I am in Toledo.'

'And have you any more orders?' he asked, mischievously.

Teresa laughed, acknowledging the thrust, but her eyes grew serious again.

'I would not have harm come to you,' she said earnestly. 'It is a weakness in my nature for I ought to rejoice when God acknowledges our strength by sending us trials, but I am always very sorry for the misfortunes of those I love. And you, my friend, I love more than most. Have I not shown it by taking an oath of obedience to you? I regard that oath as binding upon me, for when I am left to my own devices, I am like a little ass weighed down with two bushels of corn; but, under obedience, my soul is as clear and untroubled as crystal.'

'Reflecting God?' he asked.

'Rather is it like a castle,' she said, thoughtfully. 'I have thought of it so often that I see it clearly within myself. The soul is a castle of many mansions and these mansions are set around a central core which remains in darkness as we hesitate at the entrance. And we must go deeper and deeper into ourselves, discarding our layers of selfishness and pride, moving from mansion to mansion, losing ourselves in the core of ourselves until we are hidden deep in the centre of that crystal where self is lost and Christ stands waiting. At the centre of every soul, he stands waiting for us, and we must seek Him there. Isn't that a fine paradox! To lose oneself in order to find oneself? To escape from oneself by going deeply into oneself?'

'You must write about it,' said Gracian.

Teresa, mouth half-open in dismay, stared at him.

'It is a most beautiful concept,' he said. 'And you must write it down. As soon as you have finished your book of the Foundations, you must work out this new and beautiful idea and write about it.'

'Why do you want *me* to write things?' Teresa asked, crossly. 'Let learned men who have studied write things; I am too stupid. Anyway there are more than enough books written about prayer already.'

'The book will be valuable,' he said, stubbornly.

Tears of frustration sparkled briefly in her eyes.

'Father, I am sixty years old,' she said, imploringly. 'I have had trial after trial. More lie ahead of me. For the love of God, let me get on with my spinning and go to choir and do my religious duties like the other Sisters. I wasn't meant for writing; I have neither the health nor the wits for it.'

'It is a matter of obedience,' he said, watching her narrowly.

She folded her hands and bowed her head in a simple and touching gesture of submission, acknowledging his right to demand from her the pledge she had given him.

When she looked up next she was smiling.

'I see why Father Juan of the Cross appointed you as novice-master,' she said, wryly. 'There is a steel lining to *your* heart; and it is very good for me to be bruised by it. I will write another book, if I am spared to finish this one! If only I live for long enough to see the two parts of Our Order separated and at peace, then I can retire to one of my convents and be forgotten. And my books may be forgotten too, although I would like to see *The Way Of Perfection* in print.'

'Then you are not entirely devoid of worldly pride,' he teased.

'And neither have I achieved detachment,' she confessed. 'I worry about my family and about my friends. You will eat here, won't you? I will leave word with Maria of St Joseph to see that you are given your meals in private. And now I must go back to my writing. This has been a topsy-turvy day.'

As she went out, Beatriz of the Mother of God moved with her silent step back into the shadows from whence she had briefly emerged. Her hands were sweating and she rubbed them up and down her habit, blinking tears from her eyelashes. So Father Gracian was to take his meals in the convent. No doubt Mother Prioress would sit and talk to him while he ate. Maria of St Joseph was beautiful and intelligent and had been reared with love. It was natural she would find the handsome priest good company. The Mother Foundress did, though she was twice his age.

And I am younger than either of them, Beatriz thought forlornly. And I was never loved by anybody. It is to women like me God ought to send visions. Perhaps He will, if I pray hard enough! And then Father Gracian will advise me and comfort me; and the other Sisters will admire me.

Shivering, she wrapped her veil over her head and padded back to the loneliness of her cell.

CHAPTER FIFTEEN

Midnight Mass was over, and the nuns had retired to their cells to sleep for a few hours until the wooden rattle awoke them again to continue the celebrations of the Nativity. In her cell at St Joseph's Convent in Avila, Teresa knelt by her windowsill and wrote steadily. She was reminding the king of his promise to exert his influence in the cause of the Reform; a promise that must be fulfilled if the Discalced Carmelites were not to be swept away by the hostility ranged against them.

Although she wrote briskly, stopping only to push her spectacles higher up the bridge of her nose, her mind ranged back over the preceding months as tableau after tableau flashed back behind her eyes.

The last six months of the year 1576 had been, she thought, a preparation for the year that followed. At Toledo she had finished her revision of *The Foundations*, and written *Rules For Visiting Convents*. There had been good news from Paterna where the Calced nuns had voted unanimously to transfer to the Discalced discipline. There had been the children to cling to her skirts and plague her to amuse them. Sweet, wild Teresita with her long and exciting tales of the Indies! And Gracian's sister, Isabelita, whose mouth was too prim but who made up little poems and songs, modelled tiny angels out of coloured clay, elected herself Prioress and went about jangling a miniature bunch of keys, and declared that a piece of cold melon deafened her throat! Neither must she forget Antonio Gaytan's daughter, Mariana, who, when she visited the convent, still declared her intention of entering as soon as she reached the permitted age.

'My little pest!' Teresa called her, and wished that these lovable children were all that distracted her from her vocation.

But it seemed as if she scarcely turned her back upon a convent when troubles sprang up like toadstools. From Seville where Father Gracian was obediently taking his meals in the parlour, came word that Beatriz of the Mother of God had begun to experience raptures and visions. Teresa's first reaction had been one of joy that God was sending gifts to a girl who had known so little happiness. Then her natural caution had prevailed and she had written for more information, which, when it came, confirmed her forebodings. Beatriz's visions became, it seemed, more frequent and more fantastic, and had to be recounted in detail to Father Gracian. Another Andalusian novice had also begun to suffer from raptures and ecstasies which forced her, so she said, to lay aside her spinning in order to compose long accounts of her experiences.

Teresa, wondering how anybody receiving genuine favours from heaven could bear to have them known by everybody, gave orders that the two nuns were to be watched carefully and not permitted to go oftener to confession than the others. But matters had grown worse; for the two nuns, disappointed in their efforts to attract attention to themselves, began to spread discord through the convent, complaining that their Prioress occupied herself, not with the needs of her community but with long gossips in the parlour with the handsome priest. It was bad enough when such lies were confined to the enclosure but somehow rumours had spread beyond the convent, fanned, Teresa guessed, by the Calced friars.

She had written more strongly to Maria of St Joseph, ordering her never to sit and talk with Gracian while he ate his meals and telling her that the writings of the nun, Isobel, were to be sent to Toledo where Teresa herself would study them and discover if there was a grain of truth amid all the nonsense.

There was nothing but the ravings of a neurotic and over-excited imagination, and Teresa, laying aside the scrawled sheets, had felt the familiar pang of disappointment because she always longed so desperately to meet another person who could enter with her into the joy of that Heavenly Betrothal. There was Juan of the Cross, to be sure, but he was already a saint and in no position to share the interior consolations which refreshed her own spirit.

In the midst of all the anxiety it had been amusing to hear the report that the troublesome Teresa of Jesus had been ordered to the Indies. Amusing also to hear what the Papal Nuncio had said of her:

> 'A disobedient, contumacious woman who promulgates pernicious doctrine under the pretence of devotion, leaves her cloister against the decrees of the Council of Trent and the orders of her Superior, is ambitious and teaches theology as though she were a doctor of the Church, in contempt of the teaching of St Paul who commanded women not to preach.'

'When did I ever mount a pulpit?' Teresa had cried. 'And how can I presume to teach theology when I have never studied it? How can they call me disobedient when I only leave my cloister in obedience to Father Gracian, and write books only because my confessors tell me that I must? Don't they realize, doesn't *anybody* realize, that it goes against my deepest desires to have to move about from place to place, to have to write down everything in order that others may peer into my thoughts, when I am only just beginning to learn dimly what it means to be a nun?'

But, her conscience being clear, she had treated the denunciation as a joke, and returned to Avila shortly after giving Casilda de Padilla the habit. Dear little Casilda! Teresa's pen moved more slowly as she reflected upon the beautiful thirteen-year-old who had twice fled from her unconsummated earthly marriage to the convent, and twice been dragged back at the very door by her relatives. But at the third attempt she had gained the sanctuary of the enclosure, and become for the Mother Foundress, 'my angel, Casilda'.

And if it is a sin to love all my little novices dearly, then I must be content to sin a little, Teresa thought.

Certainly some of her own kin gave her little cause to love them. Her sister Juana was in debt again and she and her husband were forever begging for money without, as far as Teresa could see, much intention of paying it back. As for Pedro, shivering through his first Castillian winter since his return from the Indies, he complained, long and loud, about the cold, about his digestion and about his insomnia! Teresa had sent him a little hand brazier to warm his fingers, and spiced pastilles for his throat, but he continued to wail out letter after letter, bemoaning his condition. So different from dear Lorenzo, who, having established himself at La Serna, was determined to subject himself to religious discipline and had made himself so ill by excessive use of the whip and the hairshirt that Teresa had begged him to mitigate his austerities. To Teresita, however, she had sent the hardest discipline she could find, for the child was becoming self-willed and spoilt now that she was staying with her father again, and needed the sting of a self-administered lash to subdue the rebellious streak in her.

Even her nuns and friars caused her pain. Apart from poor deluded Beatriz and Isobel, the nuns at Malagon were behaving badly. The Prioress, Mother Brianda, who had replaced Ana of the Mother of God, did not, like her predecessor, order the nuns to slap one another but was too gentle, encouraging her spiritual daughters to behave with a sugary devotion which set Teresa's teeth on edge. And Mother Brianda was not well, which meant that Teresa's own cousin's daughter, Beatrix of Jesus, must take over as Prioress of Malagon and Beatrix was too apt to make personal attachments with her spiritual sisters.

But these were mere pinpricks compared with what Teresa thought of as the disasters of the past year. The scandalous slanders about Father Gracian, the complaints of her brother, the squabbles of her nuns, even the task of writing *The Interior Castle*, had all faded into insignificance beside the trouble that had befallen the Community of the Incarnation.

Her term of office as Prioress over, Teresa had surrendered her keys and gone back thankfully to the tiny convent which, being the first of her foundations, held a special place in her heart. In this small space, hidden from the world by shutters and spiked grilles, she could sink into comparative anonymity, obeying the Rule as the other Sisters did, earning a little money for the community by her spinning, stealing out in her rare moments of leisure to pray in the small hermitage of the inner courtyard only to be dragged back to join in the recreation, taking time out of the night to answer her immense correspondence or to work upon her book. Here her mind could expand to illimitable horizons, her heart could swell with love for the whole world, and in forgetting herself, she could retreat to the core of herself, to the innermost mansion of that crystal castle.

Then, in October, the nuns of the Incarnation had re-elected Teresa as Prioress. When the news reached her, she had wept with frustration at the prospect of going back to rule over so many Calced nuns, for though she had brought order instead of anarchy, it would be hard to leave a small, tranquil community for a large one in which the elements of discord were always apparent. Indeed she had been re-elected only by a narrow majority – fifty-five of the Sisters had voted for her while Ana of Toledo had received forty-four nominations.

The vote had been declared invalid by the Father General, Tostado, who had ordered Ana de Toledo to assume the role of Prioress. Teresa, knowing her to be a conscientious, well-intentioned woman, had accepted the decision with relief and hoped that would be the end of the matter.

It was bitter to learn from Juan of the Cross that the nuns had refused to obey but had greeted Father Tostado with yells and imprecations and shaking fists.

'It means that I have taught them nothing except personal attachment to me,' she said miserably. 'Father Tostado feels as I do that it is ridiculous for a Discalced nun to be Prioress over the Calced. Ana de Toledo will make an excellent Mother, if she is left in peace to rule.'

'Fifty-five of the Sisters voted for you,' said Father Juan.

'And did me no favour by it,' she said sharply. 'I have no desire to return to the Incarnation and I look to you, Father Juan, to quell this unseemly personal attachment.'

The little priest with the commonplace features and light, inward-gazing eyes, nodded gravely.

'There is something I must confess to you, Mother Teresa,' he said. 'The letters you have written to me – I kept them all in a leather pouch, and sometimes, when I was depressed, I have been in the habit of taking them out and reading them over, It was a great imperfection in me, but it's only recently that I could bring myself to destroy them. So you must not blame the poor Sisters too much, for they have learnt bad habits from me.'

'I find that difficult to believe,' she said with a smile that was half a sigh, for there remained between the young friar and herself a difference of temperament that would always set up a barrier. Juan of the Cross was fast disciplining himself beyond the need for human affection as he moved into the dark nothingness where his God dwelt unseen. Teresa, still bound up in human friendships, was groping towards a more personal Redeemer.

'I hold you,' he confessed shyly, 'still in great affection, my daughter.'

'And I have some liking for you, my Father,' she replied.

And the woman of sixty-two and the man of twenty-nine smiled at each other in complete, momentary harmony, knowing they were making their way along different levels to the same goal.

That had been the last time she had seen him, for a few weeks later there had come a royal summons. Philip of Spain, Emperor of the Indies and of all Spanish possessions beyond the seas, wished to meet Teresa of Jesus with whom he had already corresponded.

They met in the half-completed palace of El Escoril which reflected one facet of its monarch's complex nature for the great building had been designed, at Philip's command, in the shape of the gridiron on which St Lawrence had been martyred. Teresa, leaning upon a heavily embossed walking stick brought by Lorenzo from the Indies, walked slowly through the great, echoing rooms hung with the black and silver that were the king's favourite colours, and seemed also to reflect the two sides of his character. The black revealed the deep pessimism of the man whose grandmother had been mad Juana, and the silver ran through the gloom like the bright affection he displayed for his children and the loyalty he inspired in his personal attendants.

She knew the soul of the man before she stood before him and it was a troubled soul for which she prayed earnestly. Yet the person of the monarch inspired her with trembling shyness, though he was not much taller than herself and almost as simply attired, in a dark tunic collared in miniver, with the Order of the Golden Fleece hanging, heavily golden, around his neck.

She knelt awkwardly and rose at his quiet bidding, raising her eyes to the narrow, long-chinned face with the cold, blue eyes and lasciviously jutting underlip. This was the man who held the government of Spain in his hands, working in his monkish office for sixteen hours out of every twenty-four, employing the most efficient network of spies in the world. It was said that the smallest by-law in the remotest province had to be signed by him before it could be put into effect, so that his room overflowed with documents over which he pored by daylight and candlelight. It was said that he, who worried if he saw an animal or a child ill-treated, would travel many miles in order to preside over an auto-da-fé where as many as a thousand heretics, drawn from the dungeons of the

Inquisition, would be strangled and burnt. This was the man who had sent Torquemada into the Netherlands, who was so ascetic that he took the discipline and wore the hairshirt before any ceremonial occasion, who could with a few words deliver Teresa of Jesus into the hands of the Inquisition.

She realized that he was waiting for her to speak and wished frantically that she could think of something witty or uplifting to say, but her brain seemed as stumbling as her legs, and the pause had grown too long for comfort before she gasped out the first thing that came into her head.

'Well, sire, here is this old gad-about nun, come at your command.'

And now he will consider me a complete idiot, she thought, dismayed; but to her astonished delight the king laughed in a rusty, creaking way as if he were out of practice.

After that, they had talked like old friends though she never could remember exactly what had been said. She knew that she had outlined her idea for a Separation of the Carmelites, and that the king had stroked his long chin and promised – or half-promised – to lend his support.

She had emerged from that great instrument of torture, leaving the solitary man within the framework of his own horrific imaginings, and, when she was on her way back, thought of a dozen profound and penetrating things she might have said to him.

The king would, she was sure, seek to honour his half-promise but he was ensnared in the turgid machinery of government while the enemies of the Discalced Carmelites moved swiftly.

An attempt had already been made to force Father Juan of the Cross to return to the Calced, and for a time he had submitted to police protection until, declaring that it was impossible to carry out his duties while his footsteps were dogged by two burly guardians of the law, he had insisted upon being left alone again. His only companion was another Discalced friar, Father Gérman of St Matthew, and the two men, in their sandals and coarse habits, were a familiar sight in the streets of Avila as they went about their unostentatious works of charity, returning every night to the hut built outside the walls of the Incarnation Convent.

December had drifted in with icy flurries of snow and a keening wind that wailed through the cracks in the rust-red walls of the town. The wind and the snow had muffled the footsteps of those Calced friars who stole like thieves through that night. And thieves they were, Teresa reflected bitterly, for they came to snatch away two of God's servants.

The two Discalced friars, praying in their draughty shelter, had been seized, pinioned and dragged away; not in silence, Teresa had been glad to hear, but yelling so vigorously that lay sisters began to spill out of the convent, wrapping their mantles over their heads and peering with terrified, snow-rimmed eyes at the young men sinking beneath the hail of blows aimed at them by the hooded figures who assumed, distorted by white flakes and swirling wind, the shapes of nightmare.

They had been taken to the Calced Priory for a night and then spirited away, Father Gérman to La Moraleja and Father Juan, so it was said, to the Calced Priory at Toledo. There had been one brief report that hinted at unimaginable cruelties being practised upon the two friars by their Calced brethren.

When she reached this point in her letter, Teresa's hand shook with indignation. Father Juan and Father Gérman were accused of having incited the nuns of the Incarnation to rebel and of having refused to return to the Calced Rule. When she thought of the methods that might be used to force them to plead guilty to the charges, Teresa felt like a bird beating its wings against the bars of indifference and cruelty.

At least, none of the Incarnation Sisters could be induced to bear false witness against their confessors. Nobody could be persuaded to declare that either of the friars had interfered in the smallest degree with the elections. Now, all the nuns, whether they had voted for or against Teresa, had been declared excommunicate by an infuriated Father General.

The letter to the king was finished. She signed and sanded it and heated the wax in the candle-flame ready for its seal. She could find only the skull seal among the jumble of papers on the window sill and she used it reluctantly, disliking the symbol of death which struck her as faintly ominous.

A letter to Father Gracian was also ready to be sent – a cautious letter, giving as full an account of the situation as she dared, with her usual pseudonyms for fear the document might fall into the wrong hands. They had begun the practice of using pseudonyms almost in jest, finding pleasure in their aptness. Gracian, worried about his receding hair-line, was Eliseus or Paul; Juan of the Cross was Seneca; Teresa herself Angela or Laurentia. The Jesuits, who had always been so kind, were the Raven because of their black habits. Her dear Discalced nuns were butterflies and grasshoppers, while the Calced were eagles, cats, owls, Egyptians – anything that savoured of malice and cruelty.

Dear, dear Gracian! Glancing down at his name scrawled across the letter, her eyes blurred. She took off her spectacles and laid them near to hand. She needed them more and more frequently these days and sometimes was forced to dictate her letters to Ana of St Bartholomew who had trained herself to write swiftly and neatly. But Teresa preferred to write to Gracian in her own hand – long, gossiping, intimate letters in which she was learning to steer a delicate balance between the respect she owed him as the Superior to whom she had vowed obedience and the personal affection she felt for the man young enough to be her son.

He had signed himself, in jest, her 'loving son', and she had been not only amused but touched by the conceit.

If I had borne a son, she reflected, I would have liked him to be like Hieronimo Gracian.

Sometimes she grew a trifle weary of the company of women. After sixty years, Teresa had no illusions about her own sex. She knew most of them to be weak and vacillating, given to back-biting and tale-bearing, jealous of their small privileges. Occasionally the intensely feminine atmosphere in which she lived became suffocating, and the sound of a masculine voice, the joy of pitting her wits against a masculine mind, something greatly to be prized. But it would be a long time before she would see Gracian.

He was still living in conditions of the utmost difficulty at the Calced Priory of Seville where he slept behind a locked door and seldom ate. He was carrying out his duties, despite the slanders buzzing about his head. Indeed, Teresa feared that he scarcely noticed them. There was something naïve and trusting in the friar that was both endearing and irritating.

She must, she decided, pay one last visit to the choir. It was not fitting that the night of the Nativity be marred by constant earthly worry. Surely, on this night, the Blessed Virgin had not noticed the damp floor and leaking roof of the stable nor allowed her joy to be clouded by the knowledge of her Son's prophesied end!

Teresa got stiffly to her feet, wincing as cramp ate through her chilled muscles. Her body, she thought ironically, was becoming an intolerable nuisance. It had begun to thicken slightly round the hips and once or twice she had found herself stooping a little. Her teeth were troubling her too, decaying slowly, imperceptibly, as she moved unwillingly into old age. Sometimes, when she saw her young nuns moving swiftly and gracefully, she felt a pang of regret that she had not employed her youth more profitably.

She took up her candle and went out to the head of the narrow staircase leading down to the choir. Everywhere was so quiet that she could hear the breathing of the Sisters and the faint crackling of the snow blown against the shutters.

She paused for an instant, enjoying the silence, and then started down towards the well of the hall. At that moment, a draught of air, caused possibly by a renewed flurrying of wind, caught the flame of her candle and twisted it into a black and smoking wick.

Plunged into thick darkness, Teresa lost her balance, gripped at the handrail, and, missing it, fell heavily down the steep flight of stairs. Her heavy garments and her instinctive shielding of neck and head probably saved her life, but she landed awkwardly, wedged between the foot of the staircase and the wall, with her left arm bent at an impossible angle.

She must have cried out in her descent for she could hear startled exclamations and the pattering of feet as the nuns, roused from their sleep, hurried from their cells, carrying the little candles which burned all night by their pallets.

The candle flames ringed her round as if she were already on her bier, and shocked eyes gazed down at her from under the white coifs.

'Are you not going to help me up?' Teresa asked, tartly.

They all sprang into action at the same time, exclaiming and commiserating as they pulled and tugged her into an upright position.

'I fell downstairs,' she began.

'It must have been the devil who pushed you, Mother!' one of the Sisters cried.

'Old Hoofy? He'd do worse than that if he could,' she joked, fighting back the waves of pain.

When she tried to move her arm, the pain stabbed like hot knives and she could feel the bones scrape together. She passed her hand shakily across her brow to force back a wave of dizziness.

'Fetch Sister Ana of St Bartholomew.'

'I'm here, Mother Teresa. I was asleep!'

The little lay sister, whose ability to sleep through the loudest noise was a standing joke, pushed her way through the choir nuns, her coif awry and her face full of contrition.

'Help me to my cell and bring some linen and some hot water. And if I might be permitted a cup of wine, it would help, if I have your permission.'

They would have given her a barrel of wine if she had expressed a desire for it.

'You must have the physician, Mother,' Ana of St Bartholomew cried. 'I'll find somebody to send for him.'

'Nonsense, Sister. Leave the poor man to enjoy his night's rest. You will bind it for me now and we will send for him in the morning. And do put your coif straight! An untidy Carmelite is like a miserably married woman. The rest of you had better go back to your cells.'

'Please don't order us to go,' one pleaded, 'until we know you are not too seriously hurt.'

'If you were to die,' said another, 'we would be utterly lost.'

Teresa, sinking to her pallet and submitting to the lay sister's probing fingers, looked up in alarm at this blatant bit of personal attachment.

'I'll tell you something, my daughters,' she said, 'that will show you how important I really am. On one occasion, I was travelling to Salamanca with four or five other sisters and Father Julian de Avila. Night fell before we reached the end of our journey and we went the last part on foot, with only a donkey to pull the wagon. I still don't know how it happened but in the darkness we lost our cart, and I was separated from the others. Oh, it was a fine muddle, I can tell you. And when we did meet up again, do you know what Father Julian said? He said, "We were in such a panic, Mother, for we couldn't decide whether to look for you or the donkey first. We couldn't make up our minds which was the greater loss." Father Julian had a great deal of sense!'

PART FOUR

THE FLAME

CHAPTER SIXTEEN

They met in a warm, dark August night on their separate sides of the grille, she in her darned and patched habit with one arm held still a trifle awkwardly; he wrapped in a dark travelling cloak with a hat in his hand and a bulging canvas bag at his feet.

'But it will be more dangerous than ever for you to return to Andalusia,' Teresa was protesting. 'And to even consider venturing into Madrid when you know how they hate us there!'

'I have the king's permission,' Father Gracian reminded her.

'And will His Majesty be able to protect you when you are again amid the Calced?' she demanded. 'The Papal Nuncio annulled your post as Apostolic Visitor and gave the brief to the Calced friars.'

'The king intervened and re-appointed me,' Gracian said with a touch of sulkiness.

'And it was unwise of you to accept,' she expostulated. 'It will set them against us more than ever. If they can lay hands on you they will not hesitate. Look at poor Brother Juan of the Cross! Dragged away nearly nine months ago and not a word since as to where he is or how he is! Poor little Juan, to be forgotten and left to suffer God knows what hardships and cruelties!'

'Brother Gérman escaped,' he reminded her.

'And is now with the Discalced friars of Mancera, thanks be to God.' Teresa brightened perceptibly, then her face darkened again. 'But what use is it to me if a hundred have escaped when Juan of the Cross is still in an unknown cell, and you, the friar I value most highly, about to put yourself in the same danger? For heaven's sake, tell me about something more cheerful. How is my dear Maria of St Joseph?'

'As energetic and independent as ever!' he returned, with a grin. 'She bears up wonderfully under all her troubles.'

'She is a little too independent at times,' Teresa said. 'She does not always open her heart to me as I like my daughters to do.'

'Perhaps you are a trifle hard on her,' Gracian hinted.

'I am hard on them all,' she admitted, 'but it is necessary. I tell you, my Father, that when I am dead, somebody must take over as Foundress. I would like it to be Maria of St Joseph. Oh, she can be a vixen sometimes, but, whenever I look at her, I see that proud, lonely child in her jewelled dress swearing that one day she would follow me. And how magnificently she copes with her problems!'

'Beatriz of the Mother of God being the greatest,' he commented wryly.

'Poor little Beatriz! To hint even that you and Maria of St Joseph – ! She has expressed contrition for her slanders but I think she could scarcely help herself. Who can measure the harm an unbalanced mind may do? So many girls enter our convent because they crave security or lack the means to find a husband. So very few seem to enter for the right reasons, even though I try to choose so carefully.'

'You cannot be everywhere,' he comforted, 'especially now that your arm is bad.'

'On the contrary, it is better!' she retorted with some asperity. 'It had to be broken and re-set again and I won't pretend the pain was pleasant, but the stiffness is wearing off now and I can fix my coif without help. I have even begun to write letters again which is a great relief to poor Ana of St Bartholomew, for she has enough to do in the kitchens apart from writing to my dictation! I will write to you in Madrid and you will answer me, won't you?'

'I'll write to you at every opportunity,' he promised.

'And send it by safe messenger?'

'With all the usual pseudonyms,' he said reassuringly.

'And do not eat with Calced!' she warned. 'Keep the door of your cell locked at night and don't trust people. Your besetting sin is a tendency to think well of everybody.'

'And your besetting sin is a tendency to fuss over everybody,' he teased. 'You wish all the world to enjoy perfect happiness.'

'Not on this earth!' she corrected quickly. 'God only sends troubles to those whom He wishes to test in His service. So when I hear that a friend of mine has many miseries to bear, part of me rejoices. And part of me,' she shrugged at her own weakness, 'longs to bear all their troubles by myself!'

'You mentioned family squabbles,' he reminded her.

'Oh, family!' Teresa laughed, half-exasperated and half-amused. 'There's my poor brother, Pedro, who never ceases to complain, and Juana who seems to imagine I have unlimited funds to throw in her direction. Even Lorenzo, dear soul! worries me with his constant pleas for advice and his occasional hare-brained schemes. You know that from time to time he gets it into his head that he ought to enter religious life. My handsome brother who will cease to flirt with the ladies when he ceases to breathe, as a Discalced friar! Imagination can go no farther!'

'And your niece and nephews?'

'Are darlings,' she said emphatically, 'though Teresita is apt to be headstrong and noisy, so unlike your gentle little Isabelita, but then your sister has the same placid, friendly nature as yourself. As for Teresita's brothers; Francisco has, I think, a vocation for the religious life, but Lorencito is a wild youngster. You heard that Juana's boy, Gonzolo, is off to the Indies to seek his fortune. Well, Lorencito wanted to return to Peru with him, but Lorenzo very wisely forbade the notion. And events are proving him right for Lorencito has got a young village girl into trouble and was trying to evade his responsibilities. The young people of today are sadly lacking in moral fibre. I still hope the boy will turn out better than he has begun. At the moment he has his father's charm without his father's principles. But enough of my relatives! Tell me about your own family. Are they all well? Little Juanita?'

'Like an opening flower,' Gracian said fondly.

'Four is such a pretty age to be,' Teresa said wistfully. 'I strive for detachment but these children clutch at my heart. It makes me feel young to hear their prattle and join in their games. If only they could take the habit before the world has hardened them. I crave your youngest sister already as a member of the Community. There is such love among us here that she would never be hurt or disillusioned.'

'And would stay for ever, protected from all evil, as I would like to do, had I not a journey before me.'

Gracian rose, shaking out the creases in his cloak.

'Must you leave already? Cannot you stay a little while longer? Tell me about your new friar, Nicholas Doria.'

'The ex-banker from Genoa? Subtle and shrewd as befits a merchant.'

'And humble and charitable as befits a man of God?'

'He is more able than I am,' Gracian evaded, 'and, I believe, a valuable addition to our ranks.'

'Perhaps he is the man to plead our cause in Rome,' Teresa said hopefully. 'His Holiness is kept in ignorance, I'm certain, of the injustices done to us. If only two of our friars could make their way to the Vatican and gain an impartial hearing, we might be able to resist Tostado; for it was by his command that little Juan of the Cross was seized. Pray for that saintly friar, won't you? And take every precaution yourself to avoid falling into the hands of the Calced.'

Even when he had promised faithfully and left, Teresa stayed where she was, leaning her head wearily upon her sound hand. She was physically and mentally tired, sick of the controversies raging within and without her convents, anxious beyond measure about her spiritual family just as she was irritated beyond measure by her blood-relatives. They sucked strength out of her when she was no more than a feeble woman, full of doubts and aridities.

And some people actually regard me as a saint, she thought in wry amusement. If so, then I must be a lop-sided one! Whoever heard of a saint finding it difficult to pray, or of a saint who, granted such favours as God has given to me, used them so ill and wasted so many opportunities?

Tiredly, she dragged herself from the floor and went slowly towards the chapel, wondering as she limped along if any echo of her petitions ever reached Juan of the Cross in whatever prison he was confined.

Over the Calced Carmelite Priory at Toledo, the dark sky also brooded, lit only by the feeble rays of a few small stars. The Brothers slept in their cells, most of them conscience free, though a few turned uneasily as if, in their slumber, some inner voice reproached them. Through the cloisters Brother Juan of St Maria padded softly with his keys jangling at his waist. He was going, as he had been going every night for over a month, to take a final look at the prisoner before he retired to his own cell for the night that still remained before the Angelus roused the friars for the first prayers of a new day.

Juan of St Maria was ill-at-ease. The duty of guarding Brother Juan of the Cross was little to his taste, for though he had scant sympathy with the aims of those who were trying to make religious life more severe, he had even less sympathy with those who sought to change a man's opinions by flogging and starvation. He would have felt better if the little friar had cursed or complained but Juan of the Cross merely smiled, with eyes that looked beyond them, even though his tunic was stuck to his back with dried blood and there were times when he had to be revived before the beatings could continue.

Since Juan of St Maria had seen a clear and unearthly light filling the dark cell, he had treated his prisoner with as much kindness as he dared; letting him exercise for a few minutes in the corridor beyond the dungeon, bringing him a clean habit, hot water, razor and comb; smuggling in some apples to supplement the bread and water diet; even giving him some paper and a piece of charcoal so that he could while away the lonely hours of solitary confinement. The reluctant gaoler had not seen the writing materials since then, but sometimes he heard Juan of the Cross chanting softly to himself, and then he would lean against the wall for a few minutes, enjoying, without understanding, the words.

'Upon a darksome night,
' Kindling with love
' In flame of yearning keen –
' O moment of delight! –
' I went, by all unseen,
' New-hushed to rest the house where I had been.'

Strange words for a celibate to sing, Juan of St Maria had thought, and wished suddenly that he could analyse the look in those strange, far-seeing eyes. But the last words, with their pathetic desire, had inspired his slow mind to a series of related thoughts. Now, trembling a little at the risk he was taking, he swiftly unlocked the door of the outer cell where the two lay brothers snored gently on their pallets. The inner door led into the small bare room with the barred window set high in the wall, where the prisoner was kept.

Juan of St Maria unlocked the inner door gently and peered into the foetid gloom. It was not light enough to see the figure, but he sensed a slight movement, waited a second and then closed the door again without re-locking it. Another moment and the outer door too closed softly.

The kneeling figure in the cell rose and moved towards the door, his fingers stretched out to the bolt. The door opened again and Juan of the Cross peered across the two sleeping figures to the outer door. The temptation to hurry was almost irresistible but he paused for a minute longer to draw from his neck the little wooden cross that Teresa had given him and to place it on the floor as a mute token of gratitude for the only man who had been kind to him during his incarceration. Then he stepped to the outer door and lifted the heavy bolt. It slipped in his hand and clattered down, arousing momentarily one of the friars who turned, mumbling sleep-hazed 'Who's there?' and fell asleep again at once.

Softly, Juan retraced his footsteps to the inner cell and took up the two thin blankets which had served him as pallet and covering. Then he went back through the ante cell to the corridor beyond. In his brief walks he had already noted a small window halfway along, and now, aided by a gleam of moonlight through the half-open shutters, made his way to the broad, low windowsill, knotted the blankets and secured them to the centre staple.

He had no idea what lay below the window, but God having brought him so far would not desert him now. His hands slipped down the makeshift rope and his arms ached intolerably. His feet slipped too, swinging loose with neither rope nor ground to meet them. He closed his eyes briefly and jumped the remaining space, landing on all fours with the knotted blankets slapping against the wall above his head.

He was, he judged, trying to remember the plan of the Calced Priory, in the courtyard of a Franciscan convent in the adjoining street. It was foolish to remain where he was but his legs were shaking so violently that he stayed for a moment, gulping in the cool air and lifting his face to the sky beyond which dwelt the hidden God for whom he sang his chants of praise. In the long months of imprisonment when it seemed that heaven and earth had both forgotten him, Juan of the Cross had sung almost unceasingly just as he had sung when, a small boy, he had tramped beside his mother from one cheap lodging to the next. Others sang when they were happy, but music welled up in Brother Juan only when his spirits were weighed down in loneliness.

The first part of his escape had taken much longer than he thought. Already the sky was lightening and he could hear the clatter of pails beyond the wall as the water carrier made his early morning rounds. That wall! It rose up, high and smooth before him, with no cracks that might serve as footholds. He stared up at it with hopeless eyes, feeling all the bitterness of extreme disappointment for it had seemed up to that moment as if God were leading him to freedom. Then he bowed his head in complete and loving submission and felt beneath his feet the rushing of the great wind as it lifted him over the guarding wall and set him down in the open market-place, empty save for a small mongrel dog that trotted up with wagging tail and little yelps of friendship. He hushed it absently, fondling its ears as he looked round in perplexity, wondering where refuge might be found in the maze of unfamiliar streets.

The dog darted away a little distance and turned, head held sideways in expectation of a game. When Brother Juan began to follow, the animal turned again and continued to lope ahead, pausing frequently to wait for his stumbling human companion.

The Angelus was just sounding as Juan rounded a corner and leaned against the wall, lifting one bloodied foot to relieve the pain of the sharp stones embedded in the sole. As he turned his head, the grille and bell-rope of the convent met his gaze. It was the Discalced Carmelite Convent of St Joseph, and his eyes blurred with relief before he looked down for his four-footed guide, but the street was empty. Accepting this as he accepted all that befell him, Juan pulled upon the rope, answered the surprised 'Deo Gratias' with a muttering of his name, and fell in a dead faint across the threshold.

'Brother Juan of the Cross seeking refuge here! Are your wits astray, Sister Leonor?'

The lay sister shook her head vigorously, moving from one foot to the other in excitement.

'He is in the parlour, Mother Prioress,' she insisted. 'He has escaped from the Calced and needs sanctuary within the enclosure.'

'Within the enclosure? But we cannot allow any man, priest or not, beyond the grille unless it be to hear the confession of a nun too ill to walk!'

Ana of the Angels rubbed her forehead in perplexity, wishing she could think more clearly after a night spent in tending Ana of the Mother of God who was suffering from one of her recurrent bouts of fever.

From the cell beyond, a voice called feebly, 'I cannot take my purge until I have made confession and I am too weak to stand up!'

'And I am not strong enough to lift her,' affirmed Sister Leonor.

Averting her eyes from the lay sister's buxom frame, the Mother Prioress of the Toledo Carmel said, primly, 'In that case, you must find a friar at once to tend to her spiritual needs.'

'And so they took him in at once,' said Teresa gleefully. 'The Calced friars came later in the day and searched the chapel and parlours, but knowing the strictness of our Rule, never dreamed of his being within the enclosure. And later that same day he was smuggled out with the help of the secular clergy, may God reward them! and taken to Beas de Segura, where he may recover his strength before he resumes his duties. I have heard from Ana of Jesus and she tells me he is dictating some poetry for her, which he composed during his imprisonment. When I think of the cruelties inflicted upon that little saint, it makes my blood boil! I tell you, my daughters, it is safer to fall into the hands of the Infidel than those of the Calced!'

But her indignation at the wrongs done to Juan of the Cross bubbled over at the news that Father Gracian had been arrested in Madrid and sentenced by the Calced friars there to be flogged twice a week, to fast three days a week, and not to communicate with Teresa of Jesus.

'They show him more mercy than they showed to Brother Juan, because they hope to win him over to their side,' Teresa commented bitterly. 'Already there are rumours, which I do not believe, that he intends to seek admission to the Augustinian Order.'

She worried over Gracian more than over Juan of the Cross, for the latter had something cold and remote beneath his gentleness which repelled her motherly nature even while it called forth her uncritical admiration. Gracian was of weaker stuff and she loved him more on that account.

But Gracian's situation was overshadowed by the blow dealt to the nuns at Seville. The Papal Nuncio, acting, Teresa was convinced, out of sheer malice, deposed the redoubtable Maria of St Joseph and appointed Beatriz of the Mother of God as Prioress there.

'A reward for slandering Gracian,' Teresa said. 'That is how to advance under the Calced Rule, my daughters. Spread false and spiteful lies about your confessor and your Prioress and you will quickly find yourselves in the seat of authority. Maria of St Joseph is behaving magnificently in the midst of all this, and even poor Beatriz is acting more sensibly than I might have expected. There is hope for that soul yet, daughters. And all is not lost, for I hear from Father Doria that Sega is shortly to be replaced as General by Angel de Salazar.'

'We must pray,' said Maria of the Cross.

'Pray for strength to bear our troubles,' Teresa said fervently. 'God could remove them all tomorrow if He wished, but He desires to test us now, and so, for a little while, allows the devil to have his way. Thanks be, there is very little more that can be inflicted upon us.'

She would remember those words in the days that followed, reflecting bitterly upon the unconscious pride which had tempted her to trust her own judgment and place a limit upon the afflictions allowed by God.

At first it seemed as if her optimism was justified. Juan of the Cross was recovering from his ordeal and resuming his arduous duties more speedily than Teresa deemed prudent, but Gracian had been allowed to return to the Discalced Priory at Alcala de Henares, and she heard through Doria, happily smuggling out letters under the noses of the Calced, that Gracian was as firm in his opinions as ever, and anxious only lest Teresa might worry about him too much. And, although this concerned her least of all, her own health was much better. Her arm had strengthened, the ache in her hip grew less during a mild winter; her bouts of sickness were far fewer; and there was a decided sparkle in her eyes when she considered the progress of the struggle between the two branches of the Order.

But on Christmas Eve, when she sat spinning, remembering idly that it was a twelvemonth since her accident, Ana of St Bartholomew came, white-faced, to tell her that the Papal Nuncio with all his officials was in the larger of the two parlours and demanded to see every member of the Community immediately.

They crowded together behind the grille, pulling their veils over their faces and hiding their hands within their wide sleeves. The Nuncio, splendidly sinister in his purple robes, read out the contents of the document he held; read slowly so that the most inexperienced lay sister could understand.

Every Discalced Convent and Priory had been placed under the direct authority of the Calced and any nun refusing obedience would be at once excommunicated and expelled.

The Rule of the Discalced would be swept aside as if it had never been, and Teresa y Ahumada, who called herself Teresa of Jesus, would be imprisoned for life in a Calced Convent as soon as one could be found that would agree to take her. In future she would be forbidden to write or teach or leave the cloister and those who spoke in her defence would find themselves in a like condition.

Teresa heard them to the end, making no sound or movement. Indeed she had the confused impression that she had already died and was listening to the tolling of the bells.

For this was the death-knell of the Reform. The long years of preparation in the Convent of the Incarnation, the slow, arduous struggle from natural to supernatural, the interior visions that had spurred her to continue the dangerous and exhausting journeys in the heat of summer and the snows of winter – all these were swept away as if they had never been. Carmel would degenerate again into worldliness and comfort, and all those who had followed her, believed in her, would be punished for their foolishness. From her vow of obedience there was no escape except through the doorway of anathema, and this obedience was owed now to the Calced who would not be gentle in their treatment of those who had sought to render life more austere and devout.

When Sega had finished, she bowed and went towards the choir, walking stiffly as if she were afraid she might break. It was the hour of Matins but she knelt dumbly in her place and the tears sliding down her cheeks wetted her habit and made a little pool in the hollow worn by her knees.

Then, with a vague, wordless gesture of infinite despair, she limped back to her cell, ignoring Ana of St Bartholomew's proffered arm.

The day wore on in whispers and tears, but the Foundress remained in her cell. The lay sister, waiting at the door lest she should be required, could heard only a low, monotonous sobbing, mingled with broken sentences of 'I accuse myself – my own fault – '; and once, as if wrung from the depths, the cry, 'Where are You, Lord? Where are You now?'

Have I been deceived all these years? Led by pride and ambition to imagine I could accomplish something in the service of God? Have I truly seen those heavenly beings and heard those words of advice, or was it a delusion all the time? Am I, without knowing it, a little mad, involving others in my crazy schemes? Or is this a punishment for my unworthiness? Others have heard Your call and gone forth to do Your will, but I have failed again and again, and dragged innocent people into my wickedness. I only entered the religious life to escape the consequences of my evil nature, but one cannot escape hell even in a cloister. And I am in hell now, in the darkness and nothingness of non-existence, burnt by those unceasing fires. Through my fault, through my fault, through my own fault!

Towards evening, Ana of St Bartholomew dared to enter, kneeling by the crouching figure and begging her to come to the refectory to eat something.

'I cannot eat,' Teresa said, dully. 'I thank you, Sister, but I cannot eat.'

'In charity, Mother Teresa.' Ana's broad, peasant face was pleading. 'I am sick with anxiety for your sake. Please me by eating something.'

'In charity then.' Teresa rose slowly, reaching for her stick.

There was in her not the slightest desire to eat or drink, for who needs nourishment in hell? But Ana looked so troubled, poor soul, and it was churlish to waste food.

The others had already gulped down a frugal supper and returned to their cells. Teresa took her place at the low table and stared down at the bread on her plate, the water in her cup, the baked pear and slice of goats' cheese in the bowl. She was weak with hunger but the effort of raising the food to her mouth was beyond her.

Ana of St Bartholomew pushed the plate nearer, made an encouraging sound, and withdrew to the door. She would have liked to do more but the Foundress had retreated to a place beyond human comfort. For a moment the lay sister closed her eyes and drooped tiredly against the door. She had been on her feet since before dawn, for whatever events occurred, meals must still be prepared and dishes washed and floors scrubbed. If only Mother Teresa would eat a little and not sit with folded hands and blank eyes.

Ana of St Bartholomew jerked out of a half doze into full awareness, her startled eyes flashing the length of the table to where Teresa sat. There was another person in the refectory, standing by the table and bending over slightly to break the bread into small pieces.

The brilliance of the white tunic dazzled the lay sister's vision, and the face was half-hidden by a falling lock of hair, but she saw the hands with their exquisite shape and strength as they performed their homely task.

In such a way had the same hands built a fire on the shores of Lake Galilee, touched the head of Peter, caressed the face of a child, been raised up over the hair of the Magdalene.

But these things are not seen by such as I am, Ana thought, in bewilderment.

She heard, still unbelieving, the deep and gentle voice.

Eat now, daughter, and keep up your heart. We have come through worse than this together.

Teresa was eating the bread held out in those long fingers and there was the scent of frankincense in the air.

I am not worthy to be here, was Ana's only thought, as she began to move slowly away from the intimacy of the scene. The last thing she saw, as she gave a final, awesome glance, was the nail-pierced palm raised to her in a courteous gesture of farewell.

CHAPTER SEVENTEEN

It was rare for Teresa of Jesus to allow herself a few minutes' relaxation, but on this warm June day with the sounds and scents of high summer floating through the window, and a slight breeze ruffling the edges of her paper, it was tempting to let her thoughts drift away from the letter she was writing and roam back over the past eighteen months.

Eighteen months! Was it really only that long since she had lived through what she had believed to be the death of the Reform? To her, it seemed a lifetime, and she herself an old woman, at peace with herself and with the world. It was time for her to retire, she considered, to give way to a younger, more vigorous woman; but whenever she suggested such a thing her superiors held up their hands in amazement, pretending not to notice her limping gait or the cough that had racked her since her bout of influenza. The illness had been a severe one, leaving her limp and tired and subject to vague feelings of depression which, she was glad to discover, scarcely ruffled the deep inner contentment in which she now dwelt.

Lorenzo was suffering from depression too. In his last letter he had declared that he was not long for the world! Of course, she had written to him sharply, telling him not to talk nonsense. A little too sharply, she reproached herself, and chewed the top of her pen thoughtfully, trying to think of something amusing to fill out this second and more kindly message. Her brother would be lonely now that he had finally given in to Lorencito's pleas and allowed the boy to sail to the Indies, but the child born of that unfortunate affair was at La Serna with her natural grandfather. No doubt Lorenzo enjoyed fussing over her.

And I, thought Teresa, sit here in my convent at Segovia and dream away an hour, forgetting for a brief space the work that still remains to be done and marvelling over the mysterious changes God has effected in the hearts of those who opposed us.

It was the king himself who had come to the aid of the Reform. Moving with incredible speed for so coldly cautious an administrator, Philip of Spain had ordered Sega to cease his persecution of the Discalced Carmelites, under pain of royal displeasure. And in the spring of the previous year, Sega had retired, more or less gracefully, from the fray, leaving the newly-appointed Angel de Salazar to write encouragingly to Teresa, releasing her and her nuns from their vow of obedience to the Calced and promising as much support as he could give.

Yet the relief was not as overwhelming as she might have expected it to be before she had endured that day of bleak and hellish nothingness. Now she knew that nothing the world could do to her was as bad as the anguish of being without God. And nothing man could give her was as nourishing as the bread served up by the hands of her Beloved.

But the world too was proving very kind. One by one her Discalced friars had come out of their prisons or out of hiding, to write to her, to call upon her in the parlour, to gather around her as children gather around a mother, each one anxious to tell of his adventures and to boast of his constancy.

There were the usual small irritations to remind her that it was not yet an ideal world. Nicholas Doria and Gracian were not working together as amicably as she had hoped, and Maria of St Joseph, ordered to resume her duties as Prioress, had proved unexpectedly difficult, grumbling that she was sick of authority and felt cramped and confined in the Sevillian house. These young girls! Teresa had thought in exasperation, forgetting momentarily that Maria was past thirty. She had written sharply, ordering her to accept the responsibility and put all notions of moving house out of her head. It was ridiculous too for Maria of St Joseph to do penance by wearing a woollen tunic in the heat of summer. She had ordered her back into a thinner habit at once, and worked off the rest of her temper on Gracian who was issuing totally unnecessary orders to the nuns concerning the material of which their stockings should be made.

She thought with relief of her other Prioress, the beautiful Ana of Jesus, who ran the foundation at Beas with such disciplined efficiency and had actually managed to save up a hundred-and-fifty ducats which she had sent as a contribution to Teresa. The money had helped to pay the fares to Rome of two Discalced friars who intended to lay the case for a separation of the Order before His Holiness.

Teresa had spent two months of that previous summer at Valladolid. The occasional flare-ups of temper between Maria of St Joseph and herself worried her far less than the consistently selfish attitude displayed by Maria Baptist. Her cousin's daughter had become increasingly prudent and shrewd, which ought to have been pleasing but was not, because these qualities were used solely for the benefit of the nuns of Valladolid. They were well fed and warmly housed and the money Maria Baptist saved by charging top prices for the sisters' needlework was hoarded for a rainy day and not sent to less prosperous foundations.

I love all my daughters, Teresa decided, but I cannot honestly pretend to *like* Maria Baptist. I prefer Maria of St Joseph's quick and generous nature, even if she is sometimes rebellious, to the cool reserve of the other.

From Valladolid she had gone to Salamanca and then paid a flying visit to Toledo to hear at first hand the account of Brother Juan's dramatic arrival; but by Christmas she had been at Malagon where the nuns were preparing to move from their small, damp convent into a large, airy one.

'They are like little lizards coming out into the sunshine!' she exclaimed, watching the bright faces under the white coifs as the Sisters explored their new quarters.

That had been a happy Christmas, with everything just as she wished it to be. The new building, with its white walls and red tiled floors and dark blue crockery, sparkled in the winter sunshine, and the singing in chapel had been clear and true.

'I would like to bring little Casilda de Padilla here,' she told Mother Brianda.

Casilda, the little runaway bride, was at Valladolid. The frightened child was now a beautiful girl of eighteen; so sweet-natured that it refreshed Teresa to be in her company. She seemed perfectly content under the rule of Maria Baptist, however, and as there was no sound reason for moving her, Teresa left her where she was.

The year 1580 had opened with a surprise. Sega, who had caused them all such misery until the king's intervention, asked Teresa if she would like to make a new foundation in any place she chose. She knew very well the amount of self-will the proud Nuncio had overcome in bringing himself to make so generous an offer, and felt a rush of warmth towards him that swept away her lingering bitterness.

For this twelfth foundation, the first for four years, she had settled upon Villaneuva de la Jara. The inhabitants of this small town had been pressing her to establish a convent among them for years, but Teresa had another reason for wishing to visit the place.

There were, she learned, a community of beatas in the town; nine women who had rejected the world and lived in silence and prayer, begging their food, and bound by no formal vows. Now they had begun to realize the necessity of organizing themselves on a more practical basis, and being quite unable to agree among themselves, turned to Teresa of Jesus for help.

She would not easily forget her first sight of the thin, ragged creatures with their greasy hair and hungry eyes, as they greeted her enthusiastically and led her into the old house where they lived. The stench within was so overpowering that she groped instinctively for the clove-pierced orange she always carried on long journeys.

'We are desperate for spiritual advice,' one of the unkempt women told her. 'We will do whatever you say, Mother Teresa.'

'Then I suggest you begin by scrubbing and polishing the entire building and mending that hole I noticed in the roof,' she said crisply. 'Wash yourselves and your tunics and comb the tangles out of your hair.'

'The desert hermits,' objected one woman timidly, 'lived their whole lives long without washing.'

'Which probably explains,' Teresa countered, 'why they lived alone. My dear ladies, what possible virtue lies in being dirty? Do you think God created our bodies so that we could neglect and soil them? We have the duty while we are on earth to keep ourselves clean and respectable and to make our surroundings as attractive as possible. When we have done that, we can concentrate on spiritual matters.'

She knew they were disappointed because she had spoken flatly of practical matters instead of advising them on prayer, but she wasted no time in explaining her point of view. Instead she rolled up the sleeves of her habit and launched herself into one of the most extensive cleaning programmes she had ever enjoyed, amusing herself with the reflection that somewhere among her ancestors must have been a maid-of-all-work.

Later, when clean and tidy, and replete after an excellent meal she had paid for out of her own pocket, they sat around her in a semi-circle, she did consent to discuss interior matters; but if they had hoped to hear her enlarge on her own experiences, they were unlucky, for she kept her talk simple and impersonal.

'Begging for your living will earn you nothing but the contempt of the townsfolk,' she said briskly. 'You must earn your own bread in whatever way suits you best, appointing a treasurer to keep accounts. Dress simply if you wish, but keep yourselves clean and your clothes mended; and make sure you eat plain, nourishing food twice a day. You must have recreation too. Sing and dance and joke among yourselves, and you will return to your devotions refreshed. And don't strive to reach the heights of prayer or seek for supernatural favours. Be content to use the simple petitions we all know from childhood, and if words do not come easily, then allow yourselves merely to love God and to think how you can best please Him.'

'Most of us,' said one dolefully, 'cannot even read.'

'Common sense is far more valuable than book-learning,' Teresa declared. 'I am not well educated and I never felt the lack of it. Believe me, once people find out you can read, they will start bothering you to write books; and then your work will be interrupted and you may even lose the faculty of mental prayer. It will be of more use for you to choose a sound and kindly confessor and follow his advice. I can see to that for you if you wish.'

'Even though we are not Carmelites?' a young woman asked.

'It would not do at all,' Teresa retorted, with her infectious chuckle, 'for all the world to turn Carmelite! We must choose our own path to heaven and follow it, with discretion and moderation. Above all things, avoid extremes. It took me such a long, weary time to learn that, and I wasted a great deal of energy in my youth inflicting upon myself penance for the sake of penance which is worse, ladies, than no penance at all!'

She had left the nine beatas in a much better condition than she had found them, and journeyed nearer to the town to set up her new convent. But every pleasure had its pain, and her joy in the foundation was marred by the demonstrations of the mob who poured from the surrounding villages, demanding to see, to hear, to touch the great Foundress, Teresa of Jesus.

'God help me and forgive me, but I declare the world grows more foolish every day!' she said, crossly, peeping in dismay between the shutters at the crowds swaying back and forth as they struggled to enter the newly consecrated chapel. 'What possible good can come of their staring at an old nun?'

'You are a legend to them,' one of the Sisters said, fondly. 'They know how greatly you have contributed to the holy faith.'

'I and five thousand others,' Teresa said, with something that sounded very much like a snort. 'I wish my daughters had a ducat for every fool that comes to gape at me! Sensation-mongers!'

The crowds were so thick that she had to be smuggled out of Villaneuva de la Jara through back streets and alleys, and even then a group of children, whose bottoms her hands itched to spank, ran after the closed wagon, shouting, 'There goes the saint! God bless Mother Teresa,' and other stupidities.

It was almost a relief to be informed by her superior that she must prepare to make a new foundation at Palencia. The excuse that she was so bone-weary and in no mood for further travelling was ignored.

'And an excellent thing too,' she said with tired amusement. 'There is no better cause of death than overwork in the service of God.'

But by the time she reached Toledo again, it looked as if some other cause would snuff out her earthly existence. It began with repeated fits of sneezing, with pains in her back and legs, and an increasing difficulty in breathing. Her head ached abominably, her eyes watered, and though she was tormented by thirst she found it almost impossible to swallow.

'It is the new disease. They call it influenza,' the doctor told her gravely.

'How serious is it?' she wanted to know.

'Very serious for babies and old folk, so it is better for you to remain in bed,' he said, feeling her pulse again.

'Thank you, but I'm neither an infant nor decrepit,' she croaked indignantly.

'The contagion is easily spread. A wave of this influenza is sweeping across Europe,' he argued.

'Then I'll remain in my cell to avoid handing on the ailment,' she conceded, 'but I am not ill enough to go to bed.'

'You're a stubborn woman,' the doctor told her, with a flash of affectionate malice.

'I'm a Castillian woman,' she nodded at him. 'I will bend a little but I will not break. Now go and tend to your other patients and leave me to be sick in comfort!'

She was not left in comfort for very long. Before the day was over, she had to drag herself down to the parlour to see her brother Pedro who had come, as usual, with a long list of complaints.

'It is so quiet at La Serna that the monotony gets on my nerves,' he began, 'and when I am nervous, I get these terrible stomach-pains. I get them anyway, whenever I eat or drink anything that is unfamiliar. I miss the spiced Indian cooking. I miss everything about the Indies. I ought never to have returned to Spain. If I had money, I would go back to Peru.'

'My dear brother, the long voyage would be too much for you!' she exclaimed.

'You know that Lorenzo's boy is going out to Quito? He is like me and cannot settle here. Lorenzo didn't wish it, but Lorencito has talked him round. There's no opportunity in Spain for an ambitious young man. The place is swarming with profiteers and land-racketeers. Lorencito will go farther in the Indies than he could hope to do here.'

'Let us hope he behaves himself better,' Teresa said sharply. 'His baby daughter is at La Serna now, isn't she?'

'The mother died,' Pedro said, gloomily. 'All extra expense for Lorenzo, you see, and it's such a noisy baby. Forever yelling and crying and demanding attention.'

'Which must relieve the quietness and monotony,' Teresa said dryly.

Ignoring this, Pedro reverted to his original complaint.

'The climate of Spain is not good for me. Since my return, I have had a series of coughs and colds. La Serna is very damp, you know. I am surprised that Lorenzo did not insist upon having the property more effectively surveyed before he bought it.'

'You are not bound to live there,' Teresa said gently.

'You don't suggest that I speculate in land with my few savings, do you?' Pedro inquired, in an aggrieved tone. 'I pay my way at La Serna, I assure you. If I had more, I might be able to donate a little to your convents. But then you have many rich friends. I hear the Duchess of Alba is quite jealous of the affection the Duke confessed for you.'

'I know, and have been teasing her about it. They are both good and generous people.'

'You would not care to interest them on my behalf, I suppose?' he said, casually.

'No, brother, I could not. I have only just begged their support for the Jesuits of Pamplona. The Order there is being subjected to the most intolerable persecution, and I must do what I can for the Jesuits have always been most loyal and helpful to the Discalced Carmelites.'

'It is of no matter! I can struggle along, ill-health and all,' he sighed deeply.

'I am not very well myself at the moment,' said Teresa.

Pedro looked at her with quick alarm.

'It's not contagious, is it?' he demanded. 'There's a great deal of influenza about at the moment. With my weak chest – '

'You're not likely to catch anything from the other side of the grille,' she told him.

'Then that's all right. Nonetheless, it might be better if I went; helped you to get some rest. It's all this sitting about on stone floors,' he grumbled. 'At your age you ought to have more sense.'

In the corridor, on the way back to her cell, Teresa summoned up the energy to drum angrily on the floor with her stick, with such vehemence in her gesture that a young nun passing by stared in surprise.

'I have been talking to my brother,' Teresa burst out, 'and am now of the opinion that some of our relatives are put on this earth simply as a test of our patience and charity. At my age, indeed! Let him look to his own, for he has not worn as well as I. And what are *you* smiling about?'

'They all said you were a very great saint,' the nun stammered, 'but to tell you the truth, I haven't seen any signs of it myself.'

Teresa's irritation vanished and she beamed.

'Sister Damiana, bless you for that,' she said fervently. 'You spoke from the heart and you see me as I really am! Now, help me to my cell, before the good doctor catches me on my feet, and turn away your face for fear of infection.'

It was several days before she was about again, however, for her illness was a severe one, and only the knowledge that she was due to visit Segovia before going on to make a new foundation at Palencia spurred her to the task of recovering as quickly as she could.

The sickness had cut through Europe like a scythe, mowing down young and old.

With deep sadness, Teresa heard that it had claimed as victims three of her oldest allies, Father Rubeo, Francisco de Salcedo and Balthazar Alvarez. She grieved for the former Father Superior of Carmel who had first authorized her to found new convents; although there had been misunderstandings between them, she felt great respect for the old man whose health had never been the same since a fall from his donkey two years before. And Francisco de Salcedo, the worldly Don who had visited her in the parlour of the Incarnation and effected her introduction to her adviser, Francisco Borgia! How strange to think of the handsome courtly old widower, who had poured his money into her convents, as dead. And Balthazar Alvarez, one of her first confessors, retired some years since but still interested in the doings of this spiritual daughter, she owed him a debt of gratitude too.

But Father Gracian was well. He had escaped the outbreak of sickness and was handsomer and more charming than ever, despite his thinning hair and slightly increased weight. His imprisonment among the Calced had done him no apparent harm, and he assured her that he had not the slightest intention of leaving the Carmelites.

'Indeed, I am here to accompany you into the lion's den, Mother,' he teased.

'The lion's den?'

'We need a licence for the convent at Palencia. The archbishop has the authority to give us one.'

'Quiroga? But he is now –'

'Inquisitor-General? I know. And your books are still in the hands of the Inquisition.'

'And as no verdict upon them has yet been announced, I prefer not to remind Archbishop Quiroga of my existence.'

'Do you think he is unaware of the woman of whom all

Europe is talking?' Gracian asked.

'All Europe,' said Teresa, acidly, 'should find something better to do!' Then she laughed and relented. 'Very well, Father. I'll go with you to the archbishop to ask for this licence. He cannot eat us, I suppose.'

Far from eating them, the white-bearded prelate had received them with the utmost courtesy, granting the licence without question, pressing cakes and wine upon them, talking about the sad possibility of war with Portugal.

'Which will make a foundation at Evora impractical until the political situation has altered,' the archbishop said, gravely.

Teresa, who had discussed the possibility of such a foundation only with a few friends and supporters, looked at the head of the most efficient religious spy-network in history with alarm.

The archbishop sipped his wine and cradled the bowl of his goblet lovingly in his palm, regarding the rich, red liquid with hooded, secret eyes.

'My officials still have some writing of yours, I believe,' he said. 'I read them myself some time ago and thought them very valuable, full of sound doctrine and written in a very pleasant style. Of course there can be no question of their general publication during your lifetime, but later perhaps something might be arranged. I suppose it would be convenient if they were to be returned to you, officially approved by the Holy Office?'

So the danger of prison and the stake that had hung over her for so long was removed in a few brief sentences. She had never feared the horrors of the Inquisition for herself but it had troubled her that she might be condemned and bring ruin upon the Order she had so carefully built up. Now that danger had gone, and her books, valueless though they were, might some day be of use to one of her nuns.

Now, in the warm Segovian sunshine, she wrote again to Lorenzo, assuring him that she was in good spirits and would soon be returning to Avila. She was trying to think of some amusing anecdote with which to round off her letter when a discreet tap at the door interrupted her.

'A messenger brought it,' the nun said, in answer to Teresa's inquiring look. 'He is waiting for an answer, Mother.'

'Don't go, Sister. It's from my brother, Pedro.'

Suppressing a sigh, for Pedro's letters were always so dreadfully long-winded, she broke the seal and ran her eye quickly over the contents. When she looked up again, her face was very still.

'Lorenzo is dead,' she said, slowly. 'My brother, Lorenzo, died a week ago. He collapsed and died – of a lung haemorrhage, Pedro says. We none of us knew there was anything wrong with him. But Lorenzo sensed the coming change. He wrote to me about it, and I scolded him for being fanciful. I scolded him a great deal, I fear, and he never reproached me for it. He was a better person than I shall ever be, for he remained in the world and the world did not contaminate him.'

'I'm very sorry, Mother. Is there any answer?'

'See the messenger has something to eat. I must scribble a few lines to my brother, Pedro. He is coping alone at La Serna.'

'Did Don Lorenzo leave any family?' the nun asked, a little chilled by Teresa's calm, unemotional air.

'Two sons and a daughter. One son sailed for the Indies less than a month ago. The other is about to enter the religious life. My niece, Teresita,' she referred briefly to the letter, 'is staying with a cousin of mine, Pedro Alvarez. How strange!'

'Strange, Mother?'

'Never mind, Sister.' She laid down the letter, thinking how touching it was of her childhood sweetheart to show a preference for the girl who was so much like Teresa herself when young. 'There is a little grand-daughter too. Pedro is not fitted to care for her – his health is uncertain. She had better be taken to the convent at Avila and provision made for her there.'

'I'm very sorry to hear of your loss,' the girl said awkwardly.

'We were a large family once,' Teresa said, quietly. 'My half-brother, Juan, was killed in the French wars when I was a child. My half-sister, Maria, brought me up after my mother's death. My other brothers all went out to the Indies. Hernando, Rodrigo, Lorenzo, Antonio, Pedro, Jeronimo, Agustin.'

She spoke each name slowly as if she conjured the images of her brothers before her for a last farewell.

'Rodrigo and Antonio were killed by the natives during our conquest of Peru. Hernando rose to be a governor and died fifteen years ago. Jeronimo died of fever as he waited for the ship that was to carry him home. And now Lorenzo is gone. Only two of them left out of eight fine young men; and Agustin is never likely to return.'

'Would you like to be alone for a little while, Mother?' the other asked.

'Alone? No, Sister, at my age death is a commonplace. Time is too precious to waste in grieving.'

Teresa scribbled a few lines and signed her name firmly. As she sealed the letter, her glance fell upon the half-finished one to Lorenzo, and her lips trembled.

'He would not believe that I was dead,' she said, as if to herself. 'He sat by me for three days and nights, willing me back to life. And now he is gone, and I remain. He was four years younger than me, and he is dead, and I am still here.'

She rose, reaching for her stick and stumbling a little as her hip caught the edge of the window seat.

Why, Mother Teresa is old, the nun thought. I never realized it before, not even when she was ill, but she is an old woman. An old woman!

'Will you come with me to the chapel, Sister, when the messenger has gone?' Teresa asked.

Her voice was steady, her eyes dry, and for the first time in her life she leaned heavily upon her companion's arm, and when they reached the chapel, she pulled her veil down over her face.

CHAPTER EIGHTEEN

Beatriz de Ovalle leaned forward slightly and touched her lips cautiously with rouge. Her parents always declared that a girl of twenty had no need of cosmetics, but Beatriz felt more confident when she was shielded by a mask of artificiality. It chimed with the languid, sophisticated airs she had cultivated, the shallow, tinkling laugh, the elaborately curled hair. All these helped to conceal the fact that her dresses were sometimes shabby, her jewels more sentimental than valuable, and her shoes occasionally worn down at the heel.

She could remember times when they had had plenty of money and then, inexplicably, they would be poor again, and Mother would cry in her gentle, hopeless way, and Father would declare it was not his fault and sooner or later a bulky letter would arrive from Aunt Teresa. Mother would read the letter and cry a trifle more, and father would take out the little bag of ducats, and then for a little, they would be rich again.

'When your brother comes home from the Indies, we will all be wealthy,' Mother had said, and Beatriz, hugging her, had pretended to believe. But she did not think that either Gonzalo or her cousin, Lorencito, would become rich, and if they did, they would never bother to return to Spain.

Her black mourning gown suited her tall, slim figure and her skin was fashionably white. She was, she decided, much more elegant than her cousin, Teresita; but then fourteen-year-old Teresita wore the coarse frieze habit of the Discalced Carmelites, scraped her curly hair under a tight coif, and tried to make herself look as much like Aunt Teresa as possible.

Hearing voices in the hall, Beatriz gave a final twitch to her heavy skirts and rustled out.

'Ah, there you are, daughter.' Juan de Ovalle, who grew a little seedier and shabbier every year, put his arm about her.

The gentleman standing by him made an elegant bow, his eyes resting upon the girl with frank admiration.

'Dona Beatriz de Ovalle, may I have the pleasure of bidding you good day?'

'But not goodbye, I hope, Don Gonzalo Gonzalez?'

She gave him the tips of her fingers to kiss, fluttered her lashes, and thought fleetingly that it was a pity such a handsome caballero should be already married.

'Never goodbye, dear lady.' He too had brought the game of flirtation to a fine art.

'I have been telling Don Gonzalo about our relative, Francisco,' her father said.

'Uncle Lorenzo's son – isn't it comical? He entered a monastery at Pastrana last October and within a month had left and decided not to be a friar after all. They say my aunt's nose is put right out of joint, for Francisco gave his portion of my uncle's inheritance to the Carmelites and now, I suppose, he will have to take it back again.'

She giggled, fingers to mouth and slanting eyes sparkling.

'And you, Dona Beatriz, have you any yearnings yet for the religious life?'

'Heavens, no!' she cried. 'Do you know there are nine nuns in my mother's family already? I tell you, it's my duty to wed!'

'Fortunate the man!' said Don Gonzalo, and something in the quality of his lingering gaze made her cheeks burn.

'Will you be coming to the hunt this afternoon?' she asked, quickly.

'Indeed, yes. I am always interested in – the chase,' he said softly.

She shot a wary glance at her father but Juan de Ovalle was smiling at them both, with a faraway, ducat-counting look in his eyes.

'You will be at home this evening?' Don Gonzalo was asking.

'Yes. Of course. Where else should I be?' she asked in her turn, and gave another affected titter when he took her hand again, holding it a little longer than was necessary.

'Beatriz, go and get some wine for our neighbour. I tell you these girls have no notion of hospitality!'

That was Juana de Ovalle, hurrying through the door, her prettiness blurred and faded by time, the habitual expression of indecision and anxiety stamped on her features.

Beatriz withdrew her hand, dropped a mocking curtsey, and set off towards the kitchen, where the big vats of wine were kept. Outside the half-open door she stopped short, hearing her own name mentioned within.

'Dona Beatriz plays her cards with skill. She means to have him.'

That was the cook's voice and now the housemaid's answering treble.

'His wife is already swearing she'll be revenged on them both. She hasn't long to live and naturally wants to be safely buried before her husband goes a-wooing again.'

'If you ask me, it's past the wooing stage. They're saying in the market-place that he's enjoyed her already. At any rate, her reputation's gone.'

There was a sick, hollow feeling in the pit of her stomach, and her legs were shaking. The phrases she had heard echoed in her head. 'Means to have him'; 'Enjoyed her already'; 'Reputation gone'; 'Saying in the market-place.'

Dear God, Beatriz thought in sudden panic. What have I done that they should gossip about me in the market-place?

Morals were still strictly guarded in Spain, and any girl foolish enough to get her name bandied about would find it impossible to obtain a husband. She would have to marry Gonzalo Gonzales as soon as his wife died, and, picturing his bold glances and insinuating voice, Beatriz suddenly knew that she had not the faintest desire to wed him. It had been vastly amusing to test her power over an attractive man. But marriage, to stop wagging tongues? She knew she could never bring herself to it, and sensed too, as she collected her scattered wits and knocked briskly at the kitchen door, that she had glimpsed something sordid and ugly beneath the flowery compliments.

'So that's the situation, Father,' said Mother Teresa a few weeks later as she and Gracian talked in the parlour of the new foundation at Palencia. 'Beatriz declares she has done nothing wrong and will not be bullied into a marriage. I am inclined to believe her, but her reputation is lost. The gentleman's wife died recently and they are saying in Alba that her death was hastened by the rumours of his infidelity. I cannot imagine how it will all end.'

'All your relatives seem fated to disappoint you,' Gracian said sympathetically.

'One ought to expect it, after my long experience of human nature, but I never could cure myself of the habit of expecting the best out of everybody,' Teresa said, ruefully.

'And your nephew is married, after all the plans for his entering the Order.'

'That too was a disappointment,' she admitted. 'But his bride is a lovely girl and comes from one of the first families in Spain. Dona Orofrisia is related to the Dukes of Albuquerque and Infantazgo, and to the marquises of la Navas and de Veleda. I wish she was a little older. Fourteen is young to embark upon married life, and she is still somewhat dominated by her mother. I was not very happy by the latter's excessive interest in the amount of Francisco's inheritance.'

'I thought he gave it to the Order.'

'Originally, yes; but now that he has decided upon marriage, the money must be used for his own benefit. Fortunately, my brother made me guardian of his estates and I intend to administer them wisely until Francisco is of an age to manage his own money. I have no intention of allowing his mother-in-law to get her hands on it.'

Teresa nodded her head and folded her lips tightly. Then she brightened, laying personal worries to one side as she began to discuss matters closer to her heart.

'Tell me when the Constitutions are to be printed. Now that they have been approved, surely there's no need for delay!'

'You forget how often you yourself have suggested amendments,' Gracian reminded her.

'So much has happened since we obtained the Separation

Brief last November,' she exclaimed. 'Do you know there are still nights when I wake up, wondering how we are to obtain our independence from the Calced, before I remember that we are now quite separate! And you are, as I wished, Father Provincial.'

'The days of persecution are over,' Gracian said, smiling.

'But there is still work to be done. The Constitutions must be printed and set within the reach of every nun. Abuses will soon creep in unless we have the Rule clearly written. Only in absolute obedience to the Rule can a Carmelite fulfil her vocation of prayer.'

'Have you no faith in your prioress?' he teased.

'None at all,' Teresa said promptly. 'Even the best of them will alter circumstances to suit herself as soon as my back is turned. There's Ana of the Incarnation, determined to move to a new house though the one they have already is perfectly adequate. And even my captain of prioresses, Ana of Jesus, is too apt to believe every wild story her nuns dream up. By the bye, Father, I am taking Catalina of Christ with me to Soria as Prioress of the new foundation there.'

'The nun from the Incarnation who supported you when you were elected Prioress there? Good heavens, the woman can scarcely read or write! What possible qualifications does she have for such a position?'

'Plenty of common sense and a saintly nature,' Teresa reported. 'You will judge for yourself when you come to Soria with us.'

'To Soria? But that's impossible,' he said. 'I cannot accompany you to Soria, Mother Teresa. I am expected at Salamanca.'

'Not accompany me?' She stared at him in deep disappointment. 'But I have been counting upon your help. This work at Palencia has tired me more than I care to admit. Inés of the Cross has helped me, of course, more than *she* cares to admit! But at Soria – oh, I did so want you to come!'

'You forget that I'm Father Provincial now and must make regular visits to all the convents.'

'Father Juan de Avila would have come with me, if I had allowed it,' Teresa said, sadly. 'He is still eager for adventure.'

'He's an old man,' Gracian said.

'Yes, an old man. Too deaf to hear confessions any longer, too lame to mount a donkey. We are both old, he and I.'

'Come now,' he said uncomfortably. 'If I thought that, I would help you to the best of my ability. As it is, you are perfectly capable of going to Soria alone.'

'I will take Teresita with me,' she said, hiding her hurt feelings. 'The girl is restless and discontented – has been ever since she attended her brother's wedding. So different from your sister!'

'Teresita will be happy when she has taken her vows as Isabelita has done,' he reassured her.

'I hope so, I'm sure. These young people can be worrying.'

Noticing that he had begun to fidget a little, she dismissed him kindly and went in search of her niece, whom she found, as she found her all too frequently these days, staring through the grille of the refectory with a sulky expression on her face.

'What's wrong, my pet?' She allowed herself a childish endearment, but the sulky look deepened.

'I was wondering,' said the girl abruptly, 'exactly how rich I am.'

'Why, your father made generous provision for you,' Teresa said, a little taken aback.

'To be used as a dowry, if I wished to marry?'

'Why, yes. I can show you the account books if you wish.'

'There's no need. It's just that –'

'Just that what? Come, Teresita, if something is wrong you must let me know. Are you considering marriage? Is that it?'

'I don't want to marry,' Teresita said, flatly. 'I always wanted to be a nun, but recently – I can't explain it, aunt, but I have such a craving in me. I don't know what for, because I've always been happier here in the convent than anywhere in the world. But now the walls and the grilles are closing in on me. There are times when I want to run and run and run – now, you'll think me very wicked.'

'I think you are a perfectly normal child of fourteen, a little fearful of the vocation you have chosen.'

'Chosen? *Did* I choose it, Aunt? Or was it forced upon me? Dona Orofrisia's mother says –'

'And what does Dona Orofrisia's mother say?' Teresa asked sharply.

'She says it is a scandal that a beautiful young thing of fourteen should wear brown sackcloth and have her hair cropped to her head. She says I should have control of my own money, and meet young men, and go to balls, and – things,' Teresita finished lamely.

'Nobody pretends a life in religion is anything less than a terrible sacrifice,' Teresa said, slowly. 'And we all have doubts and fears, especially when we are young. But you are perfectly free to leave me whenever you choose. You could make your home with Francisco and his bride. They would introduce you to suitable young men, and nobody would be happier than I at the news of your marriage. But you must make up your own mind. You must search deeply into your own heart and beg God to help you to make the right decision.'

'You promised that you would take me with you to Soria.'

'And then on to Burgos.' Teresa nodded. 'Our Blessed Lord tells me that I am to make a new foundation there. But if you want to return, at any time, then you must tell me. I am hoping your cousin, Beatriz, will join us there for a while. The poor girl needs a rest and a change.'

'Away from the gentleman she doesn't want to marry?'

'Yes, sly-boots. Her parents are trying to push her into the match as well, but she has no desire for it. So you must be very kind and polite to her if she arrives.'

'I'll be an angel!' Teresita cried, with one of her swift and bewildering changes of mood.

'That might prove too great a strain for all of us,' Teresa said, dryly; but she left her niece looking, for the moment, a little happier.

It was a shock to learn some weeks later that another of her protégées had defected. So much of a shock, indeed, that at first Teresa could not believe it and sat staring at the letter with an almost comical expression of dismay.

'Casilda de Padilla has left the convent at Valladolid and joined the Calced,' she said blankly.

'Impossible!' exclaimed Catalina of Christ.

'Not according to Maria Baptist. She seems to be as surprised as I am. What in the world possessed the child? When I saw her last year she was completely happy and content. Yet, even then, she was apparently considering a change.'

'Then I call her ungrateful,' said Catalina of Christ in her blunt manner. 'She cannot have forgotten how you shielded her when she ran away from her husband, how you stood out against her relatives, how you gave her the habit with your own hands.'

'I loved that girl,' Teresa reflected. 'I truly believed – I still believe – that she had a strong vocation for our Order. I never knew a novice with a sweeter nature or a sunnier temper. Is it possible that I was mistaken?' She looked at her companion with concern. 'Casilda has joined the Mitigated Rule,

Teresita still wavers between the world and the cloister. Yet my other niece, Beatriz, who seemed destined for a life of fashionable idleness, writes informing me that she wishes to enter the Discalced Order. I told her to wait a while for I was certain this was some new whim, but now I'm not in the least sure. My skill at judging character seems to be deserting me as far as these girls are concerned.'

'You forget all the others who have not left and do not waver,' Catalina pointed out. 'You forget Leonor of St Gabriel, and Isabelita, and little Juanita, and Mariana Gaytan.'

'What a sensible soul you are!' Teresa exclaimed. 'And how right I was to bring you here to Soria as Prioress! I will tell you that I have written to Father Gracian to tell him that you are carrying out your duties admirably.'

'Did our Father Provincial have a few doubts on the matter?' Catalina inquired.

'He does not know my nuns as well as I do,' Teresa smiled, her good-humour restored.

'Neither does our Vicar-Superior,' said Catalina. 'It is months since he visited us.'

'Father Antonio of Jesus has not yet forgiven me for voting Gracian as Father Provincial, and voting himself into second position. Indeed, I swear he's taken a vow not to answer any of my letters.'

'He thinks you favour Father Gracian.'

'Naturally I favour a man who is less than forty to someone in his mid-seventies,' the Mother Foundress said testily. 'The post of Father Provincial is an important administrative one, requiring tremendous stamina and much more tact and humility than Antonio of Jesus ever possessed. He makes a far better deputy.'

'Some of us thought that Brother Juan of the Cross might prove suitable,' Catalina suggested.

'Lord bless us, no!' Teresa chuckled. 'He is the last man in the world to put in such a position. He has no taste for finance or worldly matters, and it is even becoming impossible to discuss spiritual matters with him. As soon as God is mentioned, Brother Juan falls into ecstasy and I along with him. No, as soon as Brother Juan leaves Baeza, I am sending him to Granada to make a new foundation there. Ana of Jesus will go with him for she can handle him beautifully, far more cleverly than I can.'

'Must you go to Avila before you set out for Burgos?' Catalina asked.

'I must, to settle this business of Francisco's inheritance. His mother-in-law is determined to get her hands on the money and I am equally determined to invest it wisely for him so that he will have something to fall back on when his relatives have squandered everything else. And I must see for myself how Lorencito's little girl is getting on. She is cutting her back teeth at present and that can be so painful. There is little hope of her father's claiming her now that he has married and settled in the Indies.'

'They give you no peace,' said Catalina of Christ, but she spoke smilingly, too wise to waste her sympathy upon a woman who neither asked for it nor needed it.

Indeed, the problems crowding in upon Teresa represented only a momentary ruffling of her surface tranquillity. It was becoming easier for her, not merely to deal with her troubles but to forget them completely when they proved insurmountable. She dwelt now in a close and conscious unity with the Power who revealed Himself at the centre of the crystal of her soul, within that seventh mansion where all doubt and fear ended and truth was Truth alone, brighter and clearer and steadier than any flame.

In this condition, she could love all souls equally, even if some of those same souls irritated and exasperated her upon the human plane. The days of her public and humiliating ecstasies were gone, and only Ana of St Bartholomew, who shared her cell, was privileged occasionally to see that radiance that streamed from Teresa's sleeping features, and to hear, one dark night when the Mother Foundress's head ached too badly for sleep, the clear chanting of an invisible choir, lulling them both to rest.

Teresa left Soria with reluctance for she loved the fertile, well-watered plain surrounding the town. Yet the sight of those rust-red walls rising above the fields around Avila filled her with greater delight. As a child she had longed to run away and explore strange lands as her brothers had been allowed to do. Now, in old age, she desired the shelter of those same walls.

'I would like to die here, in the place where I began,' she said to Teresita.

'Die? You're not going to die, are you?'

'Not for a while, if I can help it.' She patted her niece's hand reassuringly. 'But I will be sixty-seven next March. Even a tough campaigner like me cannot live for ever.'

'But you must promise to remain alive until I have taken my vows,' said Teresita.

'Your – does that mean you have made up your mind?'

'With's God's help,' said Teresita, and the discontent had vanished from her eyes. 'I know that I am free to choose, and, being free, I choose Carmel. Not to please you, Aunt, and not because Father expected it, not even to please myself, but because I feel a conviction very deep within me, and it makes nonsense of all my fears.'

'I will be at your profession. You have my promise,' said Teresa, and aunt and niece clasped hands affectionately.

Within a few days, even Teresita's change of heart had been relegated to the background of her mind. The Mother Foundress had flung herself, heart and soul, into the preparations for the new foundation at Burgos. She would install Tomasina Baptista there as Prioress for Tomasina possessed, above everything else, that admirable common sense so necessary in one who held authority.

She was extremely irritated therefore to be called down to the parlour one cold November day, to find Brother Juan of the Cross on the other side of the grille.

'You're supposed to be in Granada, establishing the new convent there!' she exclaimed.

'I made a detour,' he said simply. 'There is a covered wagon and two mules outside, ready to take you to Granada as soon as you are prepared to travel. It will be so pleasant, Mother, to enjoy your company upon the journey.'

'But, good heavens, I am about to set off for Burgos. I can't spare the time to jaunt up and down Spain for the sake of pleasure,' she said, crossly.

'It was to be a surprise for you,' said Brother Juan.

She missed the wistful note in his voice, the eager look of a boy bringing flowers to his mother, and felt only a stirring of temper at the impractical dreams of saints.

'At any other time I might agree,' she said, struggling for patience. 'But when the snows come the roads will be impassable. I might be trapped at Granada until spring. Surely you are capable of doing something by yourself, Brother Juan!'

'Yes, of course. It was thoughtless of me.'

'Ana of Jesus is young and will be a more amusing companion than I could be,' Teresa said. 'We will meet later, after both the foundations are made, and compare notes on our adventures.'

She dismissed him with a brisk, smiling nod and hurried away to make some final calculations on the cost of the journey to Burgos. A little later, the small friar mounted one of the waiting donkeys and rode slowly away.

He, who lived only for the love of God, had allowed himself to feel more affection for Mother Teresa of Jesus than he had ever permitted himself to feel for any other human being; he had hoped to give her pleasure by arranging the journey to Granada especially for her comfort; and she had rejected him, had shrugged away his friendship, left him to make his way alone. After a little while, he raised his head, without looking back, began to sing as he always sang when his agony of loneliness became unbearable.

'I was a trifle sharp with Brother Juan,' Teresa remembered as her own cart rumbled over the unmade roads towards Burgos. 'Fortunately it is impossible to hurt his feelings, for he is as far above earthly attachments as I am below sanctity! But I will spend some time with him when he returns from Granada and make up to him for any neglect.'

She paused, realizing that Tomasina Baptista was no longer listening but was peering anxiously through a slit in the canvas.

'What is it?' she asked.

'Floods, Mother Teresa. The entire road is completely flooded.'

'Nonsense!' Teresa began, but a glance through the slit contradicted her. A moment later, the jangling of harness and the alarmed shouts of muleteers brought them to a standstill.

'We cannot go forward,' one of the other Sisters moaned. 'We will be drowned, swept away by the current.'

'Reverend Mother, the river has burst its banks and is rising higher,' one of the outriders called. 'There is no guarantee that any of the wagons will get through to the other side. We don't know how deep the mud is.'

'We cannot turn back,' Teresa said, firmly. 'We are expected at Burgos and this is the only road to Burgos, so there's an end of the matter.'

'This is sheer stubbornness,' the man began, but she interrupted him with one of her infectious chuckles.

'We are on God's business,' she said serenely. 'We must be prepared to risk everything in that Cause.'

'Even our lives?' quavered another.

'What better way to lose them than in the service of Our Lord?' Teresa demanded, gaily. 'But you need not fear I will be reckless with your safety. We will take the lowest wagon, and I will sit up next to the driver – if one of these men will volunteer for the task. The rest of you will wait here until I am safely across. Then you will follow, calmly, reciting the Creed.'

She clambered down to the ground, pulling her veil over her face, and accepting a helping hand from the young muleteer who came sheepishly forward.

It was good to be out in the fresh air after the stuffy atmosphere of the covered wagon, and she looked about her with interest at the bleak landscape and the swirling waters ahead.

The muleteer gathered up the reins and cracked his whip over the back of the reluctant mule. Teresa clung to the side of the high seat as the wagon began to roll slowly forward. Then they were in the midst of the waters, lashed by the wind into a frenzy of small waves. The water spun around them, bubbling down into swirls of mud and small pebbles thrown up by the grinding of the wheels.

Then they were moving into the shallower water of the opposite bank. Teresa twisted in her seat to wave encouragement, felt her fingers slide helplessly along the guard rail and fell heavily into the icy water.

She was up almost at once, spluttering as she pushed aside her choking veil, limping through the muddy water with the long skirts of her habit threatening to drag her back at every step. She felt as if every bone in her body had been jarred out of place, but worse than physical discomfort was the sheer humiliation of being toppled from her seat after going so far without mishap.

Not for the first time, her fiery Castillian temper came to her aid. Those now preparing timidly to make the crossing saw her shake her fist at the sky.

'What else, Lord?' Teresa shouted. 'What else have You in store for me? Is it fair to punish me when I am doing Your Will? What more do You need of me?'

In the midst of the swirling water, the voice spoke to her, gravely and sternly, removing all comfort.

I need you to suffer, daughter. Your suffering is necessary to Me.

CHAPTER NINETEEN

Her world had shrunk to four white walls and a small, barred window through which she could see a patch of blue sky. Her bed was covered with a fresh white counterpane, and straw had been laid over the tiled floor so that when she fell into a light doze the footsteps of the Sisters would not disturb her. Ana of St Bartholomew had scarcely left her side except to go to Mass since the evening Teresa had been forced to admit that she could no longer stay on her feet.

And now I am dying, she thought, while it crossed her mind fleetingly that she should have died before, at the time when the printed Constitutions of the Rule of Discalced Carmelites had been put into her hand. Then, death would have been a triumphant climax to the long years of struggle. But her suffering had been to live on, the Reformer who was already assuming the reputation of legend. And legends, she thought, are most uncomfortable to live with.

Most of her nuns, she knew, loved and respected her, but some of them loved her more at a distance, finding it impossible to believe that the woman who had brought Carmel back to its original Rule was now perfectly content to live under that Rule, obeying the Prioress like the least of them. And there were some who did not love her at all but resented her existence, interpreting every glance of hers as a critical one and losing no opportunity in reminding her that she was grown old and useless.

And that is my ending, Teresa thought. Not the grand and glorious martyrdom I sought as a child, but a slow flickering out, like a candle that has burned for too long.

She had always imagined that at the point of death, her whole life would pass before her in retrospect; but the little girl building hermitages in the garden, the high-spirited girl in the orange dress, the young nun crawling on paralysed legs, the woman lifted up to the heights of prayer were no more than feeble images in her memory. In the forefront of her mind were the problems that still remained, the welfare of her friends, the events of the previous ten months. Even on her deathbed, there was no time for reflection.

She had intended to return to Avila as soon as she had made the foundation at Burgos, but that flooded road had been simply a foretaste of what awaited her.

They had been received kindly by Dona Catalina of Tolosa, two of whose daughters had already joined the Order. Her house was large and tastefully furnished and she had installed grilles so that the nuns could live enclosed while negotiations for the sale of a building went on. But the fall from the wagon had shaken Teresa more than she had realized. At Burgos she was never free from aching joints, and racking headache, from attacks of vomiting and from noises in her head that distracted her thoughts, making it impossible to concentrate and difficult to sleep.

She had tried to ignore her ailments, lying on the floor to talk to visitors when she could no longer hold up her head, dictating letters when she could not sleep.

But matters went too slowly, for although a licence for the convent had been obtained, the Archbishop of Burgos had delayed three months before signing it. Teresa had been at a loss to understand this totally unexpected coolness until Dona Catalina had come to her tearfully and confided that the Jesuits of Burgos had no desire for a Carmelite convent in the same district as themselves.

'They are afraid that your convent will attract revenues from their own Order,' Dona Catalina wept. 'My Jesuit confessor refuses me absolution while you and the Sisters lodge in my house.'

So, despite the good woman's protests, they had moved to fresh quarters, taking over the upper floor of the Hospital of the Conception and sweltering in the tiny, low-ceilinged rooms. On the floors below, patients tossed and turned uncomfortably on their narrow pallets while the few overworked nurses hurried up and down, fighting their hopeless battle with flies, and dirt and disease.

Within the day, veiled Carmelites moved among them, urged on by the stooping figure in the patched and frayed habit who scrubbed floors and emptied pails and laughed so merrily at her own predicament when she slipped and fell, that even those who knew themselves dying smiled too.

But, at last, the negotiations for the new building had been completed, the licence signed, and the Jesuits, for whose cause in Pamplona Teresa had never ceased to fight, quietened.

And there had been moments of brightness too. Paying a

brief visit to Dona Catalina of Tolosa, Teresa had paused to talk to the youngest of her daughters, teasing the child because of her passion for sweets and swearing they would call her Dona Roly-Poly if she grew much plumper. When she rose to leave, the round-faced Elenita had risen too, snatching her cloak from its hook and putting her hand out to Teresa.

'If you want me, Mother Foundress, I'll come with you,' she said.

'Charm,' laughed Gracian, paying a flying call to Burgos en route to Soria. 'You have more charm than an old lady ought to possess.'

'If I have, I learned it from you!' she retorted, not troubling to conceal her delight at his unexpected visit.

He was handsomer and more prosperous than ever, eager to tell her of his visitations; yet there was a little sadness mingled with her pleasure. Once, he would have asked her advice as a matter of course. Now she knew very well that he inquired her opinion as a matter of courtesy, for the soul she had formed and shaped was moving away from her, and she, like all good mothers, must make it easy for them both to break the bonds.

Yet she continued to fret about him, hearing that he had gone into Seville where there was plague raging. She had hoped that he would go to the new convent at Granada, where Ana of Jesus was letting her new authority go to her head slightly.

'Spending twelve thousand ducats on the new building!' Teresa exclaimed. 'How in the world did she acquire such a sum, and how in the world has she managed to spend it all so quickly? She must plan to let her nuns sleep between silk sheets and eat off silver plate! And my poor daughters at Avila cannot earn enough to keep body and soul together.'

She was, herself, very short of money and more than grateful to those prioresses who, with an eye to the needs of others, sent gifts to their less fortunate Sisters. Her own appetite was so poor that she was happy to send on the fruit and cakes, the fish packed in bread, the leather bottles of wine which arrived; but there were nights when, unable to sleep, she could not help picturing trout smothered in cream sauce, cucumbers pickled in red vinegar, quinces baked in their own juice, cakes dripping with honey and spread liberally with butter, slices of pink-fleshed melon sprinkled with ginger and brown sugar – all the delicacies she had enjoyed in childhood, as if in old age her mind began to play tricks presenting her forgotten desires in the shape of food.

She had written to her nuns at Medina del Campo, begging for the loan of a hundred-and-fifty ducats so that she could send something back to Avila where the Sisters of St Joseph's were practically in a state of famine. All that arrived was another interminable letter from Ana of the Incarnation, who was still senselessly determined to move her nuns into a larger building.

In the heat of July, she forced her aching limbs into a stifling wagon and set off for Palencia. Her daughters there had written in glowing terms about the generosity of the townsfolk. By going there in person, she hoped to raise some funds for her other convents. But she could stay there for only a month for Teresita had written to remind her of her promise to be present at the girl's final vows.

Her superiors, however, had different ideas. Father Gracian finally breaking his bond of dependence upon her, ordered that she proceed to Valladolid to inquire further into the defection of Casilda de Padilla.

'Let me write and tell him that you are not well enough to travel,' Ana of St Bartholomew begged, but Teresa refused. It would be good to see Maria Baptist again, for though her cousin's daughter had often disappointed her, she could never forget that it was Maria who had first suggested they found a convent of their own.

At Valladolid, she had experienced the humiliation of being completely unwanted. After the kindness of Palencia, the cold-set face of Maria Baptist had hurt her deeply. She had felt so ill at Valladolid that there were times when she could hardly drag herself down to choir, but the nuns, too much in awe of their Prioress to show any attention to the Foundress, ignored the fact; and Maria Baptist lost no opportunities in impressing upon Teresa that she held no official position in the Community.

Teresa, obediently kissing the ground as penance for having come late to a meal she could not eat, felt a deep sadness for the woman, so admirable in so many ways, in whom there was no charity, no humility, and whose jealousy was so intense that it drove her to such acts of petty spite.

She left Valladolid with orders from her superiors to go to Medina where the Vicar-Superior waited to see her. The prospect of meeting Antonio of Jesus, and healing the unspoken breach between them, compensated in some measure for the door slammed in her face at the Valladolid convent, for the resentful glare in Maria Baptist's small eyes, even for the unendurable journey in a haze of sickness and flies.

She had forgotten long before her sarcastic reply to the over-zealous Alberta Baptist who had objected to recreation.

'Go and contemplate in your cell then, daughter, and leave us to enjoy ourselves.'

But for that careless remark she must make atonement now, arriving at Medina so faint with exhaustion that the very walls wavered and dissolved before her, to be greeted by a cool unsmiling, 'Our Vicar-Superior is already awaiting you in the parlour.'

He had grown old with immense dignity, she thought, peering up at the tall, white-haired friar. He held himself like a man who knows his true worth, his thumbs hooked in his girdle, his voice richly sonorous; but her sight was not so dim that she could not see the weakly petulant mouth, the cold, remembering eyes of the man who had always wanted to be first in every sphere. At Durelo, he had hoped to be the first Discalced friar. He had expected to be Father Provincial. He had not forgotten and would not forgive her for having chosen first Juan of the Cross and then Brother Gracian in preference to himself.

'You are to leave this convent early tomorrow morning and go immediately to the Duchess of Alba's residence,' he told her.

She gaped at him foolishly and he tapped an impatient foot.

'The Duchess of Alba's daughter-in-law is about to give birth to her first child and nothing will content the Duchess of Huescar except your presence at the event. The young lady wishes to have a saint present. You and I,' his lip curled, 'know such an opinion to be nonsense, but it will not do to offend such a powerful friend of the Reform.'

Every human instinct in her cried out a protest against this intolerable command. To bring her out of her way in order to send her off again when she was too ill to eat or sleep, because he wished to pay off an old grudge, roused in her a passion of resentment. Then the resentment died, and knowing that this could not have happened had her soul been completely refined and purified, she bowed her acceptance.

When she came out of the parlour, Alberta Baptist was waiting to inform her that the evening meal had been cleared away and nothing more could be served unless Teresa wished to insist upon privilege.

'I thank you, Mother Prioress, but I am entitled to no privileges,' she said quietly and dragged herself to a cell to pray, without light or interior joy, for her Vicar-Superior because she feared greatly for his soul.

She and Ana of St Bartholomew left at dawn, having been offered neither breakfast nor refreshments for the two-day journey. The lay sister had procured some figs but the fruit was dry and full of seeds that hurt Teresa's back-teeth and although the muleteers stopped for water there was nothing else to buy, although, when they stopped in the evening, Ana took their last four reales and went off to try to find some food. She came back with two eggs and the information that no lodgings for the night were to be had. The muleteers had swaggered off to drink away the evening, and the broiling day now blew cold and menacing.

They spent the night huddled in the empty wagon, breaking open the eggs, both of which proved to be rotten, and sipping the warm water that still remained in the leather buckets. At one stage, Teresa was aware that the lay sister was crying quietly. To cheer her, she launched into a frivolous anecdote, but was interrupted by a fit of vomiting that left her so weak and shaken she had to crawl back into the wagon. She was glad it was too dark for Ana to see, for she could taste blood in her mouth. But when light dawned and their escort returned, she saw her condition reflected in her companion's horrified face.

She thought she must have slept a little during the day for she drifted in and out of periods of consciousness. They were taking her to Avila, she thought, where her father was waiting to scold her because she had taken some raisins and given them to Rodrigo.

The jolting had stopped and a man was speaking to her. She wondered vaguely who he was and what he was doing there.

'The Duchess of Huescar is delivered of a fine son, Mother, and regrets that you have been inconvenienced.'

Duchess? She dragged her mind back into the present and flicked a little humour from her misery.

'It seems,' she observed, 'that here is one more saint who won't be needed.'

They had driven on to the convent where for the first time there were other friendly faces beside Ana's. When she had eaten a little and paid her customary visit to the infirmary, she felt well enough to join in the recreation, singing a little in the voice that was always a trifle out of tune, and regretting that her legs were too stiff to dance, her fingers too swollen to pluck a guitar. It was only when she excused herself, with the remark that it was more than twenty years since she had gone to bed so early, that she knew quite certainly, from the trembling motion of her heart, that she was a dying woman.

Now, lying in the white bed, and looking, she supposed with an inward chuckle, as neat as if she were already buried, she allowed the Sisters to wait upon her, knowing they would reproach themselves later for any fancied neglect. She was not in great pain and her mind was clear, so clear indeed that it surprised her to cough up blood because surely she was still young? Sixty-seven years old, she reminded herself, and I should have died before, when the Cause was first triumphant.

Yet she could not have wished for a gentler end. The Prioress of Alba was one of the sweetest of her nuns, so tender-hearted that she would weep bitterly when forced to reproach a Sister, and so ascetic that she often went for two or three days without food. It was this Juana of the Holy Ghost who sat now by Teresa, retailing the messages that were pouring in from her convents.

'It seems that I am loved after all,' Teresa joked; then her expression grew a little troubled because it would never do to encourage such personal attachments.

'You must not imitate me,' she urged those who crowded into her cell. 'I have been a bad nun and set many bad examples.'

They were not listening to her but begging for advice. She was aware that time had passed, that she had received the Last Sacraments, that her small room was crowded with those who must bear witness to this death. An account of it would be circulated to all her Carmels; her last words would be noted, remembered. But she could only say to those present what she had been saying now for years.

'Keep the Rule, my daughters. Remember that God alone suffices, and that we do His Will by constant prayer, by constant acts of charity. Always, always keep the Rule.'

Her sins were crushing her; all the little flares of pride and temper returning like great boulders to prevent her from rising into the light. She called out, in the sudden weakness of fear.

'God will not despise a humble and contrite heart, will He?'

Antonio of Jesus was bending over her. It was good to see him, to know that he had come, had forgotten his disappointed vanity.

'Do you wish to be buried at Avila, Mother Teresa?' he was asking.

Her fading eyes twinkled and her voice held all its old asperity.

'For heaven's sake, Father, will they not spare me a bit of earth here?'

She could see her niece, Teresita, in the corner of the cell. She was sitting quietly with her rosary in her hands, but her eyes were red-rimmed.

I'm sorry to have to break my promise, Teresa thought. I longed to see you make your profession, but you will not hold it against me that I could not be there.

Her eyes passed to the worried face of little Mariana Gaytan, and she said aloud, 'Don't fret, for you will be allowed to make your vows even though I shall be dead.'

The last word had disturbed somebody. There was no sound or movement, but she saw a troubled and frightened soul. She looked straight at young Teresa of St Andrew, nicknamed by the Community 'honour of penance' because of the terrible mortifications she inflicted upon herself. The girl had never seen death before and, sensing that she herself would not live long, feared the event.

'Sister, when your turn comes, I will fetch you myself,' the Mother Foundress said warmly, and the troubled soul was still.

Surely it is time now, Teresa thought. There is nothing more for me to do here; nothing useful for me to say. I am only an ignorant woman, after all, with many sins to answer. And I am tired, so tired.

She moved her head slightly so that it rested more comfortably on Ana of St Bartholomew's arm. Outside, the brief Spanish twilight reddened the sky.

Sister Catalina of the Conception, disturbed by the sound of voices, turned her head slightly towards the door, and was frozen into that gesture as wonder and bewilderment shackled her limbs.

A long procession of men and women was entering the room,

bearing lighted tapers, crowned with jewels, clad in shimmering garments. As they stepped lightly, they sang and talked and filled the place with most joyous laughter before they vanished – where? Catalina could not tell, but she saw them make deep reverences towards the Mother Foundress and she smelled the fragrance that came from them. It seemed to her too that she recognized their faces and knew their names, although she had never seen them before. Surely that was Agnes of Rome, martyred at twelve; and the two who walked together – Perpetua and Felicity – their friendship unchanged since the day they had faced the wild beasts in the arena at Carthage. And Pedro of Alcantara; and Francisco Borgia, and the woman with glowing hair so familiar in portraits of Mary Magdalene.

The singing died and the figures were gone, and there was silence for the space of a heartbeat. Then Teresa's voice rang through the cell, vibrant and gay as if she had shed all her years.

'It is time! It is time to set forth and meet You, oh my Lord, my dear Love!'

And she went out very quietly like a candle, with three faint, lingering sighs. The nuns had sunk to their knees as Antonio of Jesus began to intone the prayers for the dead. Ana of St Bartholomew rose and went swiftly out of the room. When she returned a coverlet hung over her arm. The Duchess of Alba had sent it to serve as pall for the Mother Foundress.

Ana draped it lovingly over the motionless figure, smoothing the folds in her rough hands. It was, she thought, only fitting that so great a woman should be shrouded in cloth-of-gold.

POSTSCRIPT

The body of Teresa of Jesus was placed in a coffin and buried beneath a pile of rubble. Nine months later, inspired by the fragrance issuing from the tomb, the nuns of Alba exhumed the body and found it completely incorrupt. Father Gracian, who was present and eager for relics, cut off the left hand, reserving the little finger for himself and sending the rest to Avila.

Three years later, Gracian returned with old Father Julian of Avila, and, obeying the orders of their superiors, exhumed the body again, finding it still incorrupt and smelling of clover. The remainder of the left arm was amputated and left at Alba, the body sewed into a sheet and carried secretly to Avila where it was publicly displayed.

The nuns of Alba, supported by the Duke of Alba, petitioned the Pope who gave orders that the body was to be returned to them. Here it was exhibited for many years, a little dryer and darker, but still incorrupt.

Finally it was completely dismembered, parts of it sent to convents in Spain and Portugal, the jawbones to the Vatican; the heart left in Alba de Tormes.

In 1614, Teresa of Jesus was beatified. In 1622, she was canonized, together with Francisco Borgia, Pedro of Alcantara, and the Jesuit founders, Ignatius Loyola and Francis Xavier.

After Teresa's death, a struggle began between Father Gracian and Nicholas Doria who wished to mitigate the Rule of the Discalced.

Gracian, refusing to defend himself against fresh slanders, was expelled from the Order in 1591. On his way to plead his cause in Rome, he was captured by pirates and sold to the Turks as a slave. Ransomed in 1595, he was reinstated in the Order and went to Brussels where he lived until his death in 1614.

Juan of the Cross, who supported Gracian, was exiled in 1591 to the desert of Peñuela where he died of a broken heart later the same year, leaving some of the most sublime mystical poetry ever composed. He was canonized in 1726 and proclaimed a doctor of the church in 1926.

Ana of Jesus, the 'captain of prioresses', founded the Discalced Convent of Madrid with Juan of the Cross, encouraged him to write his *Spiritual Canticle*, and herself collected and arranged for publication all the manuscripts of Teresa of Jesus. In 1591, she was condemned to three years' imprisonment for supporting Gracian; but seven years later she was chosen to found convents at Paris and Dijon, where she met St Francis de Sales and St Jane de Chantel. Meeting Father Gracian again, she went to Brussels to found a convent there, dying in that city in 1621. Her cause for beatification was introduced in 1876, and in 1897 she appeared in vision to St Thérèse of Lisieux.

Teresa's favourite prioress, Maria of St Joseph, founded in 1585 the Convent at Lisbon, endured nine months' imprisonment for her championship of Gracian, founded Carmels in France and died at Toledo in 1603.

Ana of St Bartholomew became a choir nun and founded the Convent at Pontoise in France. She died in 1626 and was beatified in 1917.

The various members of Teresa's family prospered – both Teresita and Beatriz took the veil and died young.

The Order reformed by Teresa continued to flourish, there being Carmelite communities today as far afield as New Zealand and the United States of America. In Great Britain the first Carmel was founded in 1794. Today there are thirty-eight Carmels in this country, each small community of enclosed women praying and working according to the Rule laid down by St Teresa.

BIBLIOGRAPHY

The Life of St Teresa, by St Teresa, translated by J. M. Cohen (Penguin Books. 1958)

The Way of Perfection, by St Teresa, translated by the Benedictines of Stanbrook (Thomas Baker)

Book of the Foundations, by St Teresa, translated by the Reverend John Delton (Catholic Publishing and Bookselling Limited. 1860)

The Interior Castle, by St Teresa, translated by a Benedictine of Stanbrook (S.C.M. Press. 1968)

The Letters of St Teresa, translated by E. Allison Peers (Burns, Oates and Washburn, 1950)

St Teresa of Avila, by Marcella Auclair (Burns and Oates. 1950)

Mother of Carmel, by E. Allison Peers (S.C.M. Press. 1961)

The Eagle and the Dove, by V. Sackville-West (Michael Joseph. 1944)

Land of Stones and Saints, by F. Parkinson Keyes (Doubleday and Company. 1957)

The Mystics of Spain, by E. Allison Peers (Allen and Unwin. 1951)

Great Catholics, by Father C. Williamson, O.S.C. (Nicholas and Watson. 1938)

The Physical Phenomena of Mysticism, by Herbert Thurston S.J. (Burns and Oates. 1958)

A Stranger in Spain, by H. V. Morton (Methuen. 1955)

Spain, by E. Allison Peers (Methuen. 1930)

The Growth of the Spanish Inquisition, by Jean Plaidy (Robert Hale and Company. 1960)

The Catholic Reform, by H. Daniel-Rops (Dent. 1963)

The Intellectual History of Europe, by Friedrich Heer (Weidenfeld and Nicholson)

Maureen Peters

Maureen Peters brings the great women of history, and their times, to life. Each of her books is a vivid tapestry of the kings and courts, the passions and the tragedies that surrounded her heroines.

The Woodville Wench *30p*

Anne, the Rose of Hever *25p*

Elizabeth the Beloved *30p*

Henry VIII and His Six Wives *30p*

Joan of the Lilies *25p*

Katheryn, the Wanton Queen *25p*

Princess of Desire *30p*